DATE DUE APR 0 7

GAYLORD | | | PRINTED IN U.S.A.

P9-DTL-930

The Big Pasture

Center Point Large Print

**This Large Print Book carries the
Seal of Approval of N.A.V.H.**

The Big Pasture

Will Henry

CENTER POINT PUBLISHING
THORNDIKE, MAINE

This Center Point Large Print edition
is published in the year 2007 by arrangement with
Golden West Literary Agency.

The text of this Large Print edition is unabridged. In other
aspects, this book may vary from the original edition. Printed in
Thailand. Set in 16-point Times New Roman type.

ISBN: 1-58547-913-6
ISBN 13: 978-1-58547-913-9

Library of Congress Cataloging-in-Publication Data

Henry, Will, 1912-
    The Big pasture / Will Henry.--Center Point large print ed.
      p. cm.
    ISBN-13: 978-1-58547-913-9 (lib. bdg. : alk. paper)
    1. Large type books. I. Title.

PS3551.L393B54 2007
813'.54--dc22

2006028370

HISTORICAL FOREWORD

IN THE BEGINNING, long before the historic latter-day Texas trail drives scattered the Spanish longhorn upon every Montana hill, there was nothing in all that vast empty land save the brooding stillness of the Crow and Blackfoot buffalo pastures.

In those virgin years before the modern range wars, another fight for these last great grazing grounds took place—the brave, desperate war of the red buffalo hunter against the encroachment of the white cattleman.

It began, and ended, in a fabulous valley where the grass grew thick and rich as the cape of a herdbull in winter robe, and the water ran cold and clean the year around.

Men still wonder at the beauty of the Gallatin, though today one must look beyond the raw green wounds of alfalfa fields and the ugly brown scars of gangplow and diesel tractor to see it. What a staggering sight it must have been nearly a hundred years ago when Nathan Stark rode into its mile-high mountain paradise at the head of his snow-caked herd of Rio Brazos longhorns.

The Big Pasture is the story of this valley and its matchless grasslands, and of their invasion by Nathan Mason Stark, the first northern cattleman to bring a Texas steer into that echoing solitude where only Indian bulls had fed before.

CHAPTER ONE

STARK STOOD at the front window of the Black Nugget's banking parlor, his broad back turned to the firelit warmth of the room and to the anxiously hovering figure of Esau Lazarus.

Outside, the December snow drove wetly up Van Buren Street, splashing its big, beginning flakes across the crudely glazed panes through which the former stared. Neither man spoke, the first because he never talked before he thought, the second because he had learned better than to say anything until Nathan Stark was ready to hear it.

Accordingly, Lazarus let the silence grow, his keen mind casting back through the harsh past he had shared with Stark.

He had known the latter ten years, since, as a youth of eighteen, he had come west from Menard County, Illinois, with nothing to stake him in the cutthroat society of the mining camps beyond the physique of a grizzly and the standard poor boy's ambition to become a millionaire. But where the ambition itself was commonplace, Stark's chosen means toward its accomplishment were singularly different. He deliberately ignored the obvious glitter of the gravel bars and placer pits, calculatingly set about the hardest, most grubbing work a white man could undertake in that gold-crazed time and place—freighting in supplies by ox team all the long, hazardous way from the Missouri River settlements.

Beginning with the Denver strikes in the fifties and continuing with the Montana finds in the early sixties, the successive camps enjoyed their rawhiding jokes about the bigboned farm boy's unsmiling addiction to hard work and poor pay. While the bearded searchers after the easy-million shook their shaggy heads and had their hard-edged laughs, Stark plodded on. He never appreciated, never joined this rough good humor at his expense. He knew where he was going and how he meant to get there. Time was money. Only fools spent it laughing.

The capricious temper of the camps did not incline to weigh dead-serious thrift and a humorless mind too heavy in the goldstrike scale of civic virtues. The young freighter was soon enough and severely let alone, forced, for lack of choice, to accept the company of the one man whose business permitted no social distinctions—Esau Lazarus, the camp moneylender and self-constituted "First National Bank of the Gravel Bars."

The wise old Jew, sensitive both by gentle nature and the ancient awareness of his race to the persecutions levied upon economic enterprise by a jealous society of spend-thrift failures, had from the beginning understood and encouraged the eastern boy's grim determination "to amount to something." He had cautiously grub-staked him to his original string of worn-out wagon bulls, subsequently watched his relentless rise from nothing to the biggest freighter west of St. Louis.

But in the friendless course of those ambitious, grubbing years he had seen the camps stop laughing and start scowling when the name of Nathan Stark was mentioned. He had understood that, too. And all too well. The bearded prophets of the placers were grown sick with that ugly, unreasonable resentment lesser men always suffer over a success they do not understand and have failed utterly to predict.

Then, ten months ago, Stark had announced his "crazy scheme" to sink his life's savings into a speculation wilder than any salted mine shaft or played-out diggings in Montana. Virginia City's forecasts of financial failure were immediate and gleeful.

Stark stood by his stubborn arithmetic.

In Fort Worth, Texas longhorn steers were begging for buyers at three dollars a head in Union greenbacks. In the beef-hungry Montana camps those same three-dollar steers would be fought over at forty dollars and nobody arguing the terms being "pure Montana dust on delivery" rather than "printed Government paper on promise." All a man had to do to make a sure million was go to Texas and drive a big herd of those cheap beeves back across the 1500 miles of mountains, rivers, deserts and unfriendly redmen that stretched northward to Montana. It was that simple. All it took was a little time and a lot of intestinal fortitude.

The Virginia Citians totted up the same set of figures, came out with a gratifyingly different answer.

Stark had at last slipped his head hobbles. The lonely, tightfisted years had finally done their dirty work. He was crazier than a third-generation Siwash bedbug. The vindicated critics from the creeks were more than happy to let him know it, and to stand back and enjoy the long awaited last laugh.

Once again they grinned too soon.

Ten days ago, on the 8th of December, 1866, nine months and twenty-three days after leaving Montana with the quiet promise to do so, Nathan Stark had come back with his historic trailherd of 3000 wild-eyed Texas longhorns—the first southern cattle to set hoof north of the Oregon Trail.

Laughs were suddenly scarcer than Sunday School teachers in Virginia City's twenty-six saloons.

The herd was here. At that very moment it was peacefully spread out on the lush winter graze of the Yellowstone Forks, sixty miles northeast of the Alder Gulch diggings. Its 2500 beef steers had already been contracted for at a figure which paid back the cost of the drive ten times over. And the 500-head balance of service-age bulls and young she-stuff remained to fatten for spring and the certain serving of its planned purpose as the seedstock in Stark's "crazy dream" of making his million "running beef in the buffalo pasture."

Lazarus broke his thoughts long enough to glance quickly at Stark. The big man had not moved from the window, was still watching the two Texas ponies huddled at the Black Nugget's hitching rail. Lazarus knew why he watched them, and grew more anxious still.

In the past hour the big-hatted Texas trail crew which had brought the great herd on its long march from the parched plains of the Brazos to the fertile valley of the Yellowstone, had been paid off and cynically invited to

10

help themselves to all they wanted of Valley Tan and Montana Tanglefoot at Stark's Black Nugget bar—at six-bits the single shot, or eight dollars the black quart bottle. In the last minutes of that hour, only seconds ago now, Ben Allison, the tall San Saba boy who had bossed the drive from Mile One to its Montana terminus, had said his awkward goodbyes to Nathan Stark and walked out of the Nugget's banking room with the one thing above hard money and certain success Stark had ever set his heart on—Nella Torneau.

With the thought of the green-eyed Texas girl, the old moneylender shook his head, shut off the backflow of memory, brought his uneasy mind to bear on the immediate, restless moment. He was in time to see Stark's heavy-maned head shift slightly, his light blue eyes flick to the right, covering the street door exit of the Nugget's main salon. He moved noiselessly behind him, improving his own view.

They were coming now, laughing, bantering, slapping happily at the bracing bite of the new snow, moving up the boardwalk, past the window, toward the waiting ponies—Ben Allison and Nella Torneau, Texans both and both impatient for but one thing—to point their crowbait cowponies toward the land of the Lone Star, leaving Nathan Stark and Montana Territory as far and fast behind as a jingling mustang trot could manage.

Lazarus could not see the sharp narrowing of Stark's pale eyes as the girl legged gracefully up, laughed, leaned down, kissed her grinning escort. But he could guess it from the cat-tense way the massive blond head

11

turned to track the departing riders up Van Buren and past the corner of Wallace Street. Only when the little ponies had faded into the thickening snow and were gone, did the big man break his silence. Even then he did not turn from the window, but offered the thought as though to the outer night and the increasing cry of the wind.

"He's beaten me, Esau. Fair and square and four ways from the middle."

His companion wagged his lean white head.

"Nonsense, Nathan. You've won again. He has left you everything."

Now Stark broke off his staring into the blind swirl of the snow, came around from the window. He looked through and past the older man, his deep voice deceptively soft. *"Everything,"* he said cryptically, *"and nothing."*

Once more Lazarus let the stillness grow, weighing his reply, studying the other.

Stark was a big man, big in the brute sense that a bear or a bull is big. Still, if you knew him, you knew there was nothing whatever of ursine good nature or bovine gentleness about him. He stood six-feet-two inches in the thin leathers of his forty-dollar Cordovan boots, weighed two-hundred and twenty-three pounds under the expensive drape of his settlement-tailored broadcloths. Yet if there was an ounce of physical or sentimental fat in either that huge body or the seemingly emotionless mind that controlled it, the old Jew had never discovered it. His momentary soft thoughtfulness

12

warned Lazarus to be slow with his next words, but did not otherwise delude him.

"You say he has left you everything and nothing," he nodded. "I do not follow you, Nathan. You have the cattle, the entire territory's respect and the camp's full credit for the drive. You have eight hundred per cent on your money and the brightest future in Montana. *Is it the woman then?*"

"Yes." Stark never walked around anything. Nor stepped over it. He had a blunt honesty, as brutal with himself as with others. "I wanted her, Ben took her. It's what I meant when I said he left me nothing."

The old man squinted shrewdly at him. "Is that *all* you meant, Nathan?"

"No." When the other said it, his light eyes darkened ominously. Recognizing the familiar warning, Lazarus heeded it, said nothing. Shortly Stark concluded, his heavy voice flat as the crack of a bullwhip. "I meant to kill him."

Lazarus fought off the chill his companion's unnatural coldness under emotional stress always brought up in him. He nodded again, probing gently, knowing the merciless way the big man's mind worked, and the care that had to be taken in questioning its decisions. "Yet you did not kill him, Nathan. Why?"

"Because," rasped Stark bitterly, "in his dumb, simple way he made me let him be my friend. And do you know what he got for that, Esau? What it cost me to let down and like a man for the first time in ten years? *The only woman I ever wanted in my life!*"

Again the pale-eyed pause, and again Lazarus knew when to wait.

"I said Ben Allison left me nothing. I was wrong. He left me a lesson I'll never forget."

"Never to let another man be your friend?" queried Esau Lazarus gently.

"That," grated Stark, "and one thing more."

He turned back to the window, looked long into the blinding drive of the snow, said it softly and with the acid bitterness of gall.

"Never to love another woman."

The four horsemen rode two and two, the tall youth and the girl first, then their leathery-faced chaperons. Chickasaw Billings and Waco Fentriss, who had belatedly decided to make the long ride back home with the young couple, were a pair of entirely competent, if unlovely, *dueñas*. Both were oldsters by cowboy standards, the former grumpily "staring sixty in the offside eye," the latter piously and repeatedly "swearing to thirty-nine since he was forty-three, six years ago." Both were, equally, and in their own words, "post-graduate pear-thicket poppers," men who had been born to the musical bawl of a night-bedding herd and who hoped to be buried to the same prairie-sweet strain. The uneasy instincts of the veteran cattleman, put on current edge by the threatening weather, were showing plainly in the wiry riders' talk as they followed their youthful companions.

"I don't cotton to the whoop and holler of this here

wind," growled Chickasaw. "I done felt it before. It ain't the kind that blows nobody nothing but bad."

"It ain't," agreed Waco, eying the piling black clouds and broken moonlight above. "And I don't especially care for the look of that sky—nor for its smell. I reckon a big snow don't stink no different in Montana than in Texas."

"I reckon," grunted his companion. Then, calling sharply back. "Watch this damn trail here. She's softening up."

"Better sing out to Ben," answered Waco. "He's been so infernal busy mooning at his missus-to-be he ain't once looked at the trail since we left town."

"Leave him be," grinned Chickasaw dourly. "He ain't feeling no pain."

Waco nodded and fell silent. As the old man had said, the going was getting a mite spongy and a man had best be watching his pony's feet.

The four riders were following the Virginia City-Salt Lake stage road south. At the moment of old Chickasaw's warning to Waco, the wheel-rutted track was turning the crumbling shoulder of Rotten Rock Mountain, a shelving, decomposing granite giant guarding the north-plunging course of the Madison River far below. The road was cut into the living rock at a few anchor spots, and otherwise consisted mainly of poorly graded fills of precariously lodged detritus. Its downgrade, nearly thirty per cent here where the route pitched riverward to reach and cross over the Madison, was murderous. Much taken with his green-eyed promised one, or not, Ben Allison knew a bad place in the trail when his big gelding set his careful feet into its warning, half-frozen slush. He reined the tall black in, told the girl to drop her sorrel mare back, giving him at least three pony-lengths of lead. He had just given the black his head, starting him downward again, when it happened.

There was no warning rumble, no advance sign of the ground giving away. There was just a sudden, sickening lurch and 500 feet of mountainside came away.

Nella had time to throw her startled mare on its haunches, inches short of the caving edge. Behind her Waco and Chickasaw sat down hard on their panicky mounts. For many seconds the billowing cloud of old snow and grinding rockdust thrown up by the avalanche obscured the canyon depths. Then the rising wind swept under it, lifted, swirled and drove it momentarily free of the swift winter flood of the Madison. The same wind, in the next breath, broke a ragged hole in the lowering scud of snow clouds, letting the frosty moonlight through for a suspended heartbeat.

It was enough.

Directly beneath them the slide had piled to a thunderous rest halfway across and blocking the stream's bed. A hundred yards below the choke of the dislodged boulders, a black dot bobbed and twisted in the downstream torrent—Ben's gelding, somehow miraculously thrown free and still alive.

But in all the visible 600-yard stretch of lashing water below the rockslide dam there was no second, smaller dot. The cliffside watchers waited through the following, interminable minute of moonlight. They saw nothing.

When, seconds later, the wind slammed shut its fleeting window in the storm, old Chickasaw Billings said it as gently as he could. "He's gone, Nella. There ain't no chance on God's green prairie for it to be no other way."

The girl said nothing. They could not see her face in the darkness and, after an awkward moment of silence, Waco shouldered his mount forward. "I seen a place back yonder about a quarter-mile where I think we can get down to the river. You want we should try it, Miss Nella? I allow we ought."

This time they could make out her answer from the wordless bob of her Stetson. Both knew enough about the way she had felt about Ben, not to ask for details. Waco swung his pony around.

Through the next hopeless hour, aided by the continuing patchy breakthroughs of the winter moon, they searched the jumbled surface of the slide from river's edge to canyon apex. They worked downstream from it on foot, hand-leading their mounts and covering every yard of the Madison's tortuous west bank on out to the canyon's mouth.

Here the open water was embraced, bank to bank, with a solid sheeting of rough river ice, and here they found the black gelding where the treacherous current had relented and spewed him out. Guided by the wounded beast's pitiful whickerings, Chickasaw worked his way precariously out from the bank. Nella and Waco, holding the horses, flinched as the single shot muffled back to them through the increasing smother of the snow. Shortly, Chickasaw's wind-bent form loomed up out of the whirling flakes.

"Saddle was pulled clean off him," he grunted, trying to make it sound matter of fact, or at least as though it could not have been helped, and failing badly on both counts. "Reins was busted clean through right up by the bit rings. All he had left on him was a piece of noseband and the splitear leather." He paused, moving closer to the girl, not trying any more to fool anybody. "Our boy's under them rocks up yonder. I wisht to God there was something else I could tell you, but there ain't. Ben's gone. From you, from me, from Waco. He ain't never coming back, Nella."

For the first time since the crashing roar of the avalanche began, Nella Torneau spoke. "I know," she murmured, low-voiced. Then, lower still. "I knew it an hour ago up on the ledge."

"I reckon we all did, Miss Nella," said Waco softly.

Chickasaw let it rest there. Taking his pony's reins from his headhung friend, he swung stiffly aboard. "We'd best be going," he gruffed. "Snow's coming on for sure now." He peered up at the race of swollen black clouds across the narrow opening of the canyon above. "She's going to be a mean bad un. We'll have to hump it."

"Whichaway?" scowled Waco, holding Nella's mare as the girl mounted silently. "Me, I don't care no more, somehow."

"It's about a dead draw," grunted his companion. "Same distance to the Madison stage depot south, as back north to Virginny City. It's up to Nella, I reckon." He kneed his pony closer. "What you say, girl? We cain't set here all winter."

She nodded, her voice as suddenly sharp as the way she wheeled her mare away from them. "You boys ain't beholden to share my trail. I don't think you'd cotton to the one I figure I've got to ride now, anyhow."

"What you trying to say?" It was old Chickasaw, eying her through the dark. "That we ain't wanted nor needed no more now that Ben's gone?"

"No. Outside of Ben, you're the only real friends I've ever had."

"Well then, ma'am"—Waco now, sorely puzzled, strangely awkward—"what is it you're meaning to tell us?"

Nella tried to make her answer hard and short, but there was no hiding the choked-back sob in it. "That you'd better ride your own way and let me ride mine, that's all!" With the broken words she kicked the little sorrel up the bank and back onto the stage road, heeling her into the teeth of the wind and due north back toward the distant lights of Alder Gulch.

"Now what," said the slow-drawling Waco, "the hell do you suppose she meant by that?"

"I dunno," replied Chickasaw testily. "You cain't tell nothing about a hard woman when she's heartbroke. And, mister," he nodded acidly, "that there's a hard woman." He shifted his cud of longleaf Burley, pursed his weathered lips, spat thinly downwind. "How-somever," he added thoughtfully, "there's one sure way to find out what's cankering her. I reckon we owe it to old Ben to tail her for a spell."

"Yeah," agreed Waco. "No matter you and me never quite figured her for him, they was true in love."

"They was," said Chickasaw. "Let's go."

"We're gone," nodded the other, and put his roan scrambling up the bank after the girl's sorrel.

Chickasaw held back, reining his bony gray around, up-canyon. He looked swiftly through the inky darkness of the Madison's towering chasm and toward the invisible upstream jumble of broken granite that was all the Montana headstone Ben Allison would ever have.

"We'll look after her, boy," he called softly, "as close and best as two old cowboys can—"

CHAPTER TWO

THE FORKS of the Yellowstone was a place to gladden the eye of the oldest cattleman. There was grass there, and water, as fine as any in all the Big Pasture. There was Fort C. F. Smith, only a two-day ride over east on the Big Horn, to guard a man's herd from getting rustled and raided to death by any unhappy Absarokas and Blackfeet who might have the gall to figure they were there first and that the graze belonged to them and their precious buffalo. The Forks also lay level and open with no heavy timber or deep-cut canyons to lose stock in. It was just about perfect cow country, providing one thing—that a man got every last head of his cattle out of it right back of the first fall snow flurries, and did not bring them back in again until the new grass was three weeks green the following spring.

Slim Blanchard and Hogjaw Bivins, the two cowboys of the original trail crew, who along with Saleratus McGivern the camp cook had been persuaded by Stark to stay on with the herd and help with the beef-steer deliveries, were finding that out with a subzero vengeance as they fought their ponies free of the last drift and headed them into the wind toward the woodsmoke smell of Saleratus's fire.

"God Amighty, Slim!" gasped the hulking Hogjaw. "You ever have any idee it could get so mother-loving cold? Jesus! I don't mind the snow but this here wind ought to be arrested for carrying a knife."

Slim was a more serious man, had seen a lot of trouble in his time and saw some more yet to come.

"Save your breath, boy, it ain't funny. We're a long way from home and this snow's only starting."

"What you reckon we'd ought to do?" Hogjaw was not grinning now.

Slim waited for a dead spot in the wind, called his answer across it. "Just the opposite of what them damned steers are doing!"

"How's that?" yelled the other.

"They're drifting *with* the wind. We'd better drift *into it,* and some fast."

"You mean head for Virginny City? In this weather, man? You're crazy!"

"Crazy if we do, froze solid if we don't. Take your pick. Me, I'm cutting my stick." Slim's voice sharpened. "You see fire color just then? Off to the left?"

"Yeah. We're heading just right. Sure funny how dead-true smoke smell will hold in a wind like this."

"Cain't see nothing funny to it. Bear left, your hoss's lugging out on you."

Slim swung his mount. Seconds later the full red stain of Saleratus's campfire flared through the horizontal slant of the snow. They got off their horses in the lee of the eight-foot lean-to of unpeeled squaw-pine poles they had put up for wind shelter while they laid out and got up the walls for their winter shack. The conference with Saleratus was as salty and alum-tart as one of his own baking powder biscuits. It was a meeting of three western minds with but a single thought. It broke up in less than thirty seconds, with Saleratus loading up a gunnysackful of cold grub while Slim wrangled him a saddlemount from the string in the pole corral back of the lean-to and Hogjaw caught up and haltered the packmule. Ten minutes after they had come in from the storm, the two cowboys were back out in it again. Behind them came Saleratus towing the packmule. Within seconds the fire stain was gone, the world about them a roaring, hollow, whirling white hell.

"Well, Esau, how do we stand?" Stark looked quickly at the account book Lazarus was just closing, his intense interest in money and the things it meant reflected in the way he stabbed the question at the old banker.

"We stand very well, Nathan," replied the latter. "When the last of the beef contracts are filled you will have realized something better than one hundred thousand dollars on the Texas venture."

Stark nodded, his jaw moving forward and setting aggressively. "It's not enough. I know it isn't. You know it isn't. You don't think I'll ever make it now, do you Esau?"

Lazarus knew what he meant. Stark had always said that he would make his million before he was thirty years old, and his mark too. He had never boasted openly of the vow but was as deadly serious about it as he was about everything he said. Nathan Stark was a literal man. When he said a million dollars he did not mean nine hundred thousand. When he said thirty years old he did not mean thirty-five, or forty, or sometime—he meant thirty years old. And when he said "make his mark" he meant that he would make it higher up on history's wall than any other man in the territory; that he would be, beyond contemporary question, the "biggest man in Montana."

"I don't know, Nathan. You have a chance. A man like you always has a chance."

Stark shook his head. "I know what you're thinking. I'm twenty-nine years old. That gives me exactly one year to run a hundred thousand into ten hundred thousand. You know men, you know money, you know arithmetic. It doesn't add up, does it?"

"It might," said the old man meaningly, *"for you."*

Stark's jaw clamped down hard on the bone of his

companion's implication. "You think I would stop at nothing where money is concerned. That I would do anything, to anybody, to get where I am going. And that when a man thinks like that it changes all the odds, sand-bags all the bets and raises three kinds of hell with Hoyle—is that it?"

Lazarus got up slowly. He put the account book care-fully in its compartment, closed the rolltop of the elegant mahogany desk, locked it, handed the ornate key to Stark. "I know you, Nathan," he said quietly. "The quality of mercy is not in you. You will make your million—"

He left it thus, suspended, and moved quickly for the door. As quickly, Stark stepped in front of him. "But what?" he demanded challengingly.

"But you will never be wealthy," said the old Jew softly, and stepped around him and went out of the room.

Stark was still staring at the door when it reopened. It was a tribute to the big Montanan's perfect nerves that not even a face muscle moved as he cocked his head and inquired icily, "Don't they knock on doors where you come from?"

Nella moved on into the room, shut the door quickly. "Where I come from they don't even have doors. They hang a green cowhide over a hole in the wall."

Stark looked at her, shrugged, made it short. He was like all chance takers. He never questioned the odds, never argued the payoff price. But once he had bet into a bad hand and been cleaned down to his last blue, he was through with that set of cards from then on. He never wanted to see them again. To him Nella Torneau

24

was a played-out hand. His blunt question let her know as much.

"What do you want? And don't stall me, Nella. I've had all I want of you and Ben. So ask it and get out."

"You made me an offer once. Was there a time limit on it?"

For a rare, ugly moment Stark's face flushed darkly. As quickly the twisted look smoothed, the normal dead-heavy set of his features returned. "It ran out the minute you rode off up Van Buren Street with Ben," he nodded.

"No options?" she asked quietly.

"No options," he said.

"Any new offers?"

"None."

She returned his cold nod, started for the door without saying anything more. He was instantly ahead of her. "Wait a minute. What the devil's going on here? Where's Ben? What's happened?"

"Ben's dead," she heard herself saying.

"Where? How?"

"Rockslide. That bad grade where the stage road goes down to the river. We turned around and came back."

"Who's we?"

"Waco and Chickasaw."

"They outside?"

She shook her head, white face tightening. "They don't like you nor your whiskey, Mr. Stark. They're waiting for me up at the Big Horn. Sorry to have bothered you—" Once more she started out, and again he checked her.

25

"Listen Nella, I don't know what your game is and I don't care. You stay on your side of the street and I'll stay on mine. The camp's big enough for both of us, but get one thing straight. *You and I are all through.* You understand that? Fool me once, I'll maybe sit still for it. Try it twice and you'll wind up awful sick. Is that clear?"

Nella's full lips twisted bitterly. "Perfectly. I didn't come here to apologize, or admit I was wrong. I came back to make a business deal, straight across the board. No jokers, no wild cards. Take it or leave it. That's all."

"Not quite," said Stark. "You and I made a deal a long time ago. Down in Fort Worth, remember? If I brought you up to Montana and set you up at a fancy faro table in the Nugget, you'd buy your chips in my game. You crossed me on that and I asked you to marry me." He paused, nodding grimly. "Do you remember what I offered you, Nella?"

"That's driftwood," she murmured. "It's piled on the bank long ago."

"But you remember it."

"Yes."

"And now that Ben's gone you think you can come back here and pick up the next best offer, do you? Just like that. Cut and dried. No jokers you say, no wild cards! That's a bad laugh, Nella. You never played a straight hand in your life!"

"It breaks us out of the gate dead even," she answered sharply.

"What do you mean by that?" growled Stark.

26

"Neither did you," she said levelly.

He looked at her and laughed. Stark could laugh. It was not an impossible act for him. But usually, as with now, it was not a pleasant sound and the expression in his pale eyes did not warm it any.

"All right, we're two of a kind. Let's leave it that way." He stared at her, deliberately running his appraising glance from the floor, up. When he had finished looking at her body, he came to her face. His eyes held there. "Maybe we can make a deal after all. Who knows? I might let you in on some cold night." He moved aside, clearing her way to the door. "Goodnight, Miss Torneau. And thanks for the call—"

His mocking bow was interrupted by the second banging-open of the door within as many minutes. This time the intruder was far from feminine. He was six-feet-and-then-some tall and his name was Lucius Clarence Bivins, though to have called him by it would have meant gunplay in most cases.

Hogjaw's quick eye took in Nella, looked for and did not see Ben, fastened on Stark.

"'Scuse me, Miss Nella, ma'am. I got to see Mr. Stark if you-all don't mind."

She nodded, started out. Stark, his knife-edged mind at work, spoke quickly. "Wait outside for me, Nella. I won't be a minute here. I'll buy you a drink for old time's sake. All right?"

She hesitated, shrugged, went on out. Hogjaw stepped in and Stark closed the door.

"What the hell are you doing in here, Bivins? Who's

27

with the cattle? Slim and McGivern?"

"Nobody's with the cattle, Mr. Stark. Snow's three foot on the level up there, with more piling on by the hour. We figured either we got out while a horse could still buck trail, or we didn't get out atall."

"What about the herd?" He asked it as calmly as though the sun were out and the new grass a foot high.

"If this wind holds and them steers keep drifting with it the way they was when we cut out, you'll have to make good on your beef contracts with thawed-out steaks come spring."

"That bad, eh?"

"We figure, yeah. Slim and me done what we could with the she-stuff and the old bulls. Them mossybacked old bastards done their share, too. They was doing more riding herd of them little pink-tit heifers than me and Slim ten times over."

Stark threw up his hands, barked the question. "For God's sake what are you talking about, Bivins? What's the situation up there? How many head do we stand to lose and how many can we possibly save?"

"What I'm talking about," grunted Hogjaw, "is us and them old herdbulls driving a good part of the young cow stuff into what little river timber there is in the crotch of the Forks; mebbe four, five hundred head in all."

"Otherwise?" snapped Stark.

"Otherwise," shrugged the tall cowboy, "you're plumb out of the beef business. We was holding the steer herd out on them south flats, away from the timber. Wind come mainly north-northwest, swerving mostly

28

around to drive due east, out onto them open plains. Last we seen, the beef herd was beginning to drift with it. My guess is they'll wind up snow-drifted and blizzard-froze to the last goddam head. There ain't no shelter in that open land for five days' ride in fair weather."

Stark took it as he took everything—with his face dead-blank and his mind turning a thousand times a minute. "But there's some chance we can pull the breeding herd through?" he asked softly.

"Not that I can see, Mr. Stark. There's native hay enough under that timber cover to carry the bunch a week, mebbe ten days. You figure this storm's gonna break up and melt off that fast?"

Stark did not say what he thought, or what he meant to do. "All right, Bivins," he said. "You and the boys wait out at the bar. I've got some business to wrap up and then I'll see you. Send Miss Nella back in here and tell Esau Lazarus I want to see him right away."

Hogjaw thought about it a minute, as though he was not going to do it, then grunted, "Yes sir," and walked out without closing the door.

When Nella came in moments later, Stark was back at the street window staring into the storm. He did not turn as he heard her, waited for her to speak.

"Hogjaw said you wanted to see me."

"That's right."

"Why?"

"I've changed my mind. The offer still holds if you want it."

Nella colored deeply. Her slender jaw tensed, making

29

her curving mouth a hard straight line.

"The original offer?"

"Precisely," said Nathan Stark. "One half of everything I own, or ever will own, for your hand in legal wedlock. Wasn't that it?"

"It was."

"Well, what do you say?"

"I don't know. What changed your mind so sudden?"

"I asked for an answer, yes or no."

He put it bluntly, his flat, dust-dry voice letting her know she could take it or leave it.

For a last moment she hesitated, her mind full of doubts, empty of answers. If she married Stark now, Ben's Texas friends, and indeed her *only* friends in the frontier world, would never forgive her. Being men, and tough-minded men at that, they would not understand or accept her reason. But what if she did not marry him? Would these Texas friends take care of her, guarantee her future? They could not do so and she knew it. Waco, Chickasaw, Hogjaw, Slim, Saleratus? My God, they were just camp tramps, drifters, cow country tumbleweeds, exactly as she herself had been before knowing Ben Allison and Nathan Stark. Among them they could not rake up a stake big enough to buy cards, once around, in the smallest pot Stark ever sat to. Beyond that, she herself was destitute. Every penny she and Ben owned had gone down the side of the mountain in his moneybelt. No, it was settle with Stark, or work the street. As a moral choice there was not a great difference, but her situation was not a moral one. At least not in *her* mind. What she sought from Stark was a legal solution. It was what had brought her bitterly back to him and what he was now reoffering her. No amount of doubts, no lack of answers, no heartsinking thoughts of Ben and the happiness she had almost had could alter that fact. He had just told her she could take it or leave it, but that was a hard-eyed lie. She could not leave it.

During the long pause Stark had not moved from the window. Now he turned.

"Well—?"

She wanted to say it looking him in the eye, with her head up and as though it were a matter of her own free choice and willful whim. She could not do it, and in the end had to lower her glance and say it to the rich oriental carpeting in front of his glistening boot-toes.

"Yes."

She looked up in time to see his pale eyes darken, his wide mouth turn up at the corners. It was not a smile, not even what passed for one in Stark's humorless repertoire of expressions. It was the lip-lifting look of a prairie lobo pulling back from a bad-smelling bait and wrinkling his broad muzzle to get rid of the offending taint.

"Lazarus will be here in a minute," he said matter-of-factly. "I'll have to fetch old Judge Hacker. He's handy."

For all her having made her decision and taken her last, hard step, his quiet words brought her up sharp. She knew Hacker for a whiskey-shot Justice of the Peace and disbarred eastern attorney who, in his rare moments of comparative sobriety, furnished the firm of Stark & Lazarus with fairly reliable advice on what could and could not be gotten away with under territorial law. More to the uneasy point, she knew he maintained a rathole office in the alley next to the Nugget, slept off his overloads of Valley Tan in its unheated garret and could be, if found sober, brought back to the Nugget's banking parlor in a matter of minutes.

"You don't mean tonight, I hope," she offered uncertainly.

"Hope in one hand, spit in the other," said Stark. "See which one gets wet first."

"What do you mean?" she asked wearily.

"To get married," he nodded easily. "Within the next ten minutes."

CHAPTER THREE

WHILE ESAU went for Hacker, old Saleratus was dispatched up the street to look for Waco and Chickasaw. At the same time, Hogjaw and Slim were instructed to start an immediate canvas of the Nugget's front bar and back poker tables to see how many of the old trail crew would sign on to fight the blizzard back up to Yellowstone Forks. The dour camp cook was first returned with his birds.

Waco and Chickasaw took the jolt of Nella's wedding announcement standing up. As a matter of fact they had not had time to sit down, when Stark put it to them. "As Ben's two best friends," grunted the big Montanan, "I thought you'd want to witness Miss Torneau's marriage to me. Woman's privilege, of course, though I doubt many have changed their minds so fast."

Chickasaw, the weaselly old chaparral rat from the sunny San Saba, squinted his beady eyes at Nella, demanded to know what in the sainted name of Sam Houston Stark was talking about. The girl told him plainly and simply that she had more than her memories of Ben to worry about right now, that she was tired of letting the western wind blow sand in her eyes, that it was a bad night out, she was alone and broke and fed up with ridgerunners and saddlebums, wanted only a warm, dry place to pack her dufflebag, plus a man who could pay the bills when they came due.

The most interesting part of this exchange of intelligences was that it was accomplished in front of Nathan Stark, and as though he were among those present but just not accounted for the way fellow Texans saw things. The Montanan did not let it bother him. When Nella had finished, and before anyone else could chip in, he merely flashed his heatless grin and sided in with her cool as well water. "Neither of us has any illusions, Chickasaw." The old man was the only one of the entire crew he called by first name. "Nella's marrying me for my money, I'm marrying her for, well, let's just say personal reasons. Ben doesn't figure in it either way."

"Mebbe he does with some of us," said the old cowboy acidly.

"How so?" queried Stark.

"Mebbe some of us ain't forgot him as fast as others." When he said it he looked accusingly at Nella. "I reckon me and Waco will be going along now. Air's getting tolerable close in here. Don't smell too good." He had already started for the door, Waco trailing him, when Nella's soft voice halted him.

"Chickasaw—"

"Yes ma'am."

"Hold on a minute. I got a question."

"So—"

"So what do you think Ben would want you to do? Stick by *me,* or walk out on *Stark?*"

The grizzled cattleman shifted his Burley, his mind jumping back to that last minute up in Madison Canyon when he had looked back toward the granite slide and said goodbye to Ben. He moved back toward the girl, chewed angrily, located Stark's gleaming, deskside spittoon, hit it dead center with a defiant stream. "I reckon you got me boxed, Nella," he grudged. "We'll see you through the ceremony, but we won't be staying for the celebration."

"I'm not asking you to," she said quickly. "I only want you to stay and see the way it goes."

"We'll stay," said the old man disgustedly, "but I can tell you how it's going to go."

A good if outraged friend, Chickasaw was a real bad prophet. Well within Stark's ten minutes the wedding was performed. It did not, however, come out anything at all like the crusty old Texan had imagined. Nor, for that matter, anything at all like Nathan Stark had.

Esau had scarcely ushered the owl-eyed Hacker to the door, given him his fee and pushed him out into the main salon when Stark was letting Nella and the others know what he had meant by "personal reasons."

"I'll make it short," he nodded to the white-faced girl. "You married me thinking I was wealthy, or at least on my sure way to being wealthy. You wronged me once. You doublecrossed me just as sure as I've done you. I haven't got a goddam nickel, Nella. I'm as broke as you are, and ten thousand dollars in debt."

"What you mean?" demanded Waco, moving forward.

"Just before Nella came back," said Stark, still looking at the girl, "Hogjaw showed up with Blanchard and McGivern. This storm hit there this morning. It caught the beef herd in the open, set the steers to drifting with it."

"Good God Almighty," said the little cowboy, "you've already tooken deposit money for deliveries ain't you?"

"Not only took it, but spent it. It's what I paid you hands off with."

"How about the she-stuff?" asked Chickasaw anxiously, his ingrained love of the native longhorns of his homeland rising at once above his dislike of Stark. "They was being held separate, wasn't they?"

"Yes. The boys managed to get them into the Forks timber."

"Any chance of getting to them?"

"Bivins says no. Claims there's three feet of snow on the level up there right now. You can see for yourselves that it isn't slowing up any."

"You fixing to try anyways?" Waco now, as anxious about the cattle as his ancient partner.

"Bivins and the others are out rounding up the crew

35

right now. If most of them are game to go, we just might get those heifers out of there."

Chickasaw shook his head. "If Hogjaw says it cain't be did, it cain't. I reckon you was right in the first place, Mr. Stark."

"How's that, Chickasaw?"

"Miss Nella married a pauper."

The old cowman's short words broke the talk off the cattle, brought it back to the brief brutal ceremony just past.

The Texas girl let them all look at her, her eyes hard and dry now, and unwavering under the regard of the three silent men. At last she nodded, speaking softly and bitterly to Nathan Stark.

"Mr. Stark, as long as you deal double that's the way you're going to get dealt to. I tried to apologize for going back on my promise to you, tried to tell you how it was with Ben and me, and why that would ruin it for you and me. You wouldn't listen because your breed just can't stand to lose a solitary thing they ever put their hands on. That's not my fault, it's yours. And it's your problem, not mine."

She paused, her low voice going softer still.

"Just now you married me for one reason alone—to get back at me for turning you down. You did it knowing you were dead broke and thinking I was crawling back here and marrying you for your money. You figured when I found out you didn't have a patched-up pot left to boil coffee in, I'd be served right and left mighty damned sorry I'd done you a wrong."

Again she broke off, but this time when she continued her green eyes were afire with a new and strangely fierce light. "You've had me wrong from the beginning, Mr. Stark. You may know men but the last woman you ever understood was your mother—if you ever had one. There's only one reason in God's world I'd marry you, mister, and money's just about as far from it as you could have guessed."

Stark's broad face went white. The normal heavy tan of it drained away as if he had been doused with a full bucket of lime-wash. His frosty blue eyes blinked rapidly, as though to clear a mind that knew what it had just heard, yet was refusing to accept it.

"By God," he said slowly, *"you wouldn't dare—"*

Nella actually laughed. She made a sound of laughing, anyway.

"Like I said, Mr. Stark, you've got a lot to learn about me."

"I think," nodded the latter, "you will find that is going to work both ways." He had himself back under rein now, held hard back on the bit of his anger. *"Is it Ben's?"*

Nella nodded, dropped her eyes as she caught the unbelieving stares of Waco and Chickasaw.

"We were going to be married in Fort Worth."

"But why me?" rumbled Stark. "For the love of God, why *me?*"

"It needed a name," murmured Nella Torneau, "and needed one quick. There was a future to be guaranteed, the best one to be had. The least I could do for Ben was to get his baby a good name. I got one. *Yours.*"

37

Stark strode toward her, the blank calm of his face more threatening than any anger. "Take it then," he rasped. "Take it and get out! I've got a herd of cattle to save!"

Nella shook her head, her eyes hardening again.

"*We've* got a herd of cattle to save, mister," she corrected softly. "That herd's half mine now, remember? We made a deal. There wasn't any strings to it."

"Get out," repeated Stark flatly. "You've got what you came back for. You don't need me anymore and I sure don't need you."

Before Nella could answer, the door opened and Hogjaw Bivins clumped in. He was followed by Slim and Saleratus—and that was all. Not another cowboy of the original Texas crew showed behind them, nor were they about to. Stark understood that as soon as the three envoys got over their happy surprise at seeing Waco and Chickasaw, both of whom they had thought were long gone down the Texas trail.

"Mr. Stark," drawled Hogjaw—none of the Texans had ever left off mistering him—"I got bad news for you. I reckon old Luke Easterday said it the best."

"And how," echoed Stark acridly, "did old Luke say it?"

"Old Luke," grunted Hogjaw, very clearly contented with being a bearer of bad news where Nathan Stark was concerned, "he said he wouldn't walk thirty feet to the backhouse for you in a April shower, let alone buck a Montana blue norther forty miles on horseback in the dead of a damn Yankee December."

38

"They won't go then?"

"No sir. Not a mother's son of them."

"How about you three?"

"Not me, Mr. Stark."

"Nor me," added Slim.

"She's unanymous," said Saleratus.

"Chickasaw? Fentriss?" Stark whirled on Waco and the old man. The latter shook his head. "We ain't lost no heifers in no Forks timber," he said quietly. "I reckon you're all alone, Mr. Stark."

"I'll go." They had forgotten Nella, and her soft voice startled them. "Our deal didn't say anything about how deep the snow might get. It just said for better or for worse. Let's get a move on, mister. I'll help you with those heifers."

Watching her tired young body straighten, seeing the way she stood up and talked to Stark, her eyes holding his and her voice as quiet and calm as the big man's own, the Texas hands looked down at the rug, scuffed their boots around awkwardly. In the silence Stark's words rode in harsh and quick.

"I'm not asking your help and I don't need it. Not it, nor you. Now you and your loyal friends just head for that door and never mind looking back. You've got your baby a name and you've got the license paper there to prove it. That's all you're ever going to get from me. *Now move!*"

Nella ignored him. Behind her, the five Texas cowboys were motionless.

"Maybe," she said slowly, "you don't need me." She

caught his angry eye and held it. "But how about Waco and Chickasaw? And maybe even Hogjaw and Slim and Saleratus? There's five tophands in any man's snow-storm, mister."

Stark knew her well enough to sense she was not just talking, or stalling. She had something in mind.

"You heard what they said," he parried, watching her. "They won't work for me."

"That's right." Her nod was as careful as his. "But they might for me."

"The devil you say! It's not me they're afraid of. It's the snow."

"Think so?" said Nella. It was a last thin hand she was drawing to, but she bluffed it out. Her smoky-green eyes fastened on old Chickasaw hopefully. "What do you say, Chickasaw? Will you work for me?"

The old cowboy clamped down on his chaw stub-bornly, his bristly chin protruding. "I reckon I'll stick around till spring anyhow," he muttered. "Got to see what Ben's boy looks like." He shrugged as though the decision were of no weight one way or the other. "Might as well be busy meanwhile."

"Waco?" She turned the brilliant emerald of her eyes on the wizened little bronco buster from Uvalde County.

"Hell, I cain't leave Chickasaw to winter by his lone-some. The old fool couldn't make it through a hard freeze without he had me to look after him."

"Hogjaw?"

"Well now damn it all, Miss Nella, you know both them old mossybacks are old enough to be buried in

40

Dan'l Boone's backyard. I reckon you got to have one hand less'n sixty-eight come spring. I'll stick."

"And me," chimed in Slim dolefully. "I wouldn't be near miserable enough less'n I had to keep bunking with Lucius Clarence."

Nella nodded, the fleeting smile speaking her gratitude. "It leaves you, Saleratus," she said softly to the scowling cook.

"The hell it does!" snapped the latter. "If those four idjuts ain't got no better sense than to go along with you, I'm damned if I have. Besides, you might get another cook and the change to good food could be fatal. Somebody's been eating my grub for a year steady, he's got to be tarnal careful how he tapers off'n it. The shock is apt to kill him."

With the last of the Brazos noblemen having cast his complaining ballot, Nella faced Stark quietly.

"Now do you need me, mister?"

The big man's face was an absolute rock. He did not make a sound for five seconds while he looked first at Nella Torneau, then at the five embarrassed cowboys.

When at last he answered her, the bad-bait wolf grin was back around the corners of his wide mouth.

"I can use you," he said cynically, and turned and brushed past them, toward the door. His hand on the burnished bronze knob, he paused, his strange, light-colored eyes seeking out the Texas girl. "And believe me, Miss Nella, ma'am," he parroted the respectful vernacular of the southern cowboys with the cruel accuracy of etching acid, *"I will."*

41

CHAPTER FOUR

FOR THE FIRST two-thirds of the return journey the going was bad. After that it got worse.

When the Texas trail crew referred to the distance from Virginia City to the Forks as "forty miles," they were using a cowboy euphemism, a figure of professional speech which meant, roughly, "a good day's ride." This distance might actually be anywhere between thirty and sixty miles, depending on the "lay of the trail," the "doingness" of the horse involved and, most important, "the size of a man's hurry."

In the present case it was fifty-eight crowflight miles, over the north spur of the Madison Mountains, from the Black Nugget's front door to the snowpiled cookfire lean-to in the Yellowstone's scanty Forks timber. The way Stark and his grim little band had to ride it, going around the Madisons to hit east for Bozeman Road, it was nearer seventy-five miles—and a black, freezing-cold, snowfight every foot of the way.

They made it safely into Bozeman only because of Stark's hard knowledge of his adopted land, and because of the extra cautions of preparation that knowledge had led him to make. Each of the seven riders led a spare, ready-saddled mount. They changed horses every half-hour, a fresh pair of riders taking the lead to break trail on every change. In these almost military maneuvers, Nella Torneau was not spared. The Texas cowboys would have let her, in fact forced her, as a woman and as the seventh, odd horseman, to ride at all times in the comparative ease and safety of their six-horse lee. But Stark deliberately chose her for his trail partner in the first pairings, subsequently saw to it that she rode her entire full share of point and trailbreak time.

They got into Bozeman late the next morning, rested two hours, traded for fresh horses, resaddled, rode on. At eight o'clock that night, half frozen, utterly exhausted, having been three times lost since leaving the wagon road and following Hogjaw instead of Stark, they at last stumbled into the outer fringes of the Forks timber. Half an hour later they found the lean-to and its lifesaving supply of cut firewood, stored food, pole corrals and stacked hay for the horses.

Even so, Hogjaw's belated homing-in on the campsite was very close to being *too close.* Chickasaw and Saleratus, the senior citizens of the southern constituency, had ridden too many years down the long trail to survive eighteen hours of subzero exposure and exertion unscathed. They had to be literally "broken" out of their saddles and carried bodily into the lean-to. Waco and Slim Blanchard, younger by not enough years to argue about, had just the strength remaining to do the breaking-out and packing-in of their frozen friends. Meanwhile, Stark was doing as much for Nella Torneau and Hogjaw was fumbling up a roaring blaze of pine-knots and pitchy balsam burls.

Examination, roughly directed by Stark, revealed that Nella's hands and feet were all right, needed only the warmth of the fire to restore their slowed circulation.

The same was true of Waco and Slim and, naturally, Hogjaw Bivins. The latter, not yet twenty years old and possessed of the constitutional toughness of a timber wolf, took the weather in his six-and-a-half-foot stride and without batting a calm gray Confederate eye. Old Chickasaw Billings and Saleratus McGivern were two horses of a more ancient and less durable color. Both had to be stripped and snow-rubbed for the better part of an anxious hour before the warning dead-white began to leave their extremities and Nathan Stark ordered them blanketed and brought in by the fire.

It was crowding ten o'clock before the latter had his exhausted followers all in fair shape and sitting up and taking notice of the supper he had slung together while Hogjaw had unsaddled the ponies, rubbed each of them dry with handfuls of fragrant, handcut prairie hay, turned them loose in the cozy shelter of the pole corral.

The half-boiled beans and moldy bacon were got down in a silence broken only by the requesting or acknowledging grunts of the diners. Within minutes the last of the tin plates was licked clean and stacked by the sheetmetal sheepherder's stove, the fire banked and Stark sitting the first watch over it.

By ten-thirty the only sounds within the blanket-hung lean-to were those of the uneasily deep sleep of that last fatigue which barely precedes death by freezing. Nathan Stark, huge body still unbeaten, weary brain still struggling against the exhaustion which had claimed his fellows, crouched over the smoldering warmth of the fire. His last thought and last, slow-turning look before the

44

numbness creeping upward through his limbs reached his mind were for the hauntingly beautiful features of Nella Torneau.

At daybreak the wind fell off and the snowfall suddenly lessened. The oppressive clouds lifted up and away from the Yellowstone Forks. There was still no sun, and no hint of one. The daylight was as cold and colorless as a granite headmarker, the blizzard merely having drawn in its swollen belly to gain a second wind and, in the doing, laid bare the sullen snow-covered land for a brief uneasy hour. Nathan Stark, knowing the treacherous nature of the northern winter from having fought it for ten years along the High Plains freight routes of a dozen isolated mountain bonanzas, sniffed the dead air, scowled, set his blunt jaw, ducked back into the silent lean-to.

"Chickasaw—" He touched the old man lightly, holding his voice down. "Come along outside. I want to talk to you." To Waco and Saleratus, who had each rolled up on one elbow when he spoke to their comrade, he held up a warning hand. "Roll out," he said softly. "Get the fire going and the grub on. Let the others sleep while they can."

Outside, he put it to Chickasaw in a way that was anything but soft and easy as he had talked inside. "Listen, oldtimer," he nodded. "We've got to do whatever we're going to do within the next hour or so. This still spell won't hold. When the wind sets in again it will turn your whiskers inside out." His companion instinctively felt of

45

his straggly white beard, nodded back. "I've bent to some tall blows in my time, youngster. Get on with it. You didn't call me out here to discuss no goddam Montana zephyrs, nor to elucydate on how hard the wind whistles at these here high altytudes. What you want to know?"

Stark did not miss the unusual use of the familiar address. It was the first time the old cowboy had called him anything but mister, and he knew that somewhere, somehow, between Virginia City and the present moment, Chickasaw had changed his mind a bit—or was thinking of changing it a bit in his favor. He filed the little tribute in his mind for possible future use, answered the question sharply.

"Ben always told me you knew more about cattle than any man alive. I'm counting on that."

Chickasaw looked at him, nodded. "With him gone that may be so. You still ain't told me what you want to know."

"One thing," said Stark. "Can you get this bunch of young stock out of this timber and back up the road toward Bozeman?"

"I might," said the old man. "Why? You rather they'd freeze to death back there than up here?"

Stark's cold eyes kindled. His big hand shot out and seized the other's thin shoulder.

"Chickasaw," he muttered fiercely, "you get those heifers up Bozeman way in good shape and I'll show you something that will make your cattleman's heart hurt, it's that beautiful and unbelievable."

46

"That so? How far up Bozeman way?"

"About ten miles this side."

"Whereaway after that?"

"South by west, maybe another ten, fifteen miles."

"All right, supposing I get 'em up to the turnoff for you, then what?"

"Then, by God, they're safe. From there I can show you the way into a valley you won't believe after you see it. If we can get the cattle into it we won't lose a single head all winter."

"Yeah. Where's all this, Mr. Stark?"

"Never mind that. Can you get the herd through the drifts between here and the turnoff?"

"I can try. It's all any old wore-out stud can do."

"Trying won't cut it, Chickasaw. Not by half. I want a yes or a no. Maybe's won't save any heifers."

"They won't, Mr. Stark, that's a fact."

"Well?"

"Well, sir, I reckon likely me and the General can bring it off for you, seeing you're so set on a centerfire answer."

"You and who?" said Stark, puzzled.

"General Grant, Mr. Stark." He gestured toward the black brush of the timbered brakes. "Ain't a critter in the herd that's took a solitary step since leaving a gathering grounds outside Fort Worth, that ain't tooken it in the due process of following old General Grant."

"And who the hell," queried Stark with suddenly rising suspicion, "is General Grant?"

"If you'd paid half the mind to your cattle on the drive

47

up here that you did to that long-legged gal in yonder," Chickasaw nodded at the lean-to and Nella Torneau, "you'd know who he was." The old man eyed him. "However," he nodded speculatively, "it ain't too late." He turned and started for the pole corral and the whickering ponies.

"Come along, Mr. Stark. Grab yourself a hoss. I allow it's high time you and the General met up with one another. Likely you'll get on famous. You're both cut out'n the same bolt of bad cloth."

CHAPTER FIVE

STARK HAD by no means spent all his time on the long ride up from Texas with Nella. He had learned plenty about trailherding the wild, unpredictable, weirdly nervous Spanish longhorn. Among the many things he remembered was that in any herd, be it one of but dozens or of several thousands of head, there was always and apparently by natural selection, a single leader. This animal, who would relinquish his point position only to death or the unremitting efforts of the trail drivers to push him back in the herd, was usually an old pear-thicket mossyback of an outlaw steer— one who had escaped many previous roundups and who, finally popped out of the brush and brought into rider-bound captivity, was determined unfailingly to lead the way back to freedom. All the trailwise drivers had to do was point this one old steer in the right direction and let him ramble. The whole herd would

48

follow him till the last calf dropped.

So it was that as he rode toward the river timber with Chickasaw he had a very good idea who and what "General Grant" was. He knew, as well, that the old man had something in mind beyond introducing him to the herd's lead steer. It did not occur to him to question what the lead steer might be doing remaining with the heifers while his brother steers had drifted off before the storm. But he got that, and some other answers, fairly quick.

As they closed in on the timber he noticed Chickasaw examining the fringe trees with intent swiftness. He made nothing of that and when the old cowboy called out for him to swing his horse a bit to the left and cut into the brush "yonder by that broke-down birch," he obeyed unquestioningly.

He had not pushed his mount a dozen paces toward the brushpile behind the down birch, when it erupted in a shower of exploding snow and flying dead branches. The next instant his little Texas mustang, long trained in the Rio Pecos near thickets, spun on his near rear foot, lunged sideways to escape the blundering rush of the red-eyed monster which had materialized out of the birch tangle. The little horse was fast but the footing was faster. His digging haunches shot out from under him and he went down, crupper first, spilling Stark into a nearby snowbank.

He did not spend much time in this questionable cover. By the time the attacking longhorn had wheeled from his first charge, the big Montanan was up and running. He beat the snorting brute to the base of a low-

49

branching cedar by three jumps and a flying scramble. Safely lodged on a sidelimb ten feet above ground, he stared down at Chickasaw malevolently. The old man, not batting an eye, waved unsmilingly toward the gaunt longhorn at the foot of the tree, then broadened the introductory gesture to include the man in its branches.

"Mr. Stark—General Grant. General, meet the boss."

Stark said nothing to Chickasaw. He improved his time and his knowledge of the breed by studying the rampant General.

He was first of all, and undeniably, no steer. The castrating knife and daubing creosote stick had never been plied upon General Grant. The ugly, thick-humping bulge of his crested neck, the depth to which his brisket carried down between his knobby forelegs, the tight-ringed curls massing his wide forehead, the arrogant, fierce roll of his tiny eyes, the uplifted stumpy bristle of his tail, all spoke eloquently of his unmitigated bullhood.

The General was, in fact, an atavism of the breed, a sportive throwback to the pure blood of the Spanish fighting bulls upon which the longhorn strain had been so richly and viciously founded. His horns were the glistening black scimitars of the arena animal rather than the clumsy, contorted sweep of the longhorn's. His build was that fine-boned, immensely muscled one of his dark-skinned progenitors, his color a rusty red and black brindle, which, for pure raw ugliness, was exceeded only by the quality of his temper.

General Grant, to put it conservatively, was a fifteen-hundred-pound handful of crossbred, fuse-lit, bovine dynamite and was, beyond that, the rarest of all early western trail stock—the natural-born herdbull leader.

At the moment, however, this exceptional bit of background on the horned fauna of south Texas was escaping Nathan Stark. He was interested only in old Chickasaw Billings. "Run that muckle-dun bastard back in the brush," he ordered growlingly. "And catch up my pony."

Chickasaw studied him, nodded, shifted his cud, spat. "Yes sir," he drawled. "Right away, Mr. Stark."

When he had hazed the longhorn bull away from the cedar, he caught the big man's pony and led him in. Stark was waiting, climbed aboard without a word. Only when he had settled himself in his stirrups and quieted the nervous mustang with the slow sure talk and easy moves of the master horseman, did he turn to Chickasaw.

"Old man," he said quietly, "you put off on me again like that, just once, it'll be your last put. I don't laugh easy and I don't play games for fun."

"I don't always play for chalkies myself, Mr. Stark," said the grizzled Texan. "Though I reckon I can most the time get up a good laugh without rupturing anything permanent."

"And what does that mean in white man's English?" demanded Stark sarcastically.

"I allow I let you walk deliberate into that bull," nodded the other, "but it wasn't all in the cause of pure joy, onstrained. If we're going to get them cute little

51

heifers up the trail to that hideout of yours, you got to understand and reckon with the General. Not to mention working with him. Leastaways, you are if you're a mind to try it my way."

Stark looked at him. "I'm of a mind," he said after a long moment. "Let's get on with it."

"We're got," said Chickasaw Billings, and kicked his old gray gelding around and off toward the snowburied lean-to.

The start was made well within the hour. Fortunately the cattle were hungry and came easy. The bulk of the herd were long yearling heifers, which meant they were facing their second winter and crowding two years in age. But that first winter had been spent on their mothers' bags and on a range where snow, while known, seldom hid the grass beneath more than a few powdery inches of unpacked cover. The young cattle thus had not learned the northern art of digging for their supper and did not have sense enough to go after the perfectly good feed under the foot and a half of heavy, hard-packing Montana snow which lay throughout the sheltered meadows of the Forks timber. Consequently when the familiar figures of the cowboys loomed through the snowshrouded conifers and naked black birch and alder scrub, they practically rounded themselves up in their eagerness to be on the trail which the long journey from Texas had taught them always ended in good graze and running water.

Chickasaw handled General Grant, as he had on the original drive. The old bull seemed to know him and made no trouble when he was cut out of the milling bunch and pointed back along the Bozeman Road. He just moved out of the herd, swung his huge curly head back toward the curious heifers, lowered his six-foot horns, blew up a cloud of snowdust with an explosive, deep-lunged snort, bellowed once, came smartly about and trudged off alongside the old cowboy's escorting pony.

Behind him, the silly little heifers echoed his exhaled snort, switched their tails, milled indecisively and with typical female disorder for a brief, noisy moment, then lined out after the huge herdmaster quiet and contented as so many settlement bossy cows on their way to the back pasture milkshed. In the wake of the quarter-mile string of frisky young cattle came the remaining herd-bulls, four- and five-year-old veterans for the most part, all of them with enough age on them to know there was no hurry and that at the end of the day's drive they would catch up with the girls and, accordingly, any part of their love life they might have missed at the last camp.

With the bulls tailing the line of drive no drag riders were necessary. Those old devils might lag back, walk slow, disdainfully sniff the snowy air and in general act as unconcerned about where the heifers were going as though the latter were a collection of calved-out, dry-bagged old canner cows. In the end they were fooling no bulls but themselves, and the delicate sentiments left behind by that long forgotten bunkhouse Byron would still prevail.

> As the damn dust clingeth to
> the wind that bloweth,
> So sticketh the bull to the
> heifer that loweth,
> And it maketh no difference
> where the hell she goeth—

It was swiftly as well that this old law of the herd could be depended on to hold the rear of the drive together and following in line with the point cattle, for within twenty minutes of leaving the Forks timber every hand was desperately needed up front.

Chickasaw had detailed Stark and Hogjaw, the youngest, strongest riders, to lead the way. Behind them and in front of Waco, Slim, Saleratus, and Chickasaw himself, he had bunched the loose saddlestock to break and pack the trail the two point riders were laying. After them came General Grant and Nella, the latter ordered to keep an eye on the old lead bull and sing out the minute he might choose to wander or take off on a side trail or up some sheltered cross-gulch that might look good to him.

For the first minutes and while the wind held off, the old cattleman's plans worked smooth as frozen well water. During the past night it had blown more than snowed and their intrail from yesterday was still plainly visible. Following its already packed undersurface they were able to make good time and leave a clean wide trail for the eagerly pressing cattle. But just as a good southern grin or two was beginning to appear among the old Texas hands, the wind began to rise. They had not made another mile before Stark's earlier warning was borne out and the full blizzard shut back down around them, blind and black and suffocating as the inside of a hard-tied gunnysack. All landmarks were lost within minutes, all human instincts confused and useless shortly thereafter. Stark tried bluffing it out for a brief, blundering time, gave it up. He was riding his own horse again now, a big rawboned stud as mean and tough as the man astride him. But he was not a range-bred animal and the snow was confusing and worrying him. Cursing, Stark dropped him back to turn the lead over to Chickasaw. In his turn the aging trail driver reined in his gelding, shook his head, cupped his hands in answer to the Montanan's shout. "Ain't no use none of *us* trying it, Mr. Stark. One man ain't no different than another when he cain't see four feet and the wind is swapping ends faster'n a saddle-burred bronc."

"But good God!" Stark shoved his bay stud into Chickasaw's pony, roared his objection into the wind. "We can't stand here and hold the herd up. If they ever get stopped now we'll never get them going again."

"He's right, Chickasaw!" bellowed Hogjaw. "Somebody's got to lead on out, blind or not, or the bunch will bog down and we've lost 'em!"

"You got any deathless bright ideas about nominating yourself for that somebody?" yelled the old man testily. "You young idjut, there ain't a man living could take us sixty yards in the right direction. We got to step aside and turn it over to somebody a sight smarter than any

55

bench-legged cowboy from the Rio Brazos, you hear?"

"I hear, you bristle-backed old bastard! But it don't add up to no sudden cheers. Who the hell you got in mind leading us out'n these here frozen Montana bull-rushes? Moses or Jed Smith?"

"Neither one!" shouted Chickasaw, strangely unmoved by the youth's angry sarcasm. "You just get your damn hoss out'n the way there, I allow my candidate ought to be along any minute!"

The old man pulled his own mount aside with the yell, just as Nella loomed up through the snowswirl. "For the luvva Christ!" hollered Hogjaw indignantly. "You wasn't meaning the gal!"

"Nope!" called the bearded oldster, still unperturbed, "not her, buster." He grinned, waved stiffly, pointing to the snow-curtain through which Nella had just appeared. "Her friend, yonder."

As he spoke, a high-shouldered, wide-horned shadow bulked black and sudden into view. The next moment General Grant moved up through the storm and past the halted ponies. He did not hesitate, only glanced at the silent riders, cleared the clotting snow from his nostrils with a tremendous grunt of recognition for his old friend, Chickasaw, moved on and unconcernedly into the teeth of the screaming wind. There was no sign that he sensed or was following the old trail toward Bozeman, but from the disdainful way he went by them and the dead-sure bearing of his course on into the storm, the freezing riders took new heart.

When Chickasaw turned to them after the first of the

56

following heifers had begun to trail unhesitatingly past in the footsteps of the great brindle herdbull, he expected no arguments, got none.

"Any objections?" he yelled defiantly.

"Yeah!" It was Waco who grinned the answering yell. "What are we doing setting here? I ain't no yearling heifer but I sure as hell reckon I got as much sense as one!"

"Which is to say how much?" demanded the molasses-minded Hogjaw, always the last one to catch a conversational drift.

"Enough, by God," shouted Waco, "to put my dumb head down and follow the General!"

CHAPTER SIX

THE WIND held four hours then died as suddenly as it had sprung back to vicious life. By Stark's handsome solid-gold stemwinder it was only minutes past high noon, yet the arctic twilight of the lulling storm was as sunless and black-shadowed as a bat roost. Still, when the snow stopped a short while later, the sullen clouds lifted again, returning the sickly gray visibility which had obtained so briefly at daybreak.

To Nella Torneau it was like being born again, or given new eyes where the old had been blind from birth. A Texas girl, and a south of Texas girl at that, she was neither bred nor accustomed to the sightless terror of a High Plains blizzard. Accordingly, it had been a fight almost beyond endurance to keep from cracking under the constant screaming and battering of the invisible wind. That she had not done so was a tribute more to her disdain of Stark than to any pride of self or ironclad constitution. She would rather have died in any one of the countless drifts along the trailside, than to admit to the brutal Montanan that he could ever ride her under or make her cry out for mercy or beg to be treated like a woman—or, God forbid, like his wife.

Nevertheless, when the storm pulled back and she could see again she was surprised to note that Stark was not with the cowboy group at the head of the herd, and her quick looks right and left in search of his whereabouts were easily as anxious as they were hateful. It was not that the girl tried to fool herself any as to how she felt about Nathan Stark. Far from it. The hulking Montanan, no matter if you despised the ground he walked on, was all male and might near a yard wide. He was the kind you got behind rather in front of when the chips were down. Right now you figured the last hand was about to be dealt, and you just wanted to know or see where Stark was going to shove his stack—so that you could push your own pile right fast in the same direction.

Nella was still scanning the cattle between her and the herd-fronting cowboys for a sign of Stark, when his heavy voice hit her squarely between her tensing shoulder blades. "Right behind you, Miss Nella, ma'am," he growled sarcastically. "That is in case you could possibly be looking for your new husband."

She flushed deeply, bit her full underlip, set her

slender jaw. "You never can tell the luck of a lousy calf," she gritted out the old Texas saw. "When you ride blind you're apt to wake up caught in a driftfence with most any kind of a coyote."

Stark dropped his wolf grin. "Well, you can see now, so *see that* you follow me. You may want to hear the good news."

"Good news!" she shot back at him. "That's a laugh, mister. In the middle of this Eskimo range? Don't be funny!"

"After nine months of me, Nella, you ought to know I'm never funny." He said it flat and quiet, wheeled his mount, put the irons to him, loped him through the trampled snow to the head of the moving herd. If there was any hesitation in Nella's nervous following of his example, it was too brief to register. A watcher would have missed it had he blinked, or been hit in the eye by a snowflake.

Stark's good news was scarcely electrifying but it was better, as Saleratus McGivern dourly put it, "then a belt in the brisket with a busted whiffletree."

By some miracle of distinctive animal sense, or simple accident of blundering brute direction, General Grant had followed the Bozeman Road to within ten miles of the settlement, then veered south and west as sharp and true as though Stark had been there to turn him. He now had the herd bearing down on a range of low hills densely covered with virgin timber, the lower reaches of which spread outward across the flats to the banks of a frozen-over stream of considerable size. The ice-locked channel of this mountain watercourse led away, almost due south, into the hills and toward the flanking twin ranges of snowcapped granite which reared ominously in the lead-gray distance.

The crew listened in amazed silence as Stark told them their route lay up the river, dead into the heart of the towering mountains ahead. The amazement was caused by the simple fact that when the big Virginia Citian said "up the river" he meant it literally. The wilderness road into his secret valley was a smooth, broad ribbon of river ice swept clean of deep snow by the updraft of the mountain wind through the narrowing gorge of the stream's canyon. They would inevitably hit some bad ice and air pockets, he told them, and the loss of a few, or perhaps even many head, was almost certain. But they had fifteen miles yet to go. The only way they could make those miles in time to save any part of the weakening herd was by the glaring treachery of the river road. It was what he had had in mind when he told Chickasaw that if he could get the herd up toward Bozeman, he would guarantee to get it on into safe shelter from there. The old cowboy (with the slightest of bows to three-quarters of a ton of bad-tempered brindle bull) had done his part. It was now up to Stark to do his.

"The guarantee," he advised the shivering Texans in conclusion to this terse outline of the river drive, "still holds." He paused, added unsmilingly, "Providing, of course, nobody steps into an air pocket or out onto a stretch of sponge-ice. In that case," he caught Nella's white-faced glance with the grim words, "don't bother

60

to wave goodbye. You won't have time." He looked around the little group, nodded briskly. "Any questions?"

"Yeah, one," said Waco Fentriss, moving his pony out a step and returning Stark's look. "Where was you when the nerves was passed out?"

By four o'clock that afternoon they had made another ten miles up the surprisingly good going of the river-ice trail. The frozen surface was just wind-pitted and snow-caked enough to furnish excellent traction for the tired cattle, the low banks of the channel just high enough to make a hard climb and thus serve to keep the herd together and moving without flankers. This relieved Stark and Hogjaw of the man- and horse-killing job they had been alternating with their share of trail breaking all the way from the Forks camp, freeing them to join Waco, Saleratus and Slim Blanchard in pushing the drag to all possible speed. Chickasaw rode point so that the General would have a familiar mount and rider in front of him and not get restless or lose interest in moving ahead. The old man had asked that Nella be allowed to side him so that in case his pony should stumble him into a piece of bad ice there would be somebody to ride back and warn the others. This was good and standard drive procedure but Chickasaw's request was pure Confederate gallantry and did not fool Stark for a minute. At the same time he did not want the girl underfoot in the hard close work of the drag driving and gruffly told her to do what she damn pleased, so long as she stayed out of *his* way.

Now, riding with the old cowboy through the nightlike darkness of the late afternoon, Nella had her first chance since the grim ceremony in the Black Nugget's banking parlor to talk to either Waco or Chickasaw alone. Even so, the drive was beginning its eleventh weary mile up the deepening canyon of Stark's mystery river before she spoke.

"Why did you do it?" she said suddenly to Chickasaw. "Was it because of Ben?"

Her blunt question, coming without preface of a single other word for a solid hour before it, startled her companion. And Chickasaw was a man who did not like having his nerves jangled. Not, especially, when they were already all cinched up, belly-pinching tight, with peering ahead and trying to guess what was three-foot and what was three-inch ice.

"Why the hell did I do what? Goddamit!" he barked back. "And don't jump at a man like that without you let him know you're coming. Clear your throat, or spit, or cuss first. Then come out with it."

She knew the old man well enough to let him have his little tantrum and not charge him for it. "Why did you and the boys change your minds back in the Nugget?" she asked quietly. "One minute you were all letting on like you, none of you, would touch me or Stark with a ten-foot pole tied on to the end of a wagon tongue. Next minute you were allowing you would stick by me and set still for Stark like as though nothing had ever happened. Why? What made the big difference, so sudden?"

"The big difference," said Chickasaw slowly, but

62

without hesitation, "was that one minute you was just a hard-tail Texas tramp that Ben had got himself all hot and bothered over, and the next minute you was something entire elsewise."

"Such as what?" she demanded angrily, white teeth flashing her resentment of the moral reference.

"Such," nodded the old man, still as slow but a little softer now, "as a woman going to have a baby."

The way he said it, the fierce, defiant way he tilted his straggly beard at her, while at the same time the words themselves were so held down and self-conscious, so plainly awkward and embarrassed by the sacred subject of motherhood, let her know that she had just heard the simple truth. It was not her, or even the memory of Ben the hardcase Texas trailhands were serving. It was the unborn baby. True to the twin codes of their outrageous cowboy sentimentality and stiff-necked southern chivalry, the men would see her through, not because she was Nella Torneau, or Ben Allison's sweetheart, but purely because she was a woman and going to have a baby!

It was sweet of them. A girl had to admit that.

And generous to a fault.

It was, touchingly, no less than they would do for any stray mongrel dog that had gotten herself caught and wandered into their camp to whelp.

When she returned Chickasaw's nod her answer had an edge on it he could have shaved with.

"Thanks. It fairly tears a girl's heart out she's that grateful."

"Do me a favor," glared Chickasaw, "and forget it. It embarrasses a man bad enough just to *be* a damn fool, without he has to be *reminded* of it."

Further contest of the thin Texas tempers was cut off by the unexpected whiplash of Stark's voice curling between them. The Montanan had ridden up so quietly and swiftly neither of them had heard or seen his approach. Both jumped nervously as his bitter words broke up their own angry exchange.

"Is this a family feud, or can a stranger horn in on it?" he rasped. "Pull in your ponies."

The last was a flat order. They did not argue it. When their mounts had stopped moving Nella said, "All right, now what?"

"Now *listen,*" snapped Stark.

In the muffled stillness of the stale air they heard the new sound at once. The wind which had died at noon had not returned in the long sullen hours of the afternoon march. The silence of the storm drawn back and waiting was almost as unbearable as the hurricane shriek of its full violence. Through its strange, shrouded heaviness Stark's sound grew ominously louder. It was a rumbling, thunderous, minor-key roar, at once vaguely familiar and frighteningly alien, and fascinating in the same ambivalent way as the hoarse bass of an angry bear's growl just before the charge.

No mountain man, old Chickasaw did not at once remember where he had recently heard it, put his querulous demand with understandable impatience.

"What in Christ's name is *that?*" he huffed.

"That," mimicked Stark, "is just a little matter of no more ice around yonder bend. *And just around it.*" He swung his mount hard around as General Grant and the first of his tiring harem began to pass. "Head that bull up that low bank to the left!" he shouted to Chickasaw. "And be damn sure he doesn't double back on you. We'll see that the main bunch follows him." The old cowboy was off with the order, and he turned to Nella. *"Maybe* we will," he qualified quietly. "I told the boys to give me a minute to get up front, then start shoving them hard. It's up to you and me to cut them up that bank after the bull."

Nella had been born and brought up in the Nueces River brakes, was better than a fair country hand with wild cattle, knew at once that Stark's "maybe" was a mighty big one. "But they're dragging their hocks," she objected quickly. "They're worn plumb down. They aren't going to go up that bank, bull or no bull."

By this time their ponies were being pushed along by the crush of the main herd front. Far behind and out of view, they could hear the thin yips and high Rebel yells of Waco and his companions, as they began to put the pressure on the drag. Stark fought his pony free of the crowding cattle, yelling for Nella to follow him out. They raced their mounts fifty paces ahead of the speeding herd, to the point where Chickasaw had just sent the reluctant General up the east bank grade Stark had pointed out. Here they spun them about to face the approaching cattle.

As they did, Stark flung open his wolfskin coat,

65

clearing the heavy double-holstered Colts he habitually wore. He shouldered his mount into Nella's, shoved one of the short-barreled .44's into her hand, kept his instructions simple.

"They're going up that bank. We'll ride them up if we can. If we can't, if they start getting by us, don't waste any shots. I want to see a heifer down every time that gun goes off, you hear?"

Nella tested her stirrups, settled herself in the saddle. "You talk too much, mister. Count your own shots." She slammed the spurs to her sorrel mare, jumping her toward the cattle. Hat off, standing in her stirrups, high voice echoing the guerrilla yells of her Texas friends, she was into the herd before Stark's mount made his first leap.

The next moment the Montanan had dashed after the wild-riding southern girl. For perhaps sixty seconds both riders spun, heeled, quarter-turned and quirted their horses along the front of the shoving herd. The time, brief as it was, was enough to let them know where they stood.

Neither they nor any ten others like them were going to turn those weary, nerve-worn young cattle by yelling and hat waving. Nella realized it as soon as Stark did. She was right behind the latter as once more he fought his slipping, struggling mount free of the herd front. Her gun, too, was only the backlash of a hair trigger behind his getting into action.

The leaders began to go down. When the last of the shots echoed dully off through the growing darkness, seven or eight animals were down, two or three stumbling and about to go down. For a long, held breath it appeared that their blocking carcasses, plus the noise and flame blasts of the Colt muzzle flashes, would turn their wild-eyed sisters. Then, with a sickening rush, the lead wave of the crazed heifers began spilling over and around the dead cattle.

Stark did not hesitate. In one move he was off his pony and on one knee in the snow, his Henry Repeater unbooted, shouldered, steadied. It was one of the best guns on the frontier; the one old Oliver Winchester was patterning his brand-new lever action on.

It was a stubby, ugly, octagon-barreled little brute, holding a whole hatful of the newfangled, self-contained, copper-case cartridges in its magazine tube, and it could throw its smashing sequence of heavy slugs just as fast as a man could center his hold and lever away.

While Nella sat her mare, empty-gunned and helpless, Nathan Stark, on foot in front of five hundred excited Texas longhorns, shot down another six head of the moving cattle in less than twice as many seconds of deliberate, timed fire.

To the fascinated Nella it seemed almost beside the point that the big man's gamble paid off, that the thunderous boom of the Henry turned the trick where the lesser bark and bite of Colonel Colt's pets had so narrowly failed, and that the point and swing heifers were cutting sharply left to leap and scramble up the low bank after Chickasaw and the General, starting the whole herd after them and thus leading it safely up and out of the frozen riverbed. It did not even seem important that, had they not been turned in that last wild minute, an untold number of the leaders, pushed inexorably by the herd behind them, would have been lost in a way now frighteningly clear to the watching girl. No farther around the sharp bend where Stark had taken his stand than a schoolboy could skip a rock across a quiet millpond, a yawning crevasse gutted the river ice from shore to shore. Beyond its waiting precipice was nothing but a seething race of black open water. Yet, it was not the deadly gunwork or the slaughtered cattle, nor the wild water or the last second turning of the herd that left her staring wide-eyed through the December gloom. It was Stark himself.

She was still sitting there, still watching him when Waco and the others rope-whipped and Rebel-shouted the lagging herdbulls up the bank slope after the disappearing drag of the heifers. She was still thinking of him when he moved his pony up through the deepening night and grunted, "All right, that's the last of them. Let's go."

She followed him off into the darkness, rebellious mind and body beaten down by twelve straight hours of saddle ache and subzero cold. What little will to think remained within her provided no warmth or strength whatever. It generated only enough resistance to ask the question; left none at all to answer it. And it was quite a question.

How in God's lonely Montana world was a hundred-and-ten pounds of homesick, in-trouble Texas girl supposed to handle a man like Nathan Stark?

CHAPTER SEVEN

THE LOW, left bank up which Stark had turned the herd issued onto a level, lightly snowed grade leading directly toward the frowning mountain wall ahead. It was pitch-dark and the fronting foothills were invisible when, minutes after leaving the river, Stark rode up on old Chickasaw and the General.

"You meaning to camp agin them hillsides yonder?" the oldster greeted him. "We cain't none of us go on much longer, Mr. Stark."

"I mean to camp past the hills," said Stark.

"Past 'em?" Chickasaw gasped.

"This grade we're following takes us through a level-bottomed notch," answered the Montanan. "The notch cuts clean through to the upper valley beyond. You can't see it till you're right on top of it and you won't believe it even after you've seen it, it's that well hidden. I stumbled on it two years ago trailing a bunch of played-out wagon bulls I had turned loose the summer before."

"You mean," said the old man, "that we can drive this bunch through that range ahead yet tonight?" He said it as though he felt Stark had finally cracked, and the big Montanan's next words did nothing to dispel the impression. "We won't even have to drive them. They'll go through by themselves, if they've got ten cents worth of range savvy still working."

"What the hell you saying?"

"There's uncovered hay and open water ahead,"

69

answered Stark. "God damn it! We've made it, Chickasaw!" His voice picked up to the thought. Neither the excitement nor the profanity were typical of him, and the veteran cowboy asked quickly, "Made what, Mr. Stark?" Then, kneeing his pony over closer to his companion's, "Listen, youngster, we'd best hold up and build a fire. The hell with the cattle, we're going to lose them anyway."

Stark actually laughed. "You think I'm crazy, eh, old man? Too much blizzard, you say. Wind-beat, snow-drunk, frozen silly, that it? Well, look at those heifers come, you old mossyback! And what do you think is ailing that cowchip-colored bull of yours? He crazy, too, you think!"

Even as he spoke, Chickasaw saw General Grant's head come up, his stubby brindle tail lift. The next moment the old bull bellowed hoarsely and began to move as though the snow were burning his feet, while from the darkness behind him came the answering, high-voiced bawling of the excited heifers and the unmistakable rattling clack of hundreds of cloven hooves digging in and picking up speed.

"Get out of the way and let them go!" shouted Stark. "Up here, you old fool! Before they run over you." Chickasaw followed him up a sharp rise to a little bench overlooking the low pass through the flanking hills. "We'll camp here," continued the Montanan. "I've changed my mind. There's good wood and plenty of shelter. I'm going to scout down the grade and pick up the others soon as the herd is past. Make sure they don't get by us in the dark. You build up a blaze while I'm gone, so we'll have something to home-in on."

"All right," said Chickasaw dully. By this time he was thoroughly confused and too tired to try to straighten things out. It was coming on to snow again, making it look as if Stark was deliberately abandoning the cattle, letting them blunder on into the blizzard and die—just as Chickasaw had advised him to. But that laugh had not sounded *too* loony. And the way the General had tailed-up and taken off, plus the sudden rush of the she-stock to go after him, did not add up to Stark's being insane-asylum bait just yet. "Look sharp," he concluded, as Stark turned the bay stud to go. "It's blacker'n a bear's gut down there. Don't let your hoss lose his feet."

Abrupt as Chickasaw tried to make the warning, Stark caught the note of real concern in it. He reined his horse sharply around.

"Chickasaw, I want to tell you something. You and that brindle bull of yours. I owe you one. I won't forget it."

"You'd best forget it, Mr. Stark. You ain't beholden to me for nothing. Neither you, nor your new missus." He had no sooner said it than he was sorry. But it was too late. Stark jumped his mount back toward him. "Old man!" he rasped. "Don't you call her that again. Not to me, you understand!"

"Yes sir," muttered Chickasaw. "I reckon I didn't rightly mean it like it sounded."

"You meant it," said Stark, and turned the stud and sent him off down the icy grade at a hand gallop.

71

Behind him the grizzled cattleman climbed stiffly down from his saddle, looked off through the slanting snow, leathered face hardlined. Whatever little pothole of mutual respect had started to thaw between him and the big Montanan scummed over and froze solid as Chickasaw's scowl deepened. "Likely I did, Mr. Stark," he mumbled to himself, "likely I did. Along about now a man don't know what he means. Saving that he sure as hell ain't out here freezing his southern backside off to do you no favors!" He was still grousing and crabbing to himself when Stark and the others rode out of the storm to side the leaping, spark-showering blaze he had angrily built up. "Get down and come in," he grumped, then, belatedly noting the empty-saddled mare the Montanan led. "Good Gawd Amighty! Where's the gal?"

Stark swung down.

"That gray of yours as strong as he looks?" he demanded, indicating the other's cowpony.

"Strong as a skunk in a billy goat's beard," snapped the old man. "I asked you where was the gal?"

"She *was* with me," said Stark, moving for the gray gelding and legging up. "God knows where she is now." He put the spurs in deep. The old horse jumped out and away from the fire. "Keep that blaze booming!" Stark yelled back, and was gone as suddenly as though he and Chickasaw's bony gray had galloped through a solid snow wall.

"Goddamit, we should of gone with him!" said Hogjaw belligerently. "It ain't human to let a man go off

72

in that stuff by himself. I'm going to tag along with him, by God, Montana dude or not!"

He spun his horse, but Chickasaw grabbed his bridle's near-side cheekstrap. "Hold up, you young idjut," he growled. "How you going to tag him?"

The hulking youth looked for Stark's trail leading into the outer blackness beyond the fire's bouncing glare. The faint line of the gray gelding's hoofprints, already nearly filled, would be gone in another twenty seconds. *And that in the firelight.* Where would they be in the blind belly of the return-blizzard?

"I reckon," he gulped nervously, "that that stuff is piling up faster'n bull hockey in the bunkhouse."

"On payday, and with a new hand listening," amplified Waco cynically. "You get fifty feet out in that Montana dandruff, buster, you ain't never going to see home again."

The wizened little brazos rider spoke the literal truth. They all knew it. In the time it had taken Stark to guide them in before going back out after the girl, visibility had closed in to two or three pony lengths. It was not over six feet now, and a man had to squint to make out his friends' faces even across the sputtering flare of a pine-knot fire.

The five men said no more, went wearily about the business of breaking out the packmule and helping Saleratus get the coffee on. They were safe and they knew it. Stark and Nella were not. Talking would not change anything—for anybody.

But the gloomy silence was premature. The Texans

73

still had a little to learn about snow, and about Nathan Stark.

Thirty minutes after he had disappeared into the storm he was back. He drifted in out of the howl and swirl of the wind without a sound, Nella carried like a sleeping child in his powerful arms. The only noise was the old gray's whicker of recognition as he spotted Chickasaw hobbling around the fire to meet them.

Hogjaw was the first to reach Stark's stirrup.

"Leave me have her, Mr. Stark," he said.

Stark let the girl's slack form slide. The big cowboy carried her clumsily to the fire, with Waco stumbling ahead to throw down a blanket. While they tucked her in, Saleratus hovered impatiently behind them with a steaming tin of his famous mocha, and Slim Blanchard cursed and kicked at the fire and fanned futilely with his hat to keep the offending smoke from "clabbering up around the pore little wore-out thing." Of the five southern cowboys only Chickasaw Billings had any thought for Nathan Stark. When the others had gone with Nella, he remained standing by the gelding's wither. He waited until they had disappeared around the fire, put his gnarled hand on the big man's thigh.

"When I pull on your arm," he told him, "fall my way."

Stark only nodded his understanding, his lips too frozen to move coherently.

"Don't be afraid to lean on me a little," said Chickasaw, reaching for his coatsleeve. "You ain't the first boy's been froze to a saddle."

He yanked hard and Stark's weight sagged heavily

toward him. It was all the Montanan could do to force his numbed right leg up and across the gray's rump; he left the rest of it up to the wiry oldster. Chickasaw caught him expertly, kept him upright, supported him slowly to the fire. There, he propped him up against the packsaddle, roughly threw a blanket over him, looked around to make sure none of his companions were watching, reached inside his ragged sheepskin coat and brought forth a flat, dark bottle of Old Crow.

He uncorked it, helped himself to a long peg, started to hand it to Stark, pulled it back. Very awkwardly he wiped off the neck of the bottle, then scowlingly reoffered it to the big man.

"Hurry it up, goddamit!" he grumped defensively. "Don't let them other bastards see you. They don't know I got it."

Next morning they saw the sun for the first time in forty-eight hours. The blizzard had pulled back to rest again and a narrow strip of blue sky, perhaps a dozen miles in width, lay open above them. The wind was still howling a gale and Stark warned them not to drag their feet about breaking camp. If he knew Montana weather—and by this time, especially in view of the remarkable way he had birddogged Nella Torneau out of the riverbank drift where her falling mare had thrown her the night before, none of them were inclined to argue that he didn't—this bluebird breather was not going to last more than long enough to get them on through the pass. With possibly ten minutes left over to roll a smoke and take a look at what he had told Chickasaw would make his cattleman's heart ache.

Refreshed by ten hours' sleep in the storm shelter of the snug bench to which Stark had guided Chickasaw, and unharmed by her half-hour burial in the snowbank preceding that sleep, Nella opened her eyes to a world entirely, almost happily, different from the frightening one of the night before. She came awake just as the Montanan was issuing his bobtailed orders for breaking camp. Somehow, the familiar drone of his flat voice sounded good. On the long trail up from Texas, with Ben Allison to lean on, or in Virginia City, where a pretty girl need never want for tall male custody, she would have said she hated the least, dry syllable of it. But here, cut off from the nearest sign of civilization by sixty miles of snow and ice and merciless Montana wind, *everything* sounded different.

Her thoughts were shortly interrupted by the abrupt appearance of their pale-eyed subject.

"How do you feel?" asked Stark, standing over her and looking giant-tall against the climbing sun.

"All right. What happened?"

"Your mare went down, following me up the river-bank last night. You spent a few minutes in cold storage."

"Who fished me out?"

"Me," said Nathan Stark.

"You'd likely have done us both a favor by leaving me there."

"It was my fault. I should have watched you."

76

"Why?"

"It was my place."

She thought about it a minute, lovely eyes shadowing. "Would it have been your place if I had been Waco or Chickasaw? If one of them had been tailing you instead of me?"

"What do you think?" he said slowly. There was no invitation in it, no rejection, just the simple question. She studied him another moment, her ripe mouth losing its soft fullness. "It would," she said, answering both his and her own question.

"It would," he agreed. "You all done now?"

"All done," she echoed his affirmative head-bob and cynical tone.

"All right then, get up and eat. McGivern's kept your plate hot. You're holding up the show."

She came up out of the blankets, lithe and quick, struck a broad pose, saluted him stiffly.

"Yes sir, Colonel Stark. Right away, sir!"

He did not scowl, smile, move a solitary face muscle. He just stood there shaking his head.

"It's too damn bad that I don't have a sense of humor," he said quietly. "I think that was supposed to be funny."

He waited only long enough to see the dark blood start furiously through her cheeks, then spun on his heel and strode off.

The trail came out of the brief foothill passage without warning. One moment they were riding between low walls of dark timber, the next, their mounts broke forth

77

into a blinding world of raw blue sky and diamond-bright sunshine. The wind, which had howled after them like a wolf pack to the last turn of the narrow trail now lay dead still. The whole immense scene before them waited motionless and impossibly perfect.

"Well," said Stark to the gaping Chickasaw, "how does your heart feel?"

The old man's answer was to close his sagging mouth and keep looking. Behind him the others had no more to say, as much to see.

Viewed looking northwestward from the foothill portals of its eastern approaches, the Upper Gallatin Valley is still one of the western world's most unexcelled wonders. What it was that December morning nearly a hundred years ago, before the bite of the timber cruiser's ax or the slash of the settler's plow was a sight of incredible primitive grandeur. Still, its present beholders were not concerned with this staggering beauty, nor was Stark's short question designed to call forth any comment upon it.

What old Chickasaw saw, what all four of the other old Texas riders saw, was simply the most perfect cow pasture God ever laid out in front of five awestricken South Plains cattlemen. As far as the crowsfooted eye could follow it, the valley floor stretched away to the north and west, watered its full length by the lazy sweep of the Gallatin River, walled, east and west, where the river swung south to enter its narrowing canyon, by the sheltering windbreaks of the Madison and Gallatin Mountains. And every acre of it, every foot, every inch that was not taken up by the stream or its winding stands of virgin woodland, was covered by a thick glossy curl of priceless grass.

"Well, old man?" Once more Stark broke the breath-held quiet. "What do you say?"

Chickasaw looked out across the endless miles of thinly snowpatched, wide-open winter range, studied the distant grazing dots of the feeding herd, at last brought his farsighted squint back to bear on Stark. He shifted his omnipresent quid of longleaf Burley from left to right cheek, checked the wind, spat carefully down it as he invariably did ahead of a major pronouncement.

"I say," he muttered, wagging his head as though he still did not believe it, "that it's the *biggest* goddam piece of beef browse I ever laid eyes on in my mortal life!"

Stark's pale eyes narrowed. A look of excitement, a far, compelling, strangely fierce expression stirred the set muscles of his broad face. He shifted his gaze to sweep the stretching immensity of gray-brown mountain meadow hay. "Old man," he murmured almost gently, "you've named it. You've put the brand on it where I couldn't in a hundred years. That's what it is."

"Eh?" queried Chickasaw, confused by the sudden appearance of excitement where he had previously seen only poker-faced stillness. "That's what *what* is?"

"The Big Pasture!" said Nathan Stark, and sent his pony forward into the waiting winter sunshine.

CHAPTER EIGHT

STARK LED them five miles up the valley. He pushed his horse hard, continually cast worried glances back at the unbroken blue of the sky over the lower valley. It was clear he expected the weather to return from that direction, and he was not wrong. As they crossed the river to climb a high sunny bench on the western side, the air began to turn noticeably colder. Before they reached the top of the trail the last of the warm light was gone, the funeral gray of the three previous days reclosing its chill shroud around them. Stark's sunlight, as he had predicted it would, had lasted just long enough to give them one unbelieving look at his Gallatin Valley empire.

While the hidden range was well sheltered compared to the open flatlands of the outer valley through which they had driven the herd the day before, and while wind is always the greatest killer in a cold country, far greater than any temperature drop, none of the little party needed the Montanan to tell them they were still a long day's ride from the ranchhouse.

They had only one pack animal, Saleratus's mule, Jeff Davis. The scarred old Missouri jack was tougher than barbecued boot leather, could tote his own weight in cast iron, was regularly packed, as now, a full four hundred pounds, an easy hundred better than a run-of-the-mill mule. Still, he was carrying blankets, tarps, ropes, beans, bacon, coffee and cookpots for seven people. There was little room remaining for the things they so desperately needed now, the axes, shovels, mattocks and crossbuck saws with which to get up a temporary shelter for themselves and their saddlemounts. Saleratus had brought along, in fact, only the three basic tools of his camp-making trade: a hand ax, double-bitted felling ax, short-handled shovel. Even a Gulf Coast Texas girl could see that things were drawing up tighter than a green persimmon pucker.

Stark apparently did not share the general gloom. At least he did not show it.

Halting his followers in a quiet spot out of the wind, where the bench ran back into a steep ravine to butt against the lower bases of the Madison range, he surveyed the available weapons, issued as casually as though he had just been detailed to dig a latrine in sandy soil on a summer day.

He gave the hand ax to Saleratus and Nella, directing them to cut firewood, get a blaze going, coffee boiled and grub cooking. To long, slow-drawing Slim Blanchard he handed the shovel, with curt orders to begin right where he stood and clear the biggest square of level ground for a cabin-raising that he could manage before he fainted and fell dead. He himself, after snapping at Waco and Chickasaw to crawl back on their horses, shake out their frozen lariats and follow along, seized the big double-bitted ax, wheeled on the gawking Hogjaw, blue eyes blazing, and marked, "All right, Bivins, let's cut wood!"

For the next four hours and without respite he and the gaunt Texan staged a felling bee that would have slowed down Paul Bunyan. The ten- and twelve-inch squaw and lodgepole pines came down like stovewood rattling off a chuck wagon tailgate. As fast as they crashed, Waco or Chickasaw would rope the ragged butts, quirt their lathered mounts, snake the tall spars campward.

By noon, and a grudging break for coffee and hot boiled bean mush, they had the mouth of the little ravine choked with the untrimmed cabin timbers.

But no sooner was the last plate licked clean than Stark took up the big ax, tossed the little one to Hogjaw. Nodding toward the jam of downed pines, he jerked his thumb at the darkening northern skies, eased to his feet, grunted quietly.

"Blizzard's giving us a break. Let's use it."

They attacked the log pile, Stark cutting the bigger crosslimbs, Hogjaw following him up to take the one- and two-inch branchlets. Both men were brute strong, both sinfully stubborn. They trimmed the logs out to twelve- and twenty-foot lengths faster than the other four men could drag them away to Slim's cleared site and start them walling upward.

By four o'clock Hogjaw had had enough. He admitted the defeat by burying his ax in the untrimmed butt of the last log, stumbling politely clear of it, vomiting from sheer fatigue. After that, he tottered weakly over to the fire, slumped alongside it, white-faced. Stark finished the tree, followed him over. Reaching soberly down, he patted the big youth's hunched shoulder. "You'll toughen to it," he told him. "You didn't do bad for a growing boy."

Hogjaw was too far gone. The remark did not register. But it did on old Chickasaw Billings, just coming in from the wall-raising for a jag of coffee. Yet peer as he might at Stark's expressionless face, he could make out no least trail sign of any intended humor. If the tall Montanan had actually just broken down and shown a spark of dry good fun, a man would still have to guess at it. He never in God's snowcovered world would know it from studying that scum-ice set of features. Or be waiting for Stark to up and admit any such weakness.

Shaking off the hopeful suspicion, he downed his coffee, refilled the lone cup, handed it to the waiting Stark. The latter took it without thanks, growled down at Hogjaw, "You had any yet?"

Hogjaw shook his head. "Don't want none," he gulped. "Thanks."

Stark shoved the cup at him. "Drink it. You don't look good." To the glumly staring Chickasaw he gritted, "See that he gets it down. And a couple more to hold it there." With the rough growl, he swung off toward the cabin site. There he snapped at Saleratus to get back to the fire and start supper, Waco and Slim to fetch the pack covers and ground tarps and spare ropes, Nella to stand by until he was ready for her.

Puzzled, and aching with fatigue to her blistered fingertips, the girl waited while he and the two cowboys threw the heavy tarps over the ridgepole, lashed them, front and rear, with pegged ground ropes, to form a temporary roof. With the makeshift job done as best it could be, he gruffly ordered the exhausted Texans firewards to join their fellows. Turning to follow them, he picked up Saleratus's shovel, handed it to Nella. He indicated the windowless interior of the canvas-covered hut, his mouth straight-set as a reservation Cheyenne's.

"Man may labor from sun to sun, but woman's work is never done."

Nella hefted the shovel, looked longingly in the direction of Stark's exposed flank.

"Don't tempt me, mister."

He moved too fast for her. She did not even get to cry out, let alone kick him in the shins as she would have loved to do. Seizing her under the arms, his big hands and wrists roughly pressing the curving sideswells of her breasts, he lifted her bodily across the threshold, dumped her rudely upon the dirt floor inside.

"Woman's place is in the home. This is ours. Get busy."

"Home!" The gasp exploded out of the indignant girl as though she had been struck in the stomach. She glared around the wet-logged interior of the muddy, unlit hovel, her green eyes wide with the enormity of the suggestion. "This—this—" Words failed her, then tried weakly to amend the hesitation. "This miserable, stinking, Montana horse shed!"

A muscle flicked, moved slightly in Stark's jaw. When he spoke she knew she had hurt him, but somehow there was no expected pleasure in the success.

"Better people than you and me have lived in stables," he said, "even been born in them. I reckon, such as it is, this one will do for us. Anyway, it's ours.

Clean it out, we're moving in tonight."

She looked sharply at him, the inevitable thought rising within her at the last words.

"Who's we?" she asked, small-voiced.

He caught her meaning, guessed her fear, and his face was not good to look at.

"All of us, you damn fool," he answered flatly. Then, voice suddenly thick-burred, strangely deep. "When I come for you, girl, you'll know it. You won't have to ask any questions about it."

Nella tried to laugh, could not, attempted a sneer, had no better luck; fell back haltingly on the adventuress's favorite close-range defense—sarcasm. "God bless our happy home," she shrugged, and started shoveling.

Nella could not sleep. She lay awake a long time. Sharing a packed-earth boudoir, 12 x 20 feet, with six men, two of whom were old and snored and gasped continually in their sleep, a badly smoking fire vented only by the gaps in the canvas roofing, the constant splash of melting snow from above where the old tarps were frayed through, together with half a dozen sweaty saddles and the conglomerate contents of Jeff Davis's scattered pack, was hardly conducive to deep and immediate slumber. Not, the good Lord knew, if you were a scared girl three months pregnant who had within the past seventy-two hours lost the man she loved and married the one she hated. And not if, like Nella, you could see nothing ahead but the grim months of sharing a double bunk with Nathan Stark while the latter, his five frostbitten Texas trail drivers and five hundred half-frozen longhorn heifers fought a futile draw with the killing winds and subarctic cold of south-central Montana Territory. Indeed, she realized she would be lucky if those months with Stark were only grim, not nightmarish; if he and the men could do so well as to draw with the Montana winter, not lose outright to it.

Her slender arm thrown across her face to protect her sleepless eyes from the drip of the leaking room canvas, Nella thus pondered the future and found it frightening. She tried the past, found it even less reassuring. This left only the shivering dark of the present and when she had thought of that the tough-minded Texas girl knew she had every reason, past, present *and* future, for fearing the big man who lay breathing so deeply and quietly at her side.

No, in the lonely darkness of a mudfloored log shed, with a High Plains blizzard howling and tearing like a mad dog at the blanket-draped doorway, a girl did not deceive herself.

From her first association with him, she had been unfair to Nathan Stark. She had not liked him, had deliberately used him as a means of following Ben Allison to Montana. She had, in moral effect, promised herself to him if he would take her to Virginia City. He had soberly agreed, meticulously carried out his part of the bargain. What was more, and worse, he had never, in all the interminable months of the great trek, treated her as anything but a very proper lady, had not sought to take the slightest advantage of the obvious implications of their hard-eyed agreement.

In the end, increasingly shamed by the fact, Nella had had to admit that for all her heartless contempt for him and his grasping, humorless kind, for all the glaring, unattractive faults of his character, his bitter ambition, his ruthless self-determination, the Montanan loved her as honestly and unselfishly as had Ben Allison or any other man in her adventuresome life.

And more. He had never lied to her, never tried to appear to be anything better or worse than what he was—a wolf-sharp businessman who knew what he wanted and would go about getting it any way he could, even to the point of paying for it if he had to.

In Nella's case he had paid for it, too, but she had failed to make promised delivery.

Then she had offered to marry him simply for the dishonest purposes of providing a good name for Ben's baby and a warm, safe place to hole up for the winter, for herself.

Poker-playing reader of hard men's (and harder women's!) faces that he was, the Virginia Citian had seen through the second half of that double deal and begun the slow process of his revenge by letting her go on through with it thinking he was still well heeled and riding high, saying no word about being dead broke and in debt or about his last-ditch determination to winter on the open range in a life-and-death gamble to cash in on his last chance at Montana fame and fortune—the starving longhorn heifers and the secret snow-free pastures of the Gallatin Valley.

He was, indeed, a hard man to know. Nella had not learned too much about him in the nine months up from Texas. Only enough to guess at one dead certainty. He was a man whose given word was as good as his guaranteed bond, a man who always paid his debts in the same lethally fair Old Testament way: an eye for an eye, a tooth for a tooth, a life for a life.

And no cash discounts for being a female.

The next two days were spent in a daylight-to-pitchdark drive to complete and amplify their winter quarters. For Nella there was no more time to worry about what lay ahead. She did the work of a paid hand, was temporarily treated as one. The endless back-aching hours limped by on feet swollen with dead-end exhaustion, but with nightfall of the second day they had the permanent roof on the main cabin, an attached lean-to finished up for Stark and her, a snowshed and corral in place for the all-important saddlestock.

Stark continued doing the work of three men and a six-foot boy, gave no further hints of a possible lean streak of hard-ore humor, or small, soft vein of human compassion. Old Chickasaw decided he had been badly premature in offering him a generous cut at the treasured pint of 100-proof. Nella concluded her worst fears of him were justified. The others worked over their Burley chaws, spat into the open backhole of Saleratus's sheet-iron stove, agreed with Waco's salty summation that he'd had the slabsided son of a bitch figured right, right along. He just didn't have no more goddam give to him than a pair of resoled Mexican cavalry boots.

The morning of the third day dawned clear as a glass of San Francisco champagne. There was not a cloud puff bigger than a cotton boll in the Gallatin skies. The wind was quiet, the morning sun warm and the eye-blinking bright. The main cabin was just toasting up to the soul-melting aroma of Saleratus's sourdough flapjacks when Nella entered from the lean-to to announce that Stark was gone. "Been gone some time," she qualified abruptly.

"How's that, ma'am?" queried Saleratus.

"He never came to bed last night. His blankets weren't touched. You seen him this morning?"

"Nope. Last I seen of him was last night. He sat up in here till late. Told me to go ahead and turn in, he'd bank the fire and set the sourdough crock back of the stove. He had some thinking yet to do, he said."

"He must have been thinking about pulling out on us." Waco's dry voice cut into the conversation from the doorway. Both turned as the little cowboy kicked the snow out of his boot arches, dropped the draping blanket, came on across the room to the stove. "I was just letting the saddlestock out to graze. Noticed that big bay stud he rides was gone. And that ain't all. So's your friend, Jeff Davis."

"Naw, by God! He didn't take the mule!"

"If he didn't, somebody else did. He's gone."

"Son of a bitch!" Saleratus was genuinely upset. It was not his style to cuss in front of women, whether he considered them ladies or not. "There's crust for you! I

89

wouldn't leave my own mother borry that mule. Pardon me, Miss Nella, but goddam him to hell anyways!"

For the first time in three days Nella's eyes lit up. "No call for any pardons, Mr. McGivern," she laughed. "I share your sentiments precisely. Yours likewise, Mr. Fentriss."

"Huh?" said the wizened rider.

"I reckon he's pulled out on us, too."

Saleratus shook his head. "I dunno about that. He don't strike me as the pulling-out kind."

"Nor me, acherally," conceded Waco on second thought. "But it don't look good. Something still smells a shade high somewheres."

"Likely," agreed the dour dough wrangler. "You ready to eat, Miss Nella?"

"Sure, Saleratus." Her answer was quick and bright. "I haven't felt so good since we got the herd across the Yellowstone."

"Why for you want to go pi'zening yourself then?" demanded Waco, keeping one eye on Saleratus. "You surround one of them self-rising bellypads of Sal's you'll for sure wish you'd stayed home with Mother. I ain't saying they ain't fit to eat, but so's a bootheel if you bile it long enough."

"You criticizing my cooking?" asked Saleratus hopefully, hands poised to remove his floursack apron.

"Not ever!" declared the other piously, knowing range law as well as any bunkhouse jury-wrangler west of the Big Muddy and not wanting any least part of his companion's thankless job. "If I had my way you couldn't

90

trade me humming birds' tongues nor friggazeed pea-
cock's eyeball for your sourdoughs, Sal. And coming to
biled bootheels, I reckon as how—"

"Me," interrupted Saleratus, hefting a two-foot stove
length of knot-hard cedar, "I reckon as how one five-
foot, hundred-and-ten-pound Brazos boy better get back
to herding the hoss stock."

"And me," grinned Waco, backing for the door
blanket, "I reckon you're righter than buffler chips
round a bull waller." He ducked under the blanket and
was gone, and Saleratus turned back to Nella. He looked
from her to the leathery pair of pie-tin-sized pancakes
smoldering and smoking in the rancid grease of the two-
foot frying pan. Checking the doorway once more to
make sure the enemy had fled, he shook his head, his
mournful, hound-sad face a study in painful honesty.
"They ain't really too good this time, Miss Nella. Best
leave me warm you up a twist of yestidday's bannock
and a couple chunk's of fatback."

She moved to him quietly, put her slender hand on
his shoulder. "Saleratus," she said, her smile striking
him as quick and crinkly enough to warm your hands
by, "I could eat a stovelid smothered in burnt onions
after listening to you two just now. For a minute you
took me back to Ben and the old times down the trail.
It was almost like as though he would step through
that blanket any second—" Her voice trailed off, the
smile fading with it. Saleratus saw the trembling glint
of the tears even as she averted her face to prevent him
from doing so. The old cook gulped, gritted his

stumpy teeth, flared at her defensively.

"Well, goddamit, we all miss him! That ain't going to bring him back, gal. So don't come around here weeping and crying and hanging on me. Christ Amighty, I got my work to do and I don't need you nor nobody else to be reminding me how much better off we all was when Ben was ramrodding the outfit. Now get the hell out'n my way and don't come back till I bang on the triangle for noon dinner!"

She came back around, voice husky but smile outshining the unshed tears. "Thanks, oldtimer. I needed that." She moved for the outer door. "I'll be back in five minutes. Keep those cakes hot and put that fatback to frying."

Saleratus stared after her. "Splatter dabs and salt hawg coming up," he grumped. "No-good, green-eyed, high-flying, flirttail Fo't Wuth filly!" Then, toothless grin spreading the proud southern drawl thicker than hominy grits and hamhock gravy, "But *Texas-bred,* goddamit! *Texas-bred—!*"

CHAPTER NINE

THE MORNING HOURS moved on well enough. The bluebird weather continued to hold bell-clear and balmy, the men's spirits to mount in step with the May-bright sun. Nothing more was said of Stark.

On the theory that, given proper time, Lucifer would dream up some sort of unsavory chore for idle cowhands, Chickasaw took his three bowlegged friends and rode off up-valley to check the grazing herd. He had hoped the inspection would suggest some added time-killing task but it did not. Everything was in order with the cattle. Old General Grant and the other herdbulls had their harems spread out in the winter sunshine as contentedly as though they were bedded down sixty miles south of the Alamo. There was plenty of stock-water still available in the open, unfrozen riffles of the Upper Gallatin. The heavy snow of the past two days had not covered a stingy tithe of the rolling blue gray miles of the pasturage. There was, in fact, not a single thing the cattle needed, or that four old cowboys could do for them. As a result, Chickasaw and his fellow herd inspectors were back at the main cabin by noon. As a further result, and as soon as their brief meal was done and the ricehull cigarette papers coming out with the third, tar-black refill of the coffee tins, they began to talk down aggressively their growing uneasiness over Stark's disappearance.

After a few minutes of listening to them letting on as though they did not give a tinker's broken-down dam where the Montanan was or how long he stayed there, Saleratus rubbed a sparing fingerful of ocher-colored Copenhagen snuff into his yellowed gums, inhaled a stiff pinch for good measure, sniffed disgustedly.

"In a pig's patoot! You once-upon-a-time tophands give me a pain I'd love to locate for you." He sneezed mightily, snuffled with the lugubrious deep pleasure of the hopeless, and happy to be so, snoose addict. "Ain't one of you heroes wouldn't give your winter's pay to see the big homely bastard riding up yonder bench trail this minute."

"If you're so lonesome for the outsize slob," observed Waco, "why don't you saddle up and trail him down? I allow you can still ketch him."

"Why don't *you?*" the sallow-faced cook snapped back. "You're the one's always allowing you could track a bear through running water!"

Saleratus's angry sling sank its arrow deep in the sensitive seat of the little man from Uvalde County. Waco prided himself above all else on his legendary (according to him) ability as a tracker and trailer. But before he could get up on his hindlegs to begin to paw a little ground, the grinning Hogjaw gave his already outraged tail another twist.

"Yeah, Shorty. Sal's right. You're the one for the job, sure enough. I'll never forget how you tracked them bees through that spring blizzard up by Bent's Fort. Nor how you trailed that polluted packrat that stole that pint out'n your warbag and got himself all stunk up last New Year's. Nor yet the way you—"

Waco looked the opposition in the eye, weighed the odds against him, nodded philosophically.

"I throw in. The truth is as out of place around here as a steer on a front stoop."

"The truth," qualified his friend Chickasaw bluntly, "is that if Stark don't show soon we'll all throw in." He made a fist of his right hand, held it up for their inspection. The forefinger of his left hand racheted across the knuckles made grotesquely big by forty years of

94

flanking calves. "Any man jack of you says I'm siding his Nibs gets a cluster of these in the whiskers. But I got to say this for the bastard. He's a real ringtail *hombre duro,* and I wisht he was here."

"Hell!" snorted Hogjaw. "So he's got more guts than you could string on a six-mile fence. So what?"

"So," sneezed Saleratus, blinking away the snuff tears and knowing he had the argument tailed-up for sure, "you're all of you just looking for a dog to kick. Chickasaw's dead right. Stark's more man in a minute than the five of us put together for a hundred and forty years!" He broke off, frowning quickly as he noticed the old cattleman squinting at the sky over the distant outer valley and not listening to his agreement. At the same time the sunlight failed as though it had been blown out like a barn lantern. Saleratus cleared his throat, concluded low-voiced. "When you figure she'll hit, Chickasaw? Come dark or thereabouts?"

The other continued to study the black cloudbank rebuilding above the northern foothills.

"Thereabouts," he said.

"Going to be as bad as before?" asked Hogjaw.

"Looks worse to me," muttered Waco. "What you say, Chickasaw?"

The old man went on looking. "Put it this way," he said at last, getting stiffly to his feet. "We had best cut wood as long as the light holds."

There was no further argument. With Stark gone the grizzled foreman's judgment was the best to be had. They accepted it, worked the afternoon away piling cordwood high along the doorway wall of the main cabin.

The blizzard crashed back into the valley shortly after nightfall. It came out of the north following an hour-long lull in the wind, struck with the nerve-shredding suddenness of a hysterical woman's scream. Thirty seconds after the first shriek it was shaking the twenty-foot ridgepole like a winter-starved bear with a spring shoat by the neck. For three straight hours there was nothing but wild wind. Then, about nine o'clock, with everybody still welded by common insomnia around the sheetmetal stove, the snow began again.

Minutes later, Stark rode in.

Through the dropping wind they first heard the friendly neighing of the ponies in the corral. Then the hideous brass of Jeff Davis's answering bray was greeting his gelded corral mates and the shrill whistle of Stark's bay stallion was replying to the welcoming whickers of the half-dozen mares in the saddle string.

Followed a long tense moment in which no one spoke and the only movement was Chickasaw spitting accurately into the stove's backhole.

When the door blankets moved they all looked up nervously, expecting the tall Montanan but entirely unprepared for the homely Roman-nosed friend who followed him in.

The door opening had been cut wide and high, to allow for both light and ventilation in the windowless shed. It was amply big to pass a man who stood plenty tall above his bunions, or a packmule who measured close to fifteen hands at his load-galled withers. In the present case it was doing both.

While they stared, Stark dropped the halter rope, let Jeff Davis stand, began arming out of his snowcaked coat. He was stiff with the cold and slow about it, and before he could get out of the frozen garment Nella was at his side.

She helped him, saying nothing.

Her eyes, like those of the others, were busy with what they saw topping the old packmule's heavy load. Her mind, like theirs, was having a hard time accepting both the object and its implications. It was a bushy eight-foot silver-tip spruce, freshly cut and of a size precisely calculated to fit under the low ridgepole of the main cabin. Nella winced to the uncomfortable truth of the thought. Day and month belatedly considered, that tree could mean only one thing. In his singular way Stark had remembered a date which they, in their self-commiserating bitterness, had completely forgotten.

Today was December 24.

"When I was a boy," said Nathan Stark softly, "we always decorated the tree Christmas Eve."

Nella looked at him, not ready to believe he had ever been a boy, much less had decorated a Christmas tree.

"What on earth can we put on it?" she asked, not actually meaning to get an answer but wanting to say something, anything, to ease the embarrassment of the following silence for Stark.

"I saw a right peart stand of mountain holly this morning," volunteered Slim Blanchard, surprising him-

97

self as much as anyone. "Some of them bright red berry clusters would look smart agin the blue-green of that spruce." He wrenched the camp ax out of the wall behind the stove. "I'll mosey along and brush out a few sprigs."

"I got a whole stack of leadfoil chawing terbaccy wrappers in my saddlebags," blurted Hogjaw. "Them kind with the purple and orange premium stickers pasted on 'em. I was saving 'em to send in for a solid gold-plated toothpick with a Mexican silver vest chain and a genuwine elk's tooth on the other end." He colored deeply, thrust out his thick jaw. "I reckon them foil liners will make fair purty spangles or glitter doodads all the same. Leastways, I'll fetch 'em."

"I ain't got nothing but some shag-ends of colored string," scowled Chickasaw. "Mebbe it would do to tie some of the other junk on with."

"Always wondered what the hell you was saving that goddam twine for," chirped Waco. "Thought sure you was developing a bad draft in your belfry. Howsomever, I can see where I was wrong."

"You was born wrong," snapped the wasp-tempered oldster. "Whyfor you collect them damn seegar bands, if you're so all-fired level in the head as you take on to be?"

"Say, by God," admitted the other unabashed, "them things *is* kind of bright and shiny at that. They'd make fair to middling ornaments, sure as sheepdip don't smell rosy!"

"Right near as nifty as snuffbox tops," added Saleratus, coming on to the pace of the occasion. "I got thirty-three different kinds, and each one glossy and beautiful as a sockfoot sorrel colt."

"Dig 'em out, Sal!" laughed Waco. "By Christ, we'll just put up the goddamdest Christmas tree ever see'd north of Red River!" He turned to Nella. "Miss Nella, ma'am, happen we drag out the family jools will you hire on to drape 'em around Mr. Stark's spruce?"

The girl's happily agreeing laugh was as quick and childishly excited as Waco's question. She immediately lost herself in a running battle of cowcamp banter with Waco and the others, as the old cowboy and his grinning companions produced and piled up their various treasures for her approval and selection.

Watching them, Stark shook his head.

The spontaneous transformation from scowling, silent suspicion of his absence and return, to loud, laughing acceptance of the tree and the whole idea of pitching in to whip up a Christmas Eve shindig, was too fast and confusing for him.

He thought he could understand a small part of their feelings, or at least remember some similar reactions of his own from years too far back in childhood to fully recall. What he could not understand and could only envy them, was their ability to let that feeling out—to laugh, be warm, let their eyes shine, their voices rise. No, somewhere along the lonesome road from dirt-poor adolescence to hardfisted money-making manhood Stark had lost the way. He no longer knew how to laugh out loud without thinking about it in advance. He had forgotten how to smile without first figuring where, or what, the grin was going to get him.

All a man like him could do, he told himself, to express a gratitude he did not feel but which he knew he owed, was exactly the sort of thing he had just done—gone into Virginia City and borrowed the money from Esau Lazarus to pay the men their first month's wages in advance, plus figuring in a piddly little Christmas bonus. And even that he had done solely because he had had to go into town anyway to let Lazarus know where he was and what he would need sent out by way of supplies when the weather broke.

The fact he had forced the seventy-mile round trip in something less than twenty hours, was beside the point. He had not even thought about it being Christmas Eve until he had gotten to the head of Van Buren Street and seen the saloons and sporting houses all decorated up like a chippie on her way to church. He had stopped on the way back to cut the tree only on a last-minute whim—and to try out the new red-handled camp ax he had picked up at Keppel's Hardware Emporium for Saleratus while waiting for the proprietor of the Bedrock Barber Shop to wrap the fancy German silver straight-edge he had previously bought Waco—before going back to Brown's General Merchandise to collect the inlaid spurs for Slim, the handcarved holster for Hogjaw, the sheep-lined cold-weather chaps for old Chickasaw.

Stark nodded to himself, satisfied with his impersonal reasoning, disturbed by only a couple of small questions which seemed to be somewhat left over after all the other pieces were in unsentimental place.

Why was he standing there lying to himself like a twenty-year trooper?

And, at the same time, feeling so Sunday-go-to-meeting good about it?

It was perhaps an hour later, close to ten o'clock, when it happened.

Stark had brought back three bottles of Old Crow—"one for Christmas, one for New Year's, one for dire emergencies"—and the Christmas quart had long gone the way of all whiskey around celebrating cowboys when, raspy and hoarse above their own good-natured noise, the crew heard the hand-close braying of a strange mule.

Stark, being nearest the door, was first to reach the blanket. Nella, who had passed the bottle with the big man more than two or three times, and had felt enough of a glow to begin thinking of him in mellower terms than knifing him in his sleep some night, was right behind him. The others, perched on or propped up by saddles and bedrolls dragged up around the stove, were too engrossed arguing which one of them should sneak up behind the Montanan and "cold-cock him with a chunk of cordwood" as a prelude to freeing the New Year's quart from his warbag a week ahead of time, to worry about wandering mules or what they might be doing out on a night like the present one.

But half a second later, when Stark pulled aside the door blanket, the most saturated member of the stove-

101

side conspiracy broke off his plotting to stare, suddenly owl-sober, at the arresting tableau beyond the firelit threshold.

The potbellied travois mule stood spraddle-legged and motionless, jug head down, long ears aslant, laboring breath rasping like a rusted file. Astride him slumped an Indian boy. He was no more than eight years old. His feet were tied under the mule's belly to keep him from falling off, his small hands knotted desperately in the stiff mane to hold him upright. He was as motionless as his slat-ribbed mount, only his beady eyes giving him the touch of life. Behind him, in the travois, bundled in a mangy buffalo robe and pair of threadbare U. S. Cavalry horse blankets, lay an Indian woman.

As Stark and Nella hesitated in their surprise, the boy's lips moved soundlessly. Failing, he tried again. The second time they heard the stilted, high-voiced apology. "Me sorry, mule no good. Him lost. Woman sick. Me cold. You help maybe—" It was barely audible and thick with the guttural North Plains accent, but it was English and they understood it. "You get the kid," barked Stark. "Me and the boys will get the squaw."

Nella nodded, moved quickly forward, pulled the boy from the mule and carried him inside. As quickly, Stark and the cowboys got the travois lacings cut away, followed her with the Indian woman. Chickasaw, with a true old Texan's unsentimental western tendency to rate a head of still useful saddle or pack stock a mile and a half higher than any Indian, stayed outside to haze the little mule into the pony corral.

102

In the cabin Nella made the Indian youth comfortable by the stove while Stark and the men had a look at the unconscious squaw. They had just taken that look when Nella came over with a cup of coffee just off the fire.

Stark dropped the buffalo robe quickly back in place. "We won't need that just now," he told her. "But you'd better stay here and talk to her when she comes around. I reckon, from what she's been through, she'll be wanting another woman to tell it to."

Nella looked at him, puzzled. He drew back the edge of the robe, gave her only an instant to see the tiny wrinkled head and dark red body of the day-old infant clutched to the woman's breast. Mercifully replacing the cover, he nodded to the silent cowboys.

"You'd best see to the boy. Rub him up good with snow. He looks pretty bad frostbit. I'll take care of the baby."

They moved off and Nella touched his arm. "Let me take care of him. You go along."

He took the baby from beneath the buffalo robe, wrapped it quickly in one of the moldy horse blankets. "No, I'll take him," he insisted.

"But I'm a woman!" flared Nella, moving angrily in front of him. "He needs a woman's care."

Stark shook his head gently. "He's past the care of any woman," he said, and stepped past her and out the blanket-draped door with the dead Indian child. When he returned a moment later, she was waiting for him. "I'm sorry," she murmured. "I didn't know."

"It doesn't make any difference."

"I think it does," she said softly.

"Not to me," he said. He knew what she meant, and that she was not talking about the Indian baby. But the time when he could care whether a thing made any difference to Nella Torneau or not was buried deep in the bitter drifts behind them. "You get some coffee into that squaw now. She's coming around. Get her talking as soon as you can."

"What do you mean, 'get her talking'?"

His frosty grin flickered briefly. "As our late friend Ben Allison would say, 'my Injun nerves are jumping like upstream salmon.'"

"I still don't get you."

"This is all Crow and Blackfoot country." The grin was dead. "With maybe a few Piegans, Bloods and Big Bellies mixed in."

"So?"

"This woman's a Sioux; Oglala, from her dress and hairdo."

Nella bit her lip, paled. She was not an expert on North Plains tribes but she knew *that* tribe. It had been the Oglala, under the famed Red Cloud himself, who fought the Fort Worth herd from the North Platte to the Yellowstone, forcing the Texas trail drivers to pay a pint of white blood for every five miles made across Wyoming Territory.

"That's not good is it?" she asked quietly.

"That's what you're going to find out." Stark nodded at the Oglala woman. "Call me if she doesn't savvy English, or lets on like she doesn't."

104

She looked up at him in somehow pleased surprise. "I didn't know you spoke Sioux. I never heard you."

"Maybe you never listened," said Nathan Stark, and turned away from her.

CHAPTER TEN

AT THE STOVE, Stark found the Indian boy being very nearly killed with kindness. Chickasaw excepted, the Texans were making over him as though he were pure white and had just been found in a basket abandoned on the old homestead doorstep—with a pleading note from his sweet-innocent but unwed mother who had run off to Dallas with the handsome whiskey drummer the fall before. The cowboys were loudly arguing what to call the little fellow and Stark, feeling that as good a place as any, placed his hand on the boy's shoulder.

"Hau, tahunsa," he grunted in Sioux. "Greetings, cousin. Do you have a name yet? How do they call you in your father's tepee?"

The boy's small face darkened. "I do not have a father, *Wasicun.*" His use of the formal reference "white man" let Stark know the youngster was not accepting the "cousin" address just yet.

"But you have a name." The Montanan ignored the lad's Indian coolness. "You are Oglala. I know their customs. You are old enough to have a tepee name. What is it?"

The boy looked at him. Among the Sioux permanent names were not given until manhood and some outstanding feat of war or of the hunt suggested one. Meanwhile each child had a pet or tepee name by which he was affectionately called. *"Hau,"* he finally admitted. "It is Waniyetula."

"A beautiful name," said Stark gravely. "One that fits well on a night like this."

"What the hell you two heathens talking about?" demanded Chickasaw. "I can savvy a little Injun talk if there's signs along with it, but you're gobbling along like a couple of lonesome turkey toms and not using your hands none atall. What you speiling? Greek or Chinee?"

"Oglala. I asked him his name, that's all."

"Did he give it to you?"

"Waniyetula—Winter Boy."

"He picked a pee cutter for a night like this un, by God!" Waco broke in.

"That's what I told him."

"You sure as sin told him right!" muttered Saleratus, shivering and poking up the fire.

"Yeah, Jesus, listen to that wind!" said Chickasaw. He rolled his eyes, pointed with his thumb as the storm took the ridgepole in its teeth and shook it again. Noting the grizzled rider's anxious gesture, the Oglala boy showed his first sign of real interest. He turned to Stark, pointed a stubby forefinger at Chickasaw, rattled off a surprising streak of Sioux. The latter, seeing Stark's blank face brighten and his grim mouth ease upward at the corners, challenged him belligerently. "What's the little red bastard yapping about now? You can tell him for me that I

106

don't cotton to his cut and color neither, by damn!"

Stark eyed him, a faint glimmer of the moment's fun far back in his pale eyes. "Simmer off now. He was just saying to tell you not to be afraid of the wind. He was born in it. In a bad blizzard just like this one. He said to tell my grandfather that no harm would come to him while he was here." He paused, nodding straightfaced at the fuming oldster. "I don't know, cowboy. Looks to me like you've found a friend."

Chickasaw scowled and locked up his straggly bearded jaw and let on as though he had just had his mother insulted in a saloon. What a crust that dirty-colored little runt had! Rolling those shoe-button eyes at a man and calling him Stark's grandfather! And letting on as though he was going to take care of you! Well, by Christ, that would be just about enough of *those* buffalo chips.

"Don't come at me with that 'friend' noise," he har-rumped at Stark. "Any time you think you're getting me enrolled in the local order of Sioux lovers, you'd better check your paintpots again. Ain't never been an Injun worth three hoots in a high wind, and calling them white don't change their inside colors a damn shade!" Glaring at his grinning fellows he stomped off to a dark corner, sat down on a sacked saddle.

As soon as he had gone, Stark's mouth straightened. "Listen, boy," he told the youth, "it's time we heard your story. Is that your mother over there? Where are you from? What are you doing traveling in this weather?" He paused, frowning down at him.

"Something is very wrong here. This is the time to be in the lodge burning the fire and mending the things for the spring hunt. No Indian travels in this weather without a great reason, especially through enemy country. And the dead child, only hours old. What was the squaw doing out so near her time? Tell it with a straight tongue, boy. What were you running away from?"

The Sioux youth stared at him a long time, possibly half a minute. Stark stared him back. Finally the boy appeared satisfied with his study of the white man. He talked very fast once he started and, for an Indian, with rare excitement.

There was nerve-tingling reason for his haste.

The woman was his mother. He did not know his father. He was a fullblood, though. That he knew. His father had been a Oglala like his mother. Like Zinca-hopa, Pretty Bird, over there in the travois.

Up until one sun ago he and his mother had lived with a white man a long pony ride to the west. In a little valley over there. This man had kept a few old cattle, not many, just a few. They were *pte-wa-quins,* packing buffaloes, like the ones the white man used to haul his wagons up the old Medicine Road.

Stark's eyes narrowed. He interrupted the boy, turned to the cowboys. "The squaw's his mother. She was shacked up with a rancher over west a ways. Fellow was running a few head. Old wagon bulls, mostly, near as I can make out. Likely castoff stuff from the Oregon Trail emigrant traffic back in the fifties, from what the boy

108

says." He turned back to the Indian lad, signaled him to continue.

Winter Boy bobbed his head, went on.

Yesterday some strange Indians had come to the ranch. They had acted like friends and Jepson, that was the white man who was good to Winter Boy and Pretty Bird, had let them come into the kitchen and eat a good meal of beef and boiled beans. When they finished they had belched a lot, after the proper custom, then their leader had pulled a rusty pistol from under his blanket and shot Jepson through the head. After that they went outside and some more Indians had come out of the forest and all these had guns and were wearing warpaint like they had been on a summer raid.

Finally, after some loud talk, the Indians had gone into the corrals and shot all Jepson's cattle. Then the chief had come back and talked a lot to Pretty Bird. He ordered the house burned and told Pretty Bird she had better take Jepson's old plow mule and get out of there.

His mother had then made a travois and said they must try and reach the white man's mines in Alder Gulch before the big snow gets too deep to travel. The chief had said he would be back next day and kill them if they were still around. He was letting them go because Pretty Bird was with child and it was bad medicine to kill anything heavy with young in the winter. And besides, right at this time they had a treaty with the Sioux.

The Oglala boy took a deep breath, gritted his teeth. He chopped his right hand in front of his mouth, to signal he was cutting off his speech.

"*He-hau,* thank you," said Stark. "Only one thing. What Indians were they? What tribe? What chief?"

"Kangi Wicasi!" snapped the small Sioux. "The cursed Crows!" He shook his head. "I do not know how to say their chief's name in their thick tongue, but my mother said we would call him Slohan in Oglala."

"Buffalo Ribs, eh?" Stark's eyes narrowed. "I'll remember it."

"Good. He was a bad Indian."

By this time Chickasaw had come out of his sulk, drawn by the terse exchange. As Winter Boy spoke, the old cowboy questioned Stark acidly.

"What's the rest of his yarn, Mr. Stark? In words of one syllable or less."

"I'll try to keep it simple enough for you," the Montanan rasped back.

"Obliged," drawled Waco, edging in. "Never could stand a man that was all wind and no whistle."

Stark nodded, let them have it.

"A band of Crows wiped out the boy's ranch. Killed the rancher. Bird named Jepson. I've heard of him. Shot all his cows, burnt his buildings. Give the squaw and the kid twenty-four hours to get scarce. Crows didn't kill them because they got some kind of a short-term peace working with the Sioux right now, and these two are Oglala just like I thought."

As he hesitated, Nella, who had come up behind the group unnoticed, spoke sharply.

"This is your day to think right, mister!"

He came around scowling. "What's that?"

"What you were saying about your Indian nerves jumping like jack salmon?"

"Yeah?"

"They ought to be."

"Go on."

"The Indian woman. I just got her to talking. Her story's better than the boy's."

"How's that?"

"Your herd's next on the Crow list—!"

There was a little more to the Oglala woman's story than that. Stark found that out when he shoved Nella out of his way and stepped across the cabin to confront the stubborn-eyed squaw.

"Hohahe, kola, welcome to my tepee, my friend," he greeted her in his stilted Oglala. "The white woman says that the Kangi Wicasi are planning to burn this ranch too. And to kill me also. How is that? I have lived many years in this country at peace with the Crows. What made them attack Jepson's place. Why do they mean now to harm me as well?"

The woman turned her face away, said nothing.

"The boy has told us part of the story," he tried again. "You have only to tell us the rest of it. If there is danger for you and Winter Boy there is danger for all of us."

She looked at him then.

"I do not know you," she said softly, speaking the tribal dialect with the same bright fluency as her son. "I did not tell the pretty white squaw that the Crows

111

were going to harm *you,* or burn *your* ranch. I said no word about you at all."

He studied her, decided she definitely was not lying. "Well, then, what did you tell her?"

"Only what the Crows told me."

"And what was that?"

"What I told the pretty white squaw."

He thought about it. This woman was no fool. Nor was she playing one. She was very smart but for some reason very afraid. And of what? Not the Crows certainly. She should know they would not be in pursuit of her in this storm. Not even if they had changed their minds about letting her get to the white settlements. No, it must have been something they told her, and a man in his clammy boots had better find out just what that something was.

He sat down by her side, carefully touched her dark hand. "Your people can read a man's face like a clean track in new snow. Tell me, how do you read mine then?"

She stiffened as he put his hand on hers, relaxed when he spoke, then glanced shyly up at him as he smiled briefly. "You are very handsome," she murmured. "Big. Strong. Angry-hearted. Like *mato,* the great grizzly bear."

He colored, pulled his hand away. "That is not what I mean. Do you trust me? Do you see any bad thoughts in my face?"

She blushed in turn. Pretty Bird was quite young, not yet thirty, and her parents had named her well. For a Sioux, or for any race or color, Zincahopa was a looker.

112

"Wonunicun," she whispered. "I am sorry. No, I see nothing. Your thoughts are good."

"All right then. Tell me what I ask."

As with her bright-eyed son, Pretty Bird talked a lot once she started.

"It was the one I call Slohan who told me. After they had set Jepson's house on fire. He was the Kangi Wicasi chief and he told me a strange thing—a very strange thing. He said he was giving us the mule and letting us live because we were Sioux. Now, as you must know, *Wasicun,* that was a most peculiar thing for a Crow to say."

It was for sure, Stark knew. The Crows and the Sioux, particularly the fierce Oglala, were blood enemies, and had been as far back as Indian memory went. He signified his understanding to Pretty Bird, and she went on.

"Well, I asked Slohan about that and this is what he said.

"About thirteen suns ago there came among the tepees of his people three Oglala braves. They were from my own clan—Makhpiya Luta's family." She smiled, adding proudly, "You must know that I am of the blood, also, of Tashunka Witko. I am the younger sister of his wife, Tasina Sapewin. We are all second cousins." Stark's blond brows contracted frowningly. Those were pretty famous names she was throwing around. In Oglala, Makhpiya Luta came out "Red Cloud" and Tashunka Witko added up to "Crazy Horse." "Go on," he ordered her gruffly. "I do not want to hear about those two. I have met them."

She watched him a minute after he said it, then continued. "Well, those three braves told Slohan that a tall yellow-haired white man had crossed the Yellowstone into Crow land with a huge herd of spotted buffalo from far south in the country of the Kiowa and Comanche. Red Cloud and the Oglala had tried to stop this herd of the white man's cattle but had failed. Their medicine had been bad. Now the cattle had gotten away from them into Crow land and they could not go after them. The Pony Soldiers down at Fort Laramie were watching them too close. But nobody was watching Slohan and his Kangi Wicasi.

"Red Cloud sent greetings to his Crow brothers and asked that a truce be called between them until the white man and his stinking spotted buffalo could be driven from the Indians' buffalo pastures. Red Cloud had driven them from the Wyoming pastures. It was up to Slohan to finish the job in the Montana grazing grounds. If this white man was allowed to bring his cattle into the buffalo pastures, others would follow. They would come thick as grasshoppers in a dry year. The grass would be destroyed and the buffalo would go away and the Indian would die. It was the white man's way. Where he went, everything died."

Stark said nothing and she concluded rapidly.

"That is about all, *Wasicun.* Red Cloud called upon the Crows to find this man, to kill him and his cattle as a warning to others. He sent the three Oglala scouts to show them where the herd was hiding, up on the grass where the Yellowstone became two rivers. The Crows had gone there right away but the big snow had commenced. The cattle were gone. The white man was not there. There was no hope of trailing a thing in that snow, so the war party went home. On the way they had crossed Jepson's valley—"

Stark touched her hand again, shaking his head.

"*Haho,* thank you, Pretty Bird, that's enough now. The boy has told me the rest. You sleep now. There is no danger while Wasiya walks about."

Wasiya was the Winter Giant, the blizzard god. The woman knew his power, all right. For the first time she smiled a real smile. Turning her head away from the light of the fire, she closed her eyes. Stark pulled the old buffalo robe around her, moved toward the stove.

"Well?" Again it was the cynical Chickasaw. "What's *her* story? Was she out hunting snowbirds and lost her way in the dark?"

"Not quite," said Stark. "The same Crow bunch that did for Jepson tried for us up on the Forks. Missed us in the storm and got Jepson on their way back home. And more—"

"Yeah?" probed Waco.

"Guess who put them up to shagging us?"

"I couldn't guess how many horses made two teams," grimaced Waco. "Who?"

"Old friend of ours from over Wyoming way. Dark-complected fellow. Looked a lot like an Indian. Called himself Red Cloud."

"Naw—!" It was a chorus of cowboy disbelief, all the riders contributing to it.

"Yes," said Stark. "You bet your damn life. And here's something else you can tie your Texas ropes to hard and fast. When this snow goes out—the very first minutes there's half-good footing for pony travel—those red Crow bastards will come looking for us."

A pin dropping in the trampled mud of the cabin floor would have crashed like a sixty-foot cedar saw log. Even the sheetmetal stove seemed to be thinking it over, holding its hollow roar to a simmering mutter.

"Well," said Waco at last, letting his held breath go with the crooked grin, "at least we got till spring to worry about it."

"You think so?" asked Stark quietly.

"Don't tell me," blustered the little cowboy, "that this goddam icebox is apt to thaw out short of April and the new grass!"

Stark eyed him. *"Ever hear of a chinook?"* he said.

"A shin-what?" scowled Waco suspiciously.

"A chinook."

"Oh! Sure. It's a kind of Injun ain't it?"

"Hell no!" broke in Hogjaw superiorly. "It's a damn fish. A sort of a sammon, or some such. Injuns catch 'em arunning up the Columbier River over yonder in the Oregon country. Or maybeso it's in the Washington. Anyways, I recollect seeing a pitcher of that country sommers in a studybook. Purtier than a grass-fat steer it was, too. Blue waterfalls asplashing right and left, them neat little green Christmas trees plastered all over the place, white snow ashining atop every mountain within forty mile. Oh, I tell you, boys it was—"

116

"It's not a fish," grunted Stark raspingly. "Nor an Indian."

"Well?" demanded Chickasaw irritably. The old cattleman was upset at having Hogjaw interrupted just when he was going good. "What in the tarnal hell is it!"

"It's a wind," nodded Stark slowly. "One worse than any blizzard that ever blew." Then, cryptically, and just before he turned away from them.

"You better hope you never hear it."

CHAPTER ELEVEN

THERE WAS WORK, and to spare, for all of them that week. The herd had to be turned daily from drifting up the valley, for in the higher reaches the snow was piling badly, putting the grass out of reach for the inexperienced southern cattle. As a result they had to be worked continually to hold them on the main valley floor where the steady updraft from the lower elevations kept the short buffalo browse comparatively free of snow, and where the river's banks were gentle enough to let them down to drink, yet where the stream still had sufficient fall to prevent the ice from forming to close in the water. Too, the Gallatin's upper course supported heavy stands of ash and box elder in addition to the common conifers and in bad weather this fringe timber afforded its wonderful protection only if the stock were held within easy drive or drift of the river. It thus became the daylong job of Stark and his four-man crew to hold the active young cattle close in to the sheltering brakes. It was hard riding work. By the time the Texas cowboys loped in each day, the light was gone, with dusk shutting in swiftly. They had little will left with which to worry about Stark, his bitter young bride, Ben Allison's baby, Buffalo Rib's vow to burn them out, or any other small part of their doubtful futures in the Gallatin Valley.

For Nella's part there was noticeable improvement with the arrival of Pretty Bird and her young son. The Fort Worth girl made sure of that.

At her sharp suggestion the Oglala woman moved into the lean-to and Stark, taking the obvious hint without an eyelid flicker, moved out.

The big Montanan had, as a matter of fact, been only too glad to do so.

The whole idea of the lean-to and his sharing it with Nella had been no more than a proud pose on his part. A man did not like to have a wife and not to have her. Not when five other men were clearly watching him and wondering about it. Naturally, he had not touched the girl. And that was all right with him, as it was with her. But for the men it would not do. With him and Nella in the lean-to together they would never leave off wondering and watching, never give up guessing whether or not he and the girl were having anything to do with one another. But if he slept with them, out in the main cabin, they would not have to guess and would *know* nothing was going on. That set better with a man than to have them wondering about it. At least it did if he had an ounce of manpride left in him, and Stark had several ounces. Not alone that, but he was honest enough to admit it. And to admit, too, that the lean-to had been a bad arrangement from the first night.

Yes, for sure, he was glad to be out of it.

It had not seemed to bother Nella a great deal but it had begun to get to him. A man could not share a 6 x 8 shed with *any* woman and not know he was bunking with a female. With a woman like Nella Torneau—

But it was no use thinking about that.

A man was a man when a woman like her lay within arm's reach of him in the warm dark. He could curse her and hate her and swear he was going to yet get even with her if it took him his whole life—and all the will power he had built up in that life. And he could know he meant it too. But when he was all through reassuring himself he could still smell the fragrant heat of her body scent lingering in the close-aired silence. Still know that she lay over there, not a yard away, soft-skinned and long-limbed and satin-naked beneath her wolfskin winter robe. And, knowing that, he would not be able to think about a thing else. Or to get a wink of decent sleep the whole night through, for the hell it stirred up in him.

Yes, for double sure, Stark had been glad to get out of that lean-to.

And glad, too, for the week of doghard work the blizzard weather following Christmas Eve had brought on.

But that work was over now. The storm was letting up again, the cattle safely spread along the river timber. It was New Year's Eve, an idle day looming tomorrow.

Turning his tall bay stud into the saddlestock corral, Stark frowned. He climbed stiffly down, pulled the

119

saddle, wiped the bay carefully with the blanket, replaced the gate pole, followed the weary cowboys toward the cabin. It was full dark and he was dead, lead-foot tired. He thought dully of the Old Crow he had saved for tonight, felt a little better from that. He would break out the quart after supper. The boys would like that. Maybe they would get a little spirit going like they had Christmas Eve. Perhaps Nella would stay clear of it this time, not smile at him nor look his way, letting him put her out of mind and keep her there. Yes. Likely that was the way it would go. Everything smooth and halfway human all around, with nobody pushing anybody nor asking any favors nor a thing else save to be let alone to have a little drink and get early to bed and let it go at that.

But a man never knew. He just never did.

All he could do, or hope to do, was to set his jaw and blunder straight on ahead like he always had when he was fighting in the dark and could not see who was shooting at him.

But it was not Christmas Eve and it did not go like Christmas Eve.

The quart went around the stoveside circle once or twice, the boys fired up a bit, took a run at a couple of sick coyote choruses of "Auld Lang Syne," backed off and bogged down pretty quick, gave it up and started hunting their bedrolls. With the whiskey working inside them and the heat of the stuffy cabin outside of them they were soon enough outsnoring the blizzard.

Shortly, Nella nodded goodnight and went into the lean-to.

Stark, after a restless twenty minutes of sucking on the fireless stub of his cigar and dragging at what was left of the Old Crow, got up a little unsteadily. He turned the damper down on the stove, fumbled some wet wood in on top of the coals, started for his own blankets.

It was then that he saw it.

And stood there with the meaning of it slowly fighting its way through whiskey.

In the far end of the room Chickasaw, under the excuse that he "didn't want the smelly little red maverick sleeping with white men," had rigged up the squaw's travois as a cot for Winter Boy. The Indian lad had long ago sought his bed, but for the first time Stark now saw that he had not sought it alone. His mother was sharing it with him.

The short hairs on his neck lifted. His stomach drew in and got small.

He looked at the sleeping men, at the silent Indians, at the drawn blankets closing the lean-to entrance. The cabin was darkening fast, as the shutdown draft and the damp wood dimmed the stove's banked coals. In the lowering light he could clearly see the beckoning shine of the lean-to candle wavering beyond the blankets, and again his stomach shrank. She had not only ordered the Indian woman to sleep outside—she was still up in there and waiting for him!

The thought put the blood to pounding in his temples like the crazy race of war-dance drums. Again, furtively this time, he checked the men and the Indians. They had not stirred nor missed a snore. Wide lips loosening, he reached down for the quart, found it, tilted it, hungry eyes never leaving the blanketed doorway. He dropped the empty bottle into the soundless dirt of the floor, moved weavingly forward. At the blankets he stopped short, his hand freezing as it parted them.

Nella was seated at the packing-box dressing table Saleratus had fashioned for her, nervously brushing her hair. On the chinked logs in front of her hung the cut-crystal vanity mirror Stark had brought her as her Christmas present from Virginia City the week before. On the table itself the candle stood in its makeshift frying-pan holder, guttering fitfully amid the eroded badlands of its tallowed drippings. By its rose and saffron light Stark saw reflected in the looking glass a sight which cut off his breath, sent the whiskey hammering through him in an ugly, wild surge.

When she had begun her brushing, she had carefully wrapped herself in the heavy wolfskin robe which served her as both bed comforter and dressing gown. But the repeated movements of her raised arm had worked the fur off her shoulder and parted it in front, revealing her breasts and the rounding curve of the soft abdomen below them. But it was not this sight alone which aroused the watching man. His reddened eyes saw something else in the same moment. On its wall peg beyond the dressing table hung the girl's ankle-length cotton-flannel nightgown, the sole concession to femininity allowed her in the spartan conditions of the winter

122

camp. And with the gown hung the red wool long under-wear which, in common with the men, she had worn night and day since leaving Virginia City.

Stark growled inaudibly, deep in his throat.

She was naked under the wolfskin—and clearly meaning to stay that way—*for him!*

Still the big Montanan remained motionless, held hidden where he was by that age-old, matchlessly exciting curiosity with which a man will spy upon a par-tially disrobed woman unaware of his presence and going on about her further preparations to receive him—knowing he can have her at any minute but wanting, even then, first to see everything she will do with her body, and every suggestive movement and part of it will unconsciously show him before she realizes he is there.

But as he hesitated, so did Nella.

Suddenly, and in a way Stark did not like.

Still not knowing he was watching her, she put down the brush, glanced anxiously at the entrance blankets, looked back into the mirror at her own white face, shook as though to an unaccountable, sharp chill, pulled the wolf robe belatedly and apprehensively back up around her slender shoulders and tightly closed across her swelling breasts.

The full realization of what she was doing—*what she had already done*—confronted the Texas girl. She was suddenly very afraid.

There were no sounds in the outer cabin save those reassuring, restless ones of the sleeping men. Yet she knew instinctively that Stark was still awake. Was still waiting. And to her fear was added a swift dark shame.

He had been so decent the past week, so strong and sure and fair, no matter how callous or cruel, right from the beginning. Then there had been his strange trip to Virginia City, the Christmas tree, his awkward giving to her of the dainty mirror, secretly and when they were alone, when the others were not around and when she had already thought he had deliberately failed to bring a present for her. And now tonight. His tired, painful attempts to cheer the men, to make a little something hopeful of their common situation and future prospects. His clumsy failure with its subsequent, hard-faced withdrawal into his normal brooding aloneness. That sort of thing got to a girl—any girl—and it had gotten to her. Once it had, if you were Nella Torneau's kind of girl, you knew that regardless of how you yourself felt about it, there was only one way to let a man like Stark know he was not the only one in Montana Territory.

But that had been half an hour ago, and it had been the sort of impulsive, emotional thing which was always far easier to think up than to go through with. Now, having started it, she knew she could not finish it. Confusingly sorry for Stark, or not, she could not go on. Twisted sympathy was not enough. Neither was their common loneliness. Nor the fact, honestly admitted to herself, that it had been overlong since she had had a man and wanted one now—very much. None of those things mattered in this last minute. There were certain men for certain women, any women, moral or married or walking the street. And the shivery, too late thought

124

which struck her now was that she could never willingly submit to Nathan Stark, nor even bear the thought of his big hands being put upon her.

Stiffening, Nella glanced again at the blanketed doorway. Its draping still hung motionless. Perhaps, after all, there was yet time! Maybe it was *not* too late.

She moved swiftly from the table, her whole thought, now, to retrieve and hurry into the discouragingly formless protection of the faded red underwear and frayed cotton nightgown. She had only taken the unlovely garments from their wall peg and begun to shrug out of the close-wrapped wolfskin, when she heard the sound behind her.

She whirled like a trapped animal.

Stark was through the blankets, standing there, dark-faced, swaying from the drink and the nearness of the moment he had fought down in his mind from the first instant he had laid eyes upon the Fort Worth girl almost ten months ago.

In turning to face him, Nella had involuntarily dropped the gown and underwear to grasp desperately for the slipping wolfskin. She was too late. The heavy robe had already fallen too far. It lay now on the dirt floor at her feet. For an agonizing, dead-still, suspended second she crouched paralyzed and virgin nude before Stark.

The towering Montanan looked at that body and all the harsh force and purpose built through ten years of stern self-denial was as suddenly destroyed as Samson's strength in Delilah's tent.

He saw the muscularly slender form of a twenty-year-old girl as inherently lean and graceful as a young lioness—and saw that form now filled out in straining breast, curving belly and molded buttock with the lush, rare beauty of a child-woman three months pregnant.

The animal sound that came out of him had no words and only one meaning.

Nathan Stark had never had an unpaid woman. The drive and dedication of his lonely struggle for self and success had left no time for the other, incomparably sweeter kind. He thus faced, for the first time in his hard life, the sole situation in which a strong man's determination and cold intelligence were worse than useless things.

He made the sound again, and moved for her.

She caught up the wolfskin, cowered back into the corner behind her, shielding her nakedness with the rich fur, fiercely whispering for a mercy she knew she could not expect. "No, Stark, no—! Please! Wait! Soon. Stark, soon. But not now. Oh God, not now—"

He had her, then, like a wild senseless thing.

She fought him, continuing to plead brokenly with him to let her go. To give her only a little more time. To think of the men just beyond the blanket and perhaps awake now. To remember Ben, the baby, anything. Only to let her go this one time. To stop now. To become Stark again. To remember who he was, what she had done to him, what he was doing to her!

He did not hear her, and the tears came then as her wild pride would not let her cry out or make a resisting sound the men in the outer cabin might hear. She turned her head to the rough logs of the wall, soft body rigid and trembling, white teeth buried in her bleeding lips to keep the shame and the pain and the terror of the interminable, struggling, sweaty minutes to herself. Only long afterward, when Stark had stumbled back to his own bedroll in the main room and become at last quiet, was the sound of her muffled sobbing audible beyond the screening blankets of the lean-to.

Even then it was only Pretty Bird, the wide-eyed Oglala woman, who heard it.

Or who cared about it.

CHAPTER TWELVE

WIND WAS the surest constant in Montana Territory. Night and day, hour on hour, year around, there was some kind of a wind blowing.

On those peculiar occasions when there was not, and the time was winter, the worried Crows and Blackfeet glanced skyward and warned one another that Man Above, the Great Spirit, was boiling up a bad pot of new weather, mixing it darkly in his sacred buffalo skull headdress—in his "medicine hat" as they put it—and they stayed in their cowhide lodges and rationed their precious supplies of prairie-chip fuel very carefully. Wise white men, ones who had been long enough in the territory to raise a beard or a batch of young ones, developed a similar built-in warning system for subtle weather shifts. "Injun feel" it was aptly called, and they were as touchy to sudden fall-offs in the wind as was any red brother west of the Yellowstone.

Nathan Stark was a wise white man. He was childless but he had raised a full set of whiskers. Accordingly, when just after midnight the howl of the up-canyon blast slacked away and the cabin's ridgepole quit shaking for the first time in seven days, he rolled up on one elbow, shook the whiskey thickness out of his shaggy head, listened hard.

He was cold sober within the next thirty seconds.

Inside the cabin there were only the normal night noises of half a dozen humans in heavy sleep—the sighs, grunts, breath catching and restless turnings of tired people under the fitful anesthesia of bone weariness.

Outside the cabin there was—nothing.

Not a sound, or the whisper of a sound. A silence was out there as lifeless as the dark side of the moon. Then, as Stark listened, it began.

The first leaping shriek nearly tore the tiny building from its foundation logs. The lashing pines and cedars at the clearing's edge began to bend and scream as though they had animal life and were in mortal pain. A tremendous back pressure burst down the dampened stovepipe, spun the draft on its skewered axis. The iron door banged open, spewing a shower of hot and cold ash across the room.

Old Chickasaw came up out of his blankets fighting a live coal out of his smoldering beard. He cursed, yelled, batted the glowing ember to the floor and, in his excitement, tried to stomp it out with his bare feet.

While his following yell was still strangling him, the others were bombarding out of their bedrolls, barking their shins, falling across each other, their carelessly scattered saddles, stacked supply boxes and even, in the case of dull-witted awakener, Mr. Hogjaw Bivins, the hot stove itself. In the midst of the confusion Nella, wrapped in her wolfskin, ran out of the lean-to and joined Pretty Bird and Winter Boy where they huddled by the overturned travois. Stark, being old to this wind if not sure of it, leaped to fasten the stove door and secure the spinning damper. The next moment he had gotten Saleratus's coal-oil lamp down from its wall shelf, was striking a flaring sulphur match to it.

The wick smoked, steadied, burned clear—for about five seconds—then was dead again, snuffed out by the wind which sucked through the tightly chinked walls as though they had been those of a lattice-work summer-house down south. Stark did not relight it. Instead, he put it swiftly back on the shelf, glancing apprehensively at the swaying ridgepole above. As he did, the cabin shuddered to a succession of wild blows from without its front wall.

In clearing the building site he had ordered a lofty old patriarch of a red cedar left in place to "guide us home in heavy weather," and to "mark the front door when the snow gets over the lintel." He wished now, and cursingly aloud, that he had made Slim knock it over and snake it clear of the cabin while the snaking was good. But the way it was he could only move fast and try to

129

make himself heard above the repeated crashings of the giant tree's wind-driven spar against the rocking front wall.

"Where the hell's the water bucket!" he bellowed at Saleratus, grabbing the stampeding cook as he bumbled by in the dark. "Ahint the stove where it ought to be, goddamit!" His captive was in no mood for light social exchanges. "Where the infernal hell you think it'd be? Hanging down the old home well?"

Waco, who had just stubbed his toe on the empty Old Crow bottle, picked it up, waved it grinningly under Saleratus's offended nose. "Don't argue with the boss-man!" he shouted. "Just hand him the dipper, you old goat. Any fool can see he needs a chaser powerful bad!" Before the angry cook could answer, Stark had found the bucket, kicked the stove door open, sluiced its contents over the rekindled fire. The flames spit back resentfully, sputtered out. "Now what in God's name you aiming to do?" yowled Saleratus. "Freeze us to death afore we're decent awake!"

Stark put down the bucket, came around on him.

"If that eighty-foot cedar comes through the roof on top of that hot stove, you'll have a fire you can keep warm by all winter!" he snapped. "Besides, being frozen is the last thing you've got to worry about right now."

"What you getting at?" Waco horned in, dropping the bottle along with his grin.

"Inside half an hour," predicted Stark, "it'll be so close inside this cabin you'll be sweating like a walked-out racehorse."

130

"I reckon it's my turn now," put in Hogjaw laconically. "What does *that* mean?"

"It means you didn't hope hard enough."

"How's that?" It was the nervous Waco getting back into it.

"You remember me telling you you'd better hope you never heard a chinook?"

"Yeah. Sure. So—?"

"So," said Stark, "you're hearing one."

For the next hour the hot blast of the chinook sucked through the valley, burned across the grassy flats, roared away up the canyon of the Gallatin. The hurricane force of its high-level scream literally pinned the little group inside the cabin, the wild hammer of its furnace forging an invisible barrier of seventy-mile desert wind across the doorless entrance. A strong man might have gotten over the footsill and three staggers into the open. After that he would have been stretched out flatter than a polar bear rug, and with about the same chance of getting up and going on.

The temperature shot up like a fuse-lit rocket. Perhaps by the end of Stark's half hour no one was actually perspiring, but neither was anyone arguing with the Montanan about his slightly missed forecast. The general idea of his "fair and warmer" prediction was correct enough to convince a double-bred Missouri mule.

In the thirty minutes after the chinook struck, the snow level outside the gaping doorway sank three inches. The swirling air inside the cabin heated up to a point where

Chickasaw felt moved to observe that it was the first time since hitting Montana he hadn't been able to see his damn breath, and for Waco to allow that it was likewise the first time his teeth had let up chattering since fording the ever loving Yellowstone. Saleratus said nothing because he did not have enough teeth with which to chatter, but Hogjaw generously conceded that he was no longer shaking like a hound-dawg trying to pass peach seeds, while Slim dolorously admitted that his chine bone, which had turned blue somewhere in Wyoming, was thawing out a mite around the edges.

Nella, like Saleratus, but not for lack of a flawless set of sparkling white teeth, said nothing. She was joined in the sentiment by Pretty Bird and Winter Boy, neither Indian feeling yet privileged to take part in the white brother's council.

Stark said what he had to say with all his usual talent for putting a chill into any situation—even a chinook.

"Dish up some cold chuck," he ordered Saleratus, "and keep your ears open while you're about it. I don't want to have to go back over any of this." He swung around to face the others, reading it off to them in his dead, flat way.

"The minute the main blow slacks off, we've got to go out after the cattle. This wind may hold for days once she's dropped off, but the first big blast always lets up pretty quick. Either way, the snow will be off the flats by daylight and the big melt-off from up canyon will hit down this far about noon. When it does the river will be out of its banks and into the timber inside of ten minutes.

132

Once she's up she will stay sky-high until the chinook quits for good. And while she *is* up, you won't be able to get across her with a sixteen-hand horse on stilts."

"Uh-huh," broke in the slow-minded Hogjaw. "Where's that leave us?"

"On the far side," grunted Stark. "Unless we can round up the herd and get it crossed back over to this side before one of the two things hits us."

"Two things?" Chickasaw asked querulously.

"*You* count them," said the Montanan. "The river rise, or our Crow friends."

"It comes out two, all right," agreed Waco. "Keep adding."

"Wait a minute, cuss it!" It was old Chickasaw again, still nettled. "Whyfor we got to bring them cattle back acrost? Dammit all, there ain't half the graze on this side there is over yonder!"

"That's right. This is the short side of the valley. But if we've got them on this side all we have to do is to hold them here until the water goes up and holds them for us."

"What the hell you digging at?" complained Waco. "You've done lost *me* now, Mr. Stark."

"Better you than the herd." The way Stark said it quieted them. "I told you this wind will take all the snow off the flats by daybreak. With last summer's old hay uncovered from here to the far foothills, what's going to happen to cattle that haven't had a real square feed since the snow first hit?"

It was a bad question and Chickasaw answered it

uneasily. "I can foller you partways, Mr. Stark. Them daffy little heifers will be scattered over sixty sections come sun-up, eating their fool heads off and moving forty rods a minute for them foothills. There'll be pothole water aplenty left by this thaw, so's there'll be nothing but us to hold 'em close to the river. They'll be spread out like spring flies over a forty-mile manure pile. That I'll give you, but what I cain't see is why it should sweat us none."

"Me neither." Waco, muttering it. "Where's your dry wheel squeak in them spreading out, Mr. Stark? It don't make sense to this cowboy."

The Montanan looked at them. "I can't tell you boys a thing about cattle. We all know that. What I can tell you about is this crazy wind we're listening to."

"All right, what about it?" Waco again.

"You just saw how fast it hits."

"Yeah."

"It quits twice as fast."

"So?" Still Waco, and scowling now.

"So your cattle are fifteen miles from the river when it drops dead. The thermometer dives like a scatter-gunned duck. It hits zero. Ten, twenty, forty below. The blizzard blasts back. The cattle start to drift, the snow piling up again a foot and a half an hour. They got five miles, maybe ten. You figure it from there."

None of the old Texas hands needed a diagram after that. Each of them had earned his saddle sores long years gone. The picture Stark had just painted for them would have been glass-clear to a settlement storekeeper, let alone to a bunch of mossyback brush poppers.

"Is that all?" queried Waco, twisting his wry grin behind the sarcasm. "It don't hardly seem like enough."

"Maybe you're forgetting the number-two squeeze," answered Stark, no humor showing in the reminder and none intended.

"Huh?" The little cowboy's grin faltered.

Stark eyed him, let it come with deliberate softness. "The Crows."

Dead silence. Waco looked at Chickasaw. Chickasaw shifted his glance to Hogjaw. The latter passed the look on to Slim and the melancholy puncher shoved it along to Saleratus. Saleratus gummed his quid, spit into the cold stove, blinked, handed the browknit expression back to its originator. Waco, the unquenchable, got his grin going again, bobbed his head, made his bowlegged way across the cabin, reached his hat from the row of doorside wall pegs.

"*That's* enough," he conceded. "Let's go."

They went an hour and a half later, when the wind pulled its relentless bar from the open doorway and let them out.

It fell off as suddenly as it had started. One minute it was still raising its six kinds of blustery hell outside. The next minute it had gentled down and was ambling along up valley steady and sure as an old plowhorse following a back-forty furrow.

Leading the way with Saleratus's lantern, Stark paused only long enough to pick the old tin thermometer

135

from its wedging place between the doorjam logs. He glanced at it, handed it without comment to Chickasaw.

The old cattleman held it to the lantern, squinting to find the thin red line in the smoky coal-oil light.

"Forty-five!" he muttered unbelievingly. "And still aclimbing!"

The others heard him and their Christ Amighty's blended with his. When they had come in at dusk it had been somewhere around ten above. It was certain as a new cinch that it had not edged any higher between then and the start of Stark's crazy wind. Any way a man wanted to read that thermometer and no matter how hard he squinted at it, or how careful he had paid attention to his sums in third grade, he came out with a pretty wild answer.

The mercury in that storebought bulb had shot up thirty-five degrees in the last two hours and fifteen minutes.

They got their horses out of the corral, saddling in the dark after the lantern blew out and Stark growled that there was no time to fuss with lighting it again. They rode past the door, nobody talking. Stark checked his nervous stud only long enough to hand the dead lantern to Saleratus, who had come out with a flourbag of cold beef and bannock for their breakfast, and to warn him to keep a sharp eye on the skyline come daylight and to see that the women stayed close to the cabin once the sun was full up. The scowling cook did not ask him why, and none of the others figured he had any reason to.

Stark swung the stud, taking the lead. After a bit, Waco

wondered aloud what time it might be. The Montanan pulled his pocketwatch, checked it by the patchy moonlight. Two thirty-five in the morning. They went on.

Every gully of the east-bank drainage was running a small river. In the shallower cuts they could see it. In the deeper ones they could hear it. And could guess, in either case, that the same thing was going on all the way up the Gallatin to the high peak snowpack of the upper canyon. And could guess, too, that Stark had been plenty generous when he had set noon as the deadline for getting the herd crossed back over the main stream.

Any southwesterner who had had the back of his dirty ears dried out by twenty years of desert wind did not need to be told how a flash flood worked. Nor to be hit over the Stetson with the fact that a fast snowmelt in these mile-high North Plains hills could put on just as good a one as ever any cloudburst in the back canyons down home.

But the Gallatin was still running winter-low when they went across it ten minutes later, not hitting their horses more than hock-high at the rock ford below the cabin bench. Four hours after that, with the seven o'clock daylight breaking warm and rosy over the sawtooth spines of the Absarokas and with the herd at last safely bunched and moving in good trail order back toward the crossing, it was running up to a tall gelding's belly at the ford, already out of its banks into the brake timber in the low places. The temperature was a summer-balmy sixty-five degrees.

All the same, there was still time. They got the first

137

cattle to take the water easier than they had any reason to hope for with a big bunch of spooky young stuff like those coming two-year-old heifers. Still, with the cursing Chickasaw and his bony gray wading point and with General Grant churning along after the old cowboy faithful as a fifteen-hundred-pound long-horned lapdog, the herd youngsters took to the icy Gallatin like tired mallards to a side-slough pothole.

That is, they did for the first fifty head.

After that, things went to hell in a hand bucket.

Chickasaw and the General were just lunging out the far side, the point bunch in midstream behind them, when Stark threw his bay stud on his glossy haunches. In the same move he came clear of the saddle and full up in his stirrups. His wild yell, excited hatwave and warning hand-point beat the eyes of his companions to the west-bank skyline by only the time it took them to set their own ponies back on their hocks.

And to get their own neckhairs to standing on prickly tiptoe.

Along the snowsharp ridge behind the cabin, watchful and still and cameo-clear against the cloudless morning sky, sixteen red horsemen sat their shaggy mounts.

None of the four Texas cowboys, and certainly not Nathan Stark, was short on Indian social savvy.

A man could take one neighborly look at that bunch over yonder and know they had not come over to pay their New Year's respects. Or to borrow a cup of coffee sugar.

When it came to High Plains horseback Indians you

138

had just two kinds—friendlies and unfriendlies.

After enough years at it a halfsmart hand got so he could see the difference in the dark. In broad daylight the village nitwit could sort it out for you with his eyes shut. The daylight they were staring across right now was never going to get any broader and none of them, Hogjaw halfway excepted, was exactly what you would call stupid.

Those sixteen Indians yonder were here on business. And not meaning to shake hands before getting down to wheeling and dealing.

There was, in fact, just one small question not yet entirely transparent as to the frontier etiquette involved. An insignificant consideration which always arose in such little moments of mutual regard between white host and red guest.

Who was going to beat *whom* to the front door of the cabin?

CHAPTER THIRTEEN

IF YOU WERE JOGGING it easy, it was a ten-minute trot from the cabin bench down to the river, no more than a two-minute swim at the ford where the stream, though on the booming rise, was still within its rocky banks. But if you were giving it a rodeo ride, screwed down tight in your saddle and scratching horsehide on every jump, you could cut the crossing time to one minute, the cabin run to three and a half. Since the visiting team needed a full five minutes to slide their ponies down the thawing ridge behind the cabin and on down the gully opening on to the bench, the home boys had about thirty seconds to play with.

They played with them fast but very far from loose.

The race for the cabin door was close as a barbershop shave. The white men won it by a wilted whisker.

Chickasaw set the example by not bothering to unsaddle. Or even to take down the corral gate pole. Or, for that matter, even to sit back on his old gelding more than enough to slow him up sufficiently to hit the cabin doorway dead center.

Stark and the others followed him into the little shelter, piling off their horses and leaping to help him and Saleratus stack the open door full of spare saddles and bulging sacks of flour and beans. So far nobody had fired a shot. The Indians now lobbed in a few long ones as they swung their ponies wide of the barricaded door. But it was only a gesture of common courtesy. The red brother's thoughtful way of letting his paleskinned cousins know it was going to be a long winter for white cattle ranchers in the Gallatin Valley branch of the Crow buffalo. Also, that unless the chinook broke suddenly, or one of them got loose from the surround to ride the 125 miles it would take to bring army help from Fort Smith, the new post the Pony Soldiers had just set up over along the Bighorn, the history of the Texas longhorn in Montana Territory was going to be a short one.

As short, say, as a Kangi Wicasi scalping knife could cut a long head of light-colored *Wasicun* hair.

The trapped white men understood this.

140

When the big Montanan wheeled from wedging the last floursack into place and started barking out orders for the further securing of the Stark Ranch headquarters shack, he got nothing but heartfelt co-operation—up to a sudden jarring point.

Chickasaw and Waco, the oldest hands at trading tricks with uninvited redmen, ran through the lean-to into the attached snowshed of the pony corral and forted up there to prevent the pulling of the standard Plains Indian joke of running off the enemy's horse herd. Hogjaw and Slim took the lean-to itself, which had rifle slits cut in its north and south walls, thus providing, with the corral snowshed to the west and the cabin doorway to the east, a four-quarter field of fire for the defenders. Stark and Saleratus stayed in the main cabin and it was when the former shouted at the latter to quiet and tie the ponies, and when he turned to give the women and the Indian boy their orders, that he hit his first snag.

A man might easily have missed it in those opening seconds, with the spooked horses milling around inside and the Crows firing wild and whooping it up outside. But he could see it now, and feel it too. And the jolt it gave him went right down to his watersoaked bootsoles.

Other than for himself and Saleratus, the narrow room was empty. Nella, Pretty Bird and Winter Boy were gone. God knew where or how or when.

God, that is, and Saleratus McGivern.

"I tried to tell you, goddamit, but you wouldn't listen!" The camp cook secured the last horse, cursed on defiantly. "Stomping and bellering and swinging your broad

141

behind around like a brindle bull in a box car. What the hell ails you? Don't you figger we ever got shot at by a Injun afore? Cripes, boy, we was fighting Comanches when you was counting your toes and puking up your maw's milk. Why, goddamit, we—"

"Shut up, you old fool!"

Stark had him by the neck of his red flannel undershirt, lifting him clear off the floor.

"Where is she? You put off one more smart word on me McGivern and I'll strangle you right where you're dangling!"

He eased off, dropping him back to the floor, big hands shaking. "I'm sorry," he managed thickly. "What happened here, Saleratus? Where's my wife? For God's sake what's she done? Where's she gone?"

He had not heard Stark call Nella his wife before and it slowed the old cook for a moment. But the big man's hands started for his undershirt collar again and he bounced right back, still defiant.

"You'd ought to know better than anybody else where she's gone or what she's did! You was the last one talked to her. All I know is she stayed out here in the cabin with the squaw after you left. Sounded to me like she was crying." He glared accusingly at Stark, hurried on. "Anyways, her and the squaw talked for a long spell. I drifted off, not listening. When I rolled out about five, like usual, they was gone. Took a sack of grub, her mare and the Injun mule. Nothing else. Their blankets was cold. No way in God's world of telling how long they'd been gone."

142

Stark started to say something, was interrupted by a single rifle shot from the pony corral. He leaped to the door, could see nothing of the Crows, waited tensely. After a moment he heard Chickasaw calling in from the horse shed, then Hogjaw's drawling relay from the lean-to was reaching him.

"The old man says to tell you he caught one of 'em sneaking back up the gully. Like maybe he was heading back home for reinforcements."

"Good. He scare him or center him?"

He could hear Hogjaw passing on the question, and Chickasaw grumping the answer back at him.

"You hear that Mr. Stark?" said Hogjaw.

"No, what'd he say?"

"Got a alibi like always, the old goat. Says Waco bumped him jest as he was squeezing off."

"Shot wide eh?"

"Yeah." There was a significant pause. "By purty near three inches. Got him in the left eye instead of the right." Stark's hard mouth relaxed.

"Tell him to stop wasting lead on those long shots, Bivins." Then, the faint smile dying and, with it, the brief warmth in the flat voice, he turned back to Saleratus. "After a bit I'll go after her. I'll need a sack of grub."

"Sure, Mr. Stark. When you figger to go? Along about dark?"

Stark scowled. "I said I'd need a sack of grub. Get it."

"Christ Amighty, you ain't going now!"

"No. In about five minutes. The stud's still blowing

from the river run."

Saleratus dropped his jaw, shook his head. "You're crazy. Idiot-eyed, nuthouse crazy."

"I don't think so, old timer." He said it very quietly.

"What *do* you think, Mr. Stark?" It was just as quiet.

The Montanan's wide mouth went ugly. The grin, this time, was the one Saleratus was familiar with. The one he and the rest of the trail crew had learned not to love in the nine months up from Texas. The one that started out like a trapwise wolf sniffing a strychnine bait. And ended up like a Sioux buck honing his pet war hatchet.

"I think," said his companion softly, "that *nobody* runs out on a deal with Nathan Stark."

Stark was not an Indian fighter. Not in the trained sense that Chickasaw and the others were from the hard experience of being born and raised under the Kaddo and Comanche terms of a Texas boyhood.

The big man had learned the language of the Sioux because his freight routes lay through their lands. He had naturally been in a few wagon surrounds during his years up and down the North Platte and knew what it felt like to get hit by a broadhead buffalo arrow. He knew, too, how much lead to give a hard-running war pony and how high you had to hold over to drill a sitting buck out past a hundred yards or so. But to call him an Indian fighter in the proud, professional meaning the name had in his day and time would have been an insult to the long-haired members of the tobacco-chewing buckskinned brigade who really deserved the designation.

144

And if there was any least doubt remaining as to his amateur standing, he now dispelled it with his blunt decision to ride out through a long dozen ready-and-waiting Crow raiders, in broad daylight.

The dumbstruck cowboys argued hard. There was no dissuading him. Twenty minutes after his terse order to Saleratus, he untied the tall bay stud, fastened the grub-sack to his saddlehorn, made what every one of them considered his farewell address.

"Now don't break in on me again," he warned them. "I'm going after the girl and all I want from you is a lot of listening and a little covering fire. You can give me the first right now and the second in about sixty seconds." He paused, staring around the silent circle. None of its members moved. Or said a word. He went on.

"We know our friends are in the timber over to the south there. I'm going out of here, due north, down the bench to the river and right on out along it. Neither Nella nor that squaw knows any other way into here and that's the way they would have to have gone out. The Crows didn't come that way, or they would have bumped into them. They came through Eagle Gap, for sure. That's the way I used the other day when I went into town for supplies and they know it as well as I do. But they know all about the river road, too, don't worry. The Gallatin's their prize buffalo pasture. They hunt it every spring. So when I make a run for the lower valley they're bound to try and beat me to it. For if they don't, and I get into it ahead of them, they know they'll never head me short of Bozeman." Again he paused and this time Chickasaw stepped quickly into the little silence.

"They won't need to worry none about beating you to Bozeman. It's a long five miles to that foothill pass we come in through. They'll ride relays and run you into the ground before you're out of sight down the valley."

"If I didn't think I could make it, I wouldn't be trying it." Stark meant it literally. It was not in the make-up of his kind to play hero or consider dying to prove a moral point. "Those raunchy Indian scrubs will never get within bullgun range of Blue Grass."

Blue Grass was the bay stud, a halfblood Kentucky racer that had cost Stark a month's freighting profits as a yearling colt in the Missouri settlements. The bullgun was the big-caliber, rifled Sharps buffalo gun used by the white market hunters in supplying the army and other frontier outposts with fresh meat. It would carry up to 1200 yards, cripple at 800, kill clean at 600. The derisive tone in which Stark made his reference showed his dangerous contempt both for the Crow ponies and their riders' smooth-bore trade muskets.

"The hell they won't!" Waco broke the third pause. "Why not wait for dark and *sneak* out? That way you can at least spare us the embarrassment of *seeing* them cut your hair."

"Wait for dark?" grunted the Montanan unsmilingly. "I mean to be back by that time. And," he added, "bringing with me what I went after."

Seeing it was no use, Chickasaw scowled and threw in the hand for all of them.

"If you are back, which you won't be," he muttered

darkly, "have that damn Sioux squaw to make a hooty owl noise or a bullbat twitter so's that we'll know it's you. It ain't healthy to sashay in out of the dark on five old boys from Fort Worth."

"All right, make it the owl hoot. It's not nighthawk season in these parts." Stark led the bay stud to the door. The others moved quickly in behind him, cocking their rifles. He flicked his heatless grin back at them. "Ten gets you five you don't get to fire a shot," he nodded.

"What the hell you mean?" snapped Chickasaw.

"When they see me go out of here, they've got two choices. They cut straight across the bench after me, running right angles as a shooting-gallery rabbit to your line of fire, or they detour the bench by way of the timber and the river, giving you nothing but snowdust to shoot at."

"Yeah, by God," said Waco admiringly. "And giving you a nice five-minute headstart. Pretty smart, Mr. Stark. I reckon maybe we've been selling you a little short all along."

Stark swung up on the stud, held him down with one hand. The hotblooded stallion was a sixteen-hand horse, would weigh better than twelve hundred pounds, had the disposition of a boar grizzly with his foot in a rusty wolf trap. The Montanan handled him like he was a halter-broke barnyard filly.

Leaning down, he caught Waco's eye.

"You're catching on, cowboy," he told him quietly, and kicked the big stud out the door in a shower of flying mud and melting snow.

147

CHAPTER FOURTEEN

THAT JANUARY 1, 1867, was a beautiful New Year's Day. Overhead, the sky was an inverted teacup of cloudless china blue, the early sun shining as brightly as a child's smile. Underfoot, the snowfree banks of the Gallatin were clean and springy. Across the timber-dark ridges of the Madisons the soft breath of the chinook flowed gently. The temperature was in the mid-sixties, the morning stillness as clear and sparkling as hand-blown glass. But for Nella Torneau, safely through the foothill pass and five miles down the Bozeman trail, the blizzard might as well still have been blowing. Try as she might, the Texas girl could not keep her mind on the bright way ahead, could not prevent it casting uneasily back along the gloomy one behind.

She was done with Stark. That much she knew. But beyond the angry fact of her desertion things were not so bitterly apparent.

She had the Montanan's name for Ben's baby and old Judge Hacker's shaky signature on a legal paper to prove it. She had her youth, her looks, more than her share of the fortitude it took a single girl to get along on the frontier. She had found a faithful servant in Pretty Bird, a shy admirer in young Winter Boy. She would be in Bozeman by nightfall, make Virginia City the next day, would somehow, after that, scrape up the money for stagefare back south and a new start down home where a woman was still something a man took his hat off to—

148

no matter who she was or what she might have been.

What, then, was spoiling it all?

Was it running out on her old Texas friends? On the salty old cowboys with whom she had shared nine months of tough trail? Who had followed her into the blizzard with Stark for no better reason than to look after Ben's baby and to see a job through for which they had signed on nearly a year and fifteen hundred miles ago? Was it the memory of Ben himself? Or the worry over his child, now beginning to make its life felt so close beneath her anxious heart?

Or was it herself?

Nella knew she was not a good woman. She was a willing victim of her own impulsive, demanding emotions. One who had always yielded to the passions which surged so fiercely within her strong young body. And one who, from her first surrender as a child of fifteen, had warped her willing life deliberately away from the humdrum moral patterns of home and fireside which so dominated her settlement sisters. No, she was not a good, not even a half-good woman. And she was not proud of it. She was, right now, heartily sick and ashamed of it. Even as she had already been those long months ago when she had tried to refuse Ben Allison's honest love. And tried, so desperately, to tell him of her shabby deal with Nathan Stark, to talk him away from wasting his gentle time on a camp tramp who was not fit to touch his work-soiled hands, let alone share his clean blankets.

But being sick and ashamed of something did not

solve it. Nor did it explain a single thing, and certainly it did not explain the way she felt about Stark.

Or did it?

The frown lines between her arching brows deepened suddenly. The rest of the unwanted thought froze the curve of her soft mouth, hard and ugly.

Maybe—no matter how she hated him—the pale-eyed Montanan was more of her kind than any man she had ever known!

"No—!"

The sharp denial came out of her like a cry of pain, and Pretty Bird halted the travois mule.

"What is it, Sha'hin?" The Oglala woman spoke a remarkably correct, if halting, English; a tribute, certainly, to her years with rancher Jepson, a book-reading, settlement-educated man who had clearly had a deep feeling for his Indian mistress. But, with Sioux simplicity, the latter had given Nella a descriptive Oglala name, "Red Hair," and invariably called her by it. "What is in your mind?" she now concluded, dark face puzzled. "Are you still afraid? Still thinking of *him,* back there?"

"Of course not!" Nella forced the brittle smile. "It's just too nice a day to keep quiet, I guess. Don't mind me, Pretty Bird. I always think out loud."

The Sioux squaw shook her head. Her answering smile was as gentle as the white girl's had been harsh. "Your tongue is crooked, Sha'hin. I am waiting. My ears are uncovered."

"Nonsense! I can't tell you something I don't understand myself!" said Nella irritably. "I reckon the way

150

you would put it, my heart is bad, that's all. I just don't feel right about running away. Not from anything, and surely not from *any* man!" The smile again, still sharp and with an unconscious twist of superiority in it now. "I suppose that doesn't make good sense to you—not to an Indian woman, I mean."

She was sorry the moment she heard herself say it. She had not intended it at all the way it sounded, started hurriedly to explain it away.

Pretty Bird held up her slim hand.

"A woman is a woman, Sha'hin." She got down from the mule, smiling the rest of it softly.

"Let us rest here a little while. Winter Boy will gather the wood and we will make a small fire. We will have some coffee and I will tell you an Oglala story."

"What kind of a story?" Nella asked idly. She was grateful for the chance to stretch her aching legs, swung down off her sorrel mare giving no second thought to the offhand query.

"A love story," replied her companion, waiting carefully until Winter Boy had moved away. "About two good men and a bad girl. Listen."

"My ears are uncovered, go ahead." Nella made cynical use of the Indian phrase, seated herself on a handy log, got ready to be bored by a childish Sioux folktale. Pretty Bird nodded, began talking, her graceful, fluent hands moving constantly, after the poetic habit of her people, in descriptive illustration of her tale.

A long time ago, it seemed, there was an Oglala chief's daughter, a willful, headstrong girl not yet twenty and a great beauty. She had fallen in violent love with a poor young brave who had no ponies to tie in front of her father's lodge. There came, shortly, a certain night in early summer. A soft, wicked night in which the sky was charcoal-black, the moon low and red as a dying dance-fire ember. Before long the young warrior's seed, so passionately planted, was growing frighteningly. The girl's lean belly became distended and her doeskin campdress could no longer hide the secret of her fierce surrender. Yet her young man still did not have the ponies which were the price of safety for both of them, and in a desperation raid to get them from the horse herd of the enemy—the hated Kangi Wicasi—he was killed.

To escape being beaten and stoned from camp, the harsh price of moral trespass among her people, the girl saddled a favorite pony and fled west into the alien land of the Crows. The Sioux would not follow her into the Kangi Wicasi buffalo pastures. There she would be safe. There she would seek security and some kind of a future for herself and her unborn child.

After many weeks and in the first great storm of winter, she came to a white man's cabin. Fearfully, she sought its shelter.

The rancher was a cold, stern man, but a hard worker and, in his thoughtless white man's way, a cruelly honest mate. And he had much to offer a lonely, frightened girl in a strange enemy land—a snug cabin, fat cattle, rich lands—and he shared what he had with her, giving her no less than her fair part, and no more. Of course he had his way with her, at once and by brute force, taking what he wanted as a man's right where she could let him have it as a woman's love gift.

For a long time she hated him for it. She kept thinking all the while about her warrior who was dead. But the years fled swiftly by. Two, three, seven, then eight. The warrior's son grew tall and strong and at last he was to have a little brother or sister. But also, at last, the Crows had found the rancher's hidden valley, and they came into it with their hearts bad for him and his few spotted buffalo.

That was all of the story, said Pretty Bird abruptly. Sha'hin, her paleskinned sister, knew the rest of it.

The Sioux squaw fell silent when she had finished, her dark eyes full of pain, and far away.

Nella had to repeat her low-voiced question three times before she heard it. "It was Jepson's child, then, we buried beyond the cabin?"

"Yes. A little girl. I knew she was dead when you took her from me." Then, after a moment, with savage intensity. "They killed her. It was not Wasiya, not the Winter Giant. It was them. The Crows. Them and that Slohan. That son of a sick she-dog, that Kangi Wicasi devil, that Buffalo Ribs! Aye, Sha'hin," her voice fell strangely soft, *"I will remember him."*

Nella nodded nervously, disturbed by the Indian woman's piercing, far-off stare, yet unable to remove her own thoughts from the obvious parallel of her own and the squaw's love stories.

"Why did you tell me your story, Pretty Bird?" she asked presently. "Was it because Jepson was like Stark?

153

Your dead warrior like mine? Are you afraid I will change my mind and go back to a man who treated me like Jepson did you? Are you warning me to hurry on while there's yet time? What is it you're trying to tell me?"

"I heard you crying there in the dark last night, back in that cabin," said the squaw. "I saw him come out of your room and I knew what he had done to you. I thought of myself and I should have warned you then. But you came weeping to me with your own story of an unborn son who would never see his true father, and I was soft and did not tell you."

"Tell me what, for heaven's sake!" demanded Nella impatiently. "That I'd made a bad bargain with Stark? That I'd been four kinds of a damn fool? That I hated him and forever would hate him and couldn't get away from him halfway far nor fast enough?"

"No, not that." Pretty Bird shook her head. "A woman always thinks of herself, Sha'hin. That's our trouble. We are all alike that way. But a man is very different. He sometimes thinks of others."

"What on earth are you talking about?"

"Love," said the Oglala woman simply,

"Oh, make sense!" Nella flushed, green eyes flashing. "Love hasn't anything in God's world to do with Stark and me!"

"Not with you, no."

"What do you mean, 'not with me'?"

"With him, my sister, *with him."* Then, spreading her hands, and very softly, "He loves you, Sha'hin. As true

and strong and fierce as the heart of an eagle. A blind squaw could see it with her eyes shut. You have driven it into him deep and hard as a buffalo lance behind a running bull's shoulder, and it will kill him if you do not pull it out."

"Oh, my God!" laughed Nella mirthlessly. "You couldn't be more wrong! And what about you? What about Jepson? Don't tell me *that* turned into love at the last minute!"

"The very last," said Pretty Bird slowly.

"When the Crows killed him, something died in me. Until then I had not even known it was alive. I tried to tell him about it then, but he did not hear me. I had waited too long."

"I'm sorry," murmured Nella, coloring deeply. "I always say the wrong thing at the right time."

"Do not be sorry," warned the Indian woman unsmilingly. "Do not be like me."

Nella glanced at her darkskinned companion, not sure she understood her somber admonition.

"What do you mean?" she asked quickly.

"Do not waste eight years dreaming about a warrior who is dead," said Pretty Bird, and got up and went to meet Winter Boy.

CHAPTER FIFTEEN

BEYOND THE FIRST FRINGE of timber at the south edge of the cabin clearing, the Crow raiders sat comfortably around a pineknot fire. It was a big fire, as Indian fires went, but then there was plenty of wood in this place and plenty of time in which to burn it. They wanted the cornered white men to know that; to know they were in no hurry at all, had no intention, whatever, of leaving without seven *Wasicun* scalps, dangling from their saddlehorns and drying in the chinook's wind.

There was another, practical, reason for the fire, of course. There was always a practical reason for what the *Shacun,* the redman, did. In this instance it was to roast a fine strip of tenderloin and backfat ripped from the yet warm carcass of the prime young heifer they had shot and dragged up from the river. It was this unfortunate animal, and her herd sisters, which the Crows were now discussing.

Perhaps a dozen of the fifty head caught in midstream by their sudden appearance had reached the east shore. The others had been swept away downstream to either drown in the roiling flood, or land far below. The balance of the abandoned herd had fallen into a mill on the west bank, presently quieted down and begun to spread out and graze.

Watching them, one of the braves wanted to know if he and some of his fellows should not cross over and begin shooting the cattle, while the others held the white men in the cabin. One of his comrades soberly reminded him that they had not brought enough powder for the spotted buffalo, this time, but only for their palefaced owners. The cattle could wait. They could come back and get them another time. Besides, their chief was not after meat this trip. He was after *hair.*

The chief said nothing, only sucked on his short stone pipe and watched the cabin.

He was a tremendous man, a magnificent specimen of a justly proud and haughty people. The Crows were the tallest of the North Plains tribes. Six feet was a common height among them, and the brave who towered over that mark was commonplace. They were a lightskinned people with clean features, many of them gray-eyed and brown-haired, with a marked tribal tendency to premature graying among the men. The silent chief was a striking example of all these racial qualities; a six-and-a-half-foot, silver-haired young giant of perhaps thirty years of age, broadchested, barrel-ribbed, big boned, and handsome enough to make a maiden weep in any language.

In addition, for an Indian, he had a remarkably quick smile and a spontaneous, good-natured laugh. Good-natured, that is, if you were an Indian. If you were a white man, he was about as friendly as a wounded wolf.

But he was among friends now, and as the second brave assured the first that they could come back for the cattle later on, he flashed his handsome grin right along with his quick headshake.

"We will not have to come back for them," he shrugged. "The way they are spreading out they will be far from the river trees when the hot wind goes and the Winter Giant returns." Again the bright smile and eloquent shrug. "Why waste good powder? They will surely die anyway."

"Aye," said a third brave. "And if they do not, there is

157

always the spring. The ponies will be fatter then and we can bring the squaws and make a real big dance out of it."

Stark's herd thus simply disposed of, the tall raiders returned their attentions to its owners.

Across the clearing the cabin lay still and quiet in the early daylight. Not a sound had come from it since the single shot, nearly half an hour ago, which had dropped their gully-sneaking comrade. The uneasy seconds tip-toed across the Crow silence. The chief smoked. The meat on the roasting stick dripped and burned. The warriors watched the cabin.

Suddenly their slitted eyes widened.

And that was all.

As Stark's rangy bay stud burst from the open doorway and raced across the bench, not one of his red watchers ran for his tethered warpony. It was a full five seconds before any of them even moved, and then it was only their chief reaching to knock the fireless dottle from his pipe against the wind-fallen cedar which braced his broad back.

"Tagwa'hoso'wa," grunted Buffalo Ribs. "He is caught in our trap. *Netowa.* He has killed himself."

It was the simple Indian truth, and his braves only nodded and continued to watch the dwindling figures of the fleeing white man and his Kentucky-bred stallion.

When Stark had said the Crows had only two choices when he made his run for it—to go after him across the bench, or by way of the river—he had been wrong by exactly one, totally unexpected third choice.

158

They could refuse to go after him at all.

Which was precisely what they were doing, and for a perfectly logical redskin reason.

The brave whom Buffalo Ribs had sent up the gully behind the cabin was a decoy. It was not meant that he should be killed, but that was the chance an Indian always had to take against the cursed, incredible shooting eye of the white brother. But prematurely sent to the Land of the Shadows, or not, the unlucky Crow had served his chief's purpose. While the attentions of the white defenders had been drawn off by his brave dash to the east, three picked warriors on the fastest ponies had slipped away to the west and, hidden by the rise of the cabin bench, sped down the banks of the Gallatin toward the lower valley, outwardbound on the long way home.

It was beside the point that they had not been dispatched to set a trap for Stark, but only to ride home and return with enough help to rush the cabin without waiting out the uncertainties of the Chinook. The fact remained that, fast as their special ponies were, they could not keep long ahead of that tall bay stud the white man rode. The Indian arithmetic of the situation was hardly figured down to the fine decimal points, but it was devastatingly simple.

Somewhere between now and the noonhigh sun, and between the outer mouth of the foothills and the white man's village at Bozeman, that big blond man on the red-bay horse would ride right up the pony rumps of Buffalo Ribs's three best braves.

Beaverhead, a warrior well named for his prominent front teeth and sagacious intellect broke his eyes from the distant galloping dot, nodded solemnly to the grinning Buffalo Ribs.

"Aye," he agreed slowly. *"Netowa."*

Where the river trail narrowed to enter the foothill pass it climbed steeply, giving an unobstructed view of the valley below. Stark slowed the stud, taking advantage of this first opportunity to scan his backtail. He was not too happy with what he saw, or rather with what he did not see. Nowhere along the wandering course of the Gallatin's banks was there a sign of Indian pursuit. Either the Crows had not followed him at all, or they had given up and turned back. Where this might have relieved a complete tenderfoot, it did nothing but disturb the big Montanan. While he was not, say, in old Chickasaw's class as an Indian authority, he knew enough of the red brother's skirmishing habits to realize they never let an enemy out of a trap unless they had a good, which was to say a deadly, reason for doing so.

Alerted by the strange stillness behind him, he put the stud on down the river trail, holding down his speed but redoubling his caution. He cleared the pass without incident, lost a little of his wariness, eased Blue Grass back onto his rolling gallop. A mile—two—five—fell behind. Still, nothing. No sight of Crow pursuit to the rear, nor of the fugitive women ahead.

He began to feel better. He was superbly mounted, heavily armed—two Colts and a Henry Repeating Rifle,

160

with ample ammunition for both—and was not weighted down by the ordinary frontiersman's dread of wartrailing hostiles. It was not that he disdained the red horsemen, nor that he underrated them. But his respect for them was as unemotionally logical as everything else about him. Take away their flashy feathers and gaudy gee-gaws, wash off their warpaint and discount their grotesque buffalo horn, wolf- and bear-skull head-dresses, and underneath you had just another man. And Stark had yet to meet the man he feared. Red or white.

An hour later he still had not met him. But he had been introduced to three reasonable red facsimiles: a slant-eyed trio of Crow scalp hunters who, if they did not literally scare him to death, certainly slowed him up enough to make him wonder if his will was in order.

Seventy-five feet south of the cooling ashes of Pretty Bird's deserted coffee-fire, a dense copse of low spruce grew almost to the edge of the river trail. Its natural thickness was further tangled by a dozen old dead and down cedars and by a solid ground cover of mountain holly and dwarf evergreens. From the impenetrable fringe of this dark screen three pairs of glittering black eyes watched the lone white man top the upriver rise, guide his tall bay stallion toward the ember-smudge of the fire spot.

"He comes! He comes!" whispered White Wolf excitedly. "By the gods, Big Belly, it is a good thing you heard his horse coming across that rocky place back along the trail."

"*Wi'pyawa,*" grunted Big Belly, "let him come." The

161

fat brave was a noncommittal man, not a talker like his two companions.

"It is a funny thing," observed the third Crow idly. "A very funny thing."

"What is that, Broken Nose?" asked White Wolf softly. "What is so funny now?"

"Oh, the way they will put that iron on their horses' feet," said the other brave. "On a quiet day like this, or even better, at night, you can hear it ring off a rock half a mile upwind."

"Be quiet," ordered Big Belly tersely.

"Yes," chided the garrulous White Wolf, "be quiet. And do not talk aginst that iron on that stallion's feet out there. It gave us time to get in here, and to bring them with us, too!" With the loose grin, he jerked his thumb over his shoulder. Broken Nose glanced in the direction of the gesture, nodded happily.

They did make a pretty picture back there in the trees a ways—the white squaw and the Oglala woman and her skinny brat—tied up as they were, with those fine gags in their mouths and their eyes bugging out like a bullfrog's from the fear and the fright sickness that was in them. Broken Nose had done that tying and he was proud of it. Proud, too, of the way he had nosewrapped the sorrel mare and the old travois mule, so they could not make a welcoming noise to the studhorse and thus warn the white man.

"Look out now!" His pleasure was interrupted by Big Belly's sibilant warning. "He is coming to the fire. Watch carefully now."

"Aye," added White Wolf, grinning the quick agreement as he raised his rusted smoothbore, "now is surely the time—!"

Big Belly's hand shot out, clamping the eager brave's gunbarrel. *"Pe'musayane!"* he hissed. "Not yet! He may pass by here on foot!"

The burly Crow had scarcely uttered his warning, when Stark pulled in the stud to fulfill its canny prediction. Swinging down, he moved swiftly to the firebed, kicked its charred remains aside, knelt to feel for warmth beneath them.

His silent watchers saw him nod quickly, knew from that he had found what he sought, would realize he was very close behind whoever had made that fire. While they wondered what he was doing following the white squaw and her Oglala companions, they waited his next move. Obligingly, he made it in their direction.

Beginning at the fire and hand-leading Blue Grass, he circled outward, seeking across the rocky ground the resumption of the fugitives' trail. On his fourth cast he was sixty feet from the fire, less than twenty from the Crow ambush.

He heard the cracking thrash of the tangled brush behind him, whirled in time to count his attackers and to throw up one arm to ward off the warclub of the first of them, dodge the second and wheel to face the third. The last thing he remembered was the flash thought that he had never seen such a tremendously fat Indian. Then Big Belly's war-ax haft was caving in the side of his head, and he knew no more.

When he opened his eyes the sun was ten o'clock high and the birds were singing beautifully. But not in the trees. He had to shake his ringing head three times before they quit chirping and let him think straight.

He was lying flat on his back in a muddy snow puddle, ten feet from the rekindled fire. Squatting by the blaze, stuffing himself with the last of the cold beef Saleratus had given him and gulping down the remaining dregs of Nella's coffee, was the mountainous Crow who had stretched him with the war ax. When he raised his head to look for the other two, one of them put a foot in his face and shoved him back down in the mud. Obeying the hint, he lay still. But by rolling his eyes upward he could make out the fat one's two friends standing behind him with their gun muzzles held just right to blow his brains out should he not choose to put them to a better use.

One of his guards, a rather pleasant-looking murderer, grinned and said something to him in Crow. He shook his head weakly, answering in Sioux, the common tongue of the High Plains tribes.

White Wolf smiled again, spread his hands apologetically. "We are sorry to keep you waiting," he grunted in reasonably good Oglala. "But Big Belly was hungry and besides we wanted you to catch your horse. He got away from us and we do not have a spare pony just now."

"*He-hau,* thank you," growled Stark. "Is it all right to sit up now?"

"Oh, sure. Take a look around. Just don't move very fast."

164

He raised himself gingerly, took White Wolf's advice, had his look around.

"Good morning," said Nella. "You're just a shade late for coffee, but we're glad to have your company."

His head was clearing fast now, his strength beginning to pound back into him. He played it poker-straight, keeping his voice and his face dead flat, as though he had never seen her before in his life and was not happy to be doing so now.

"Do any of our friends understand English?" he asked.

She got the idea, dropped her cynical smile.

"I don't think so. At least they wouldn't talk to me. Try Pretty Bird. She was spieling some Sioux with them."

He looked past Nella and her mare, to where the Oglala woman and her son sat the travois mule.

"How about it, Pretty Bird?"

The squaw twisted her dark mouth, rasped back at him in angry Sioux. "You *Wasicun* dog, I would not tell you anything!" Then, as menacingly, but in her precise English. "I do not think so. I think you can talk, all right."

"I'll tell you what I think," gritted Stark. "We'll never have a better chance to find out than right now."

"What do you mean?" said Nella anxiously.

"I mean *before* they get around to tying me aboard Blue Grass. I'm no authority on community life among the Crows, but I know gambling odds and I wouldn't give you one to a hundred for our chances once they pack us back to their pardners up yonder at the cabin."

Listening to them, Big Belly's suspicious scowl deep-

165

ened. "That is enough of that!" he called in Sioux. "I do not like talkers."

"Watch the fat one," said Stark deliberately to Nella. "He's the one I'm working on."

"Did you hear me, *Wasicun?*" growled Big Belly. He got up from his haunches, grunted, belched, gestured with his war ax. "Or do you want another taste of this?"

"Your wind is as big as your belly!" sneered Stark, answering in Sioux. "You bellow like a bull but you are only a paunchy old cow. Who would be afraid of such a pile of rump-tallow?"

The world over, no fat man likes to be reminded that he is a fat man. Additionally, the Indian, of all men, resented any insinuation that he was something less than a male among males.

Big Belly started for Stark.

"Get low on your mare!" the latter called to Nella. "They're not the world's worst shots!"

"Don't try it, Stark!" Even with Big Belly looming in front of him, he caught the sudden, naked concern in Nella's plea, and the thrill of it ran through him, hot and dark. The next instant the fat brave was driving the war ax down at him and he was laughing harsh and ugly and his big hands were flashing upward to seize the whistling weapon in midair.

He rolled backward with the blow's momentum, pulling the ax and its wielder down upon him. Bunching his thighs he drove his feet up into the Crow's paunch catapulting his three hundred pounds over his head and into the dumbstruck braves behind him. As Big Belly's

166

flying bulk crashed into them Broken Nose, in the act of shooting at Stark, triggered his piece wildly into the open sky above. White Wolf's interrupted aim was a little better, but not much. Another few inches higher and he would have shot Stark through the head. As it was his gun went off with its sights full of Big Belly's great buttocks. The huge brave fell atop his two henchmen, roaring in blind pain and grasping his wounded hindquarters. Before he could find his feet, Stark was in the middle of the dogfight.

He seized Broken Nose by his long braids, hauled him to his feet, broke the haft of Big Belly's war ax over his head. Broken Nose did not object. He just slumped down in the mud and stayed there. Stark leaped over Big Belly, figuring him to be badly hurt and out of it for the moment. In the same move, he made a sliding, diving grab for the elusive White Wolf.

But the thin talkative Crow was the least valorous of his brothers. And the most disposed to test the validity of the old adage built up around surviving today in the hopes of finding a better fight tomorrow—preferably one, in the present case, about three long pony rides away.

Too, a man could not depend for certain upon Big Belly's reaction to being shot through the rump. The fat brave was not a generous fellow and might possibly read something personal into the mishap. In either event, White Wolf was satisfied that the best climate for him at the moment, all things considered, lay to the west. He wasted no time in taking his leave. In fact, he was already aboard his pony and departing for points beyond Bozeman by the time Stark, recovering from his missed lunge, was stumbling to his feet wiping the mud out of his eyes.

Cursing and spitting blood from his gravel-torn lip, he turned to attend to Big Belly. He was in time to observe three things: the haunch-shot buck was back on his feet; was hauling out Stark's two staghandled Colts, which he had previously appropriated as legitimate prizes of prairie warfare; was holding them trained on his white brother's beltbuckle while he limped in close to his help-less target to make sure he did not miss with the unfamiliar weapons.

About this time Stark observed a fourth thing.

And got ready to act accordingly.

Nella Torneau, bound hand and foot aboard the sorrel mare, had turned the perfectly trained little cowhorse with her knees and had her pointed squarely at Big Belly's back. The next moment her high Rebel yell had the little mare churning mud like a sixteen-second rope-horse coming out of Chute Four. The sorrel swerved in the last jump, refusing to run even an Indian dead-down, but her twisting haunch slammed into the Crow's shoulder, knocking him sprawling at Stark's feet. The Montanan stomped his face in with the arch of his boot, stepped over his relaxing bulk, caught up the sorrel mare, cut Nella free.

"I *was* going to let you ride back that way," he said unsmilingly.

"Why?" For once her face was as sober as his.

"I figured you'd earned it."

"How so, Stark?"

"We had a deal, you ran out on it. To me that added up to bringing you back."

"And now?" There was something very subdued, almost hopeful, in the way she asked it.

He looked at the slashed rawhide thongs in his hand, then up at her. Nodding slowly, he tossed the severed bindings aside. "There's no ropes on you now," he said, and turned away from her.

She watched him anxiously as he freed Pretty Bird and Winter Boy, then whistled up the nervously circling Blue Grass. The big stud came in to him at once, gentling down and nuzzling and bunting at him with his soft nose. Stark swung up on him, ran down and caught up the remaining two Crow ponies. Without a word he handed one of them over to Pretty Bird, the other to Winter Boy. Taking the travois mule, he led him to where Broken Nose lay still unconscious. He scooped up the tall brave, dumped him, limp as a gutted coyote, across the old mule's packsaddle, bound his hands to his feet under the patient animal's belly. Nella was still watching him, still thinking desperately of what he had meant by his parting remark when, leading the burdened mule, he headed Blue Grass back toward her.

There was no doubt he had just told her she was free to go. To Bozeman, to Texas, to hell, to anyplace. Just as long as it was a far piece of buffalo pasture away from Nathan Stark.

She had not expected that, had no cynical answer

ready for it. Had, additionally, no luck digging one up in the little time it took him to come up to her.

"Well, where do we go from here?" she tried brightly, attempting to bluff it out with the standard dazzling smile and caustic hard humor. But Stark was not buying any bright smiles or Texas-sharp sarcasm that January morning. He let her know as much in one flat phrase, not trimming it with any answering grins.

"*I'm* going back."

There was no invitation in it, no hint of what she should do, or of what he thought she should do.

"What about us?" she asked small-voiced, and taking advantage of the arrival of Pretty Bird and Winter Boy aboard their borrowed ponies to hide behind her inclusion of them in the wavering question.

"Well," said Stark, to all three of them, "what about you?"

His answer did not come from Nella but from the charcoal-eyed Oglala woman. She gestured quickly to indicate she spoke for Winter Boy, murmured with head-down shyness. "We will go back with you, White Eyes." She used the Oglala name which Red Cloud had given Stark, and which the famed Sioux chief had taken from the faded, almost colorless blue of the Montanan's eyes. "It is the law of my people. You saved our lives."

"No, you owe me nothing, Zincahopa," he told her gently. "I give your life back to you."

Pretty Bird shook her head. When she spoke again she looked at him in a way no man could miss. "I do not want it, White Eyes. It is yours now."

Stark colored deeply. He set his jaw, fighting down the embarrassed anger the handsome squaw's worshipful glance stirred up in him.

Damn these Indian women! One kind word or off-hand pat on the head from a white man and they would follow him home, handlicking and tail-tucked as a lost dog. To cover the awkward pause he turned to the boy, demanding gruffly, "How about you, son?"

"I go where my mother goes," muttered the Oglala youth sullenly, not looking at him and letting his Indian scowl tell the white man it was maternal, and no other loyalty, which forced him to say it.

Now they had come down to it.

It was Nella's turn.

No stalls, no brilliant smiles, no sharp tongue, no green-eyed female bluffs, no defensive flares of hot Texas temper would do it now.

Stark had deliberately played her into a corner she could not slide out of. He had laid his cards on the table, face up, and called her, cold.

She could buy more chips, or get out of the game.

She brought her eyes up, meeting and holding his waiting gaze, her long look and slow words strangely soft.

"I'll play those," she said. "Let's go."

CHAPTER SIXTEEN

STARK LEFT the unconscious Big Belly where he lay. Wounded and afoot, many miles from his companions upstream and his home village on the Big Hole River westward across the Tobacco Root Mountains, the gluttonous brave was helpless to do them immediate harm. Chickasaw or Waco, he knew, would have stuck a Colt muzzle in the helpless Crow's ear and quit worrying about him. But Stark could not do it that way. Ruthless as he was in a called fight or a close business deal, he had a moral prejudice against murder such as few frontiersmen of his time possessed. This same inherent, if hard-eyed, regard for fair play which had led him to captain the dread Virginia City Vigilantes in their hanging of Henry Plummer now forced him to spare the life of Big Belly. As for the other Crow, the one who had gotten away down the Gallatin, there was no use worrying about him. He *knew* what he would do. It was only a question of whether or not the escaped brave could return with the whole warrior strength of Buffalo Ribs's main band before the chinook quit blowing, and the big snow came back. If he could—

But the hell with that, Stark thought. He had other, more pressing maybe's to sweat about. Such as sneaking back into the Upper Gallatin without being caught at it. And such as timing his arrival at the cabin with full nightfall. And getting Pretty Bird to stage an owl hoot that would fool the Crows but not old Chickasaw. And—

Again, he broke the stride of his runaway thoughts, reining them short-up.

He turned in the saddle, gave a last look at the little caravan behind him. It was waiting in silent order: Nella

172

first, leading the travois mule and the captive Indian: Winter Boy and his mother handclose behind her, holding the retrieved guns of the Crows on the now conscious Broken Nose. He waved back to them, swung the bay stud up the Gallatin.

Pretty Bird returned his wave, tapped the breech of her borrowed muzzle-loader significantly, called out to the jolting, squirming Broken Nose.

"Move around all you want, but do not make a noise. I am a better shot than your friend White Wolf. You will not get it where he gave it to Big Belly."

"That is not a good thing to say to me, my Oglala sister," objected the Crow. "You make a bad joke on your Kangi Wicasi brother."

It was Winter Boy's turn to flourish his new gun. He did so with all the vast dignity of an eight-year-old warrior. "My mother does not joke!" he piped importantly. "You better be quiet like she says when we get into the valley up there."

"*Aii-eee!*" wheedled the head-down captive, addressing his plea to Pretty Bird. "We are Indians, cousins in the blood, as brother and sister, you and I. The boy is as my son, I am as his father. What could you be dreaming of doing to me, to your old friend Broken Nose?"

"I have a better question for you, old friend Broken Nose," said the Oglala squaw quietly.

"Aye, sister?" cried the brave hopefully, "Name it, name it!"

"What were *you* dreaming of doing to us?" asked Pretty Bird.

There was no more talk from the Crow brother just then. Even by the time Stark had led them safely into the north timber below the cabin bench and was waiting for the daylight to go and for it to become dark enough for an owl to be out hunting—and hooting his disappointment at the lack of white snow to see a brown deermouse against—Broken Nose had yet to make his first noise.

But at that point the Montanan stopped trusting his red guest's respect for Pretty Bird's marksmanship, and haltered his slack mouth with a rawhide bit. The crude gag in place, they waited.

They were still a mile from the cabin, a distance demanded by the fact the chinook was moving up-valley and might, should they venture closer, carry the scent of their horses to those of the Crow raiders, or to their own in the cabin corral. It was a bad nervous two hours until sunset, yet there was no other way for it. They had to suffer and sweat the endless minutes through. They had come too far, too hazardously, to push their luck by inviting any disastrous exchange of social whickers between their mounts and those above.

The winter twilight came at last. Swift minutes later the black thumb and finger of the January night snuffed out its remaining sunless, gray light. Stark made ready for the last mile.

All the mounts except the sleepy old travois mule were tethered and left behind. He hated to abandon Blue Grass but Nella's sorrel and the two Crow ponies were mares and the big stud's presence would keep them quiet. With the plan he had in mind, to offer the captive brave to Buffalo Ribs as the price for calling off the siege, he realized he was as good as giving the beautiful stallion to the Crow raiders. Yet there was no other way around what lay ahead of them. They had to go the rest of the way in afoot. And go fast. With a gin-clear sky and an early moon they had, at best, half an hour of darkness in which to make their move. After that, the cabin bench would be lit up by a glare of moonlight bright enough to read the fine print in a catalogue guarantee.

Unhesitatingly, he turned over the final lead to Pretty Bird. From here in, it was Indian work. Let an Indian do it. He followed the squaw, rifle ready, coat removed to clear the staghandled Colts taken back from Big Belly. Behind him came Winter Boy, assigned to lead the mule. The shaggy beast knew his Oglala smell and would follow him close and quiet as an old campdog. Nella walked rear guard, her short carbine unslung and on cock.

They made the first half-mile, up the steep river trail to the lip of the bench, without incident. The rest of the journey lay in two ticklish stages: the first quarter-mile along the edge of the thin bench timber to a point opposite the cabin; the last 400 yards across the open benchtop itself—and in that final stretch there was no brush, no rock, no cover of any kind bigger than a bat's shadow to shelter their sneak-in.

They were able to get up to the jumpoff spot undetected. But they had used up precious time doing it.

There were perhaps five of their original thirty minutes remaining, when Stark turned to Pretty Bird and grunted, "Go ahead, give it your best try." The Oglala woman nodded, sent out the first mournful complaint of the great horned owl launching himself from his lofty cedar perch to float the forest aisles for his evening meal.

After a restless wait, she repeated the soft *taa-hoo, taa-hoo,* knowing the white men in the cabin could not risk any acknowledgement of the call but that they must be given enough time to realize the persistence of her imitation marked it as Stark's agreed signal.

Therein lay the cause of the restlessness.

What a white man could figure out for a clearly repeated sign, so could a red. In the time a cowboy might take to react, a Crow could be long on his way.

Could be?

No.

Was.

"What was that?" said Buffalo Ribs, coming up off his blanket by the raiders' fire where, full of Stark's good beef, he and his fellows were resting.

"An owl," shrugged the drowsy Beaverhead. "You are getting old, brother, when you cannot tell an owl—even in your sleep."

"Who is on watch out there?"

"Iron Hand and Gray Bull, I think. Maybe Four Horses is with them. I forget."

"I am going," grunted the chief. "Arouse the others and come quickly."

When he reached the three wakeful braves on guard at the timber's edge, he growled suspiciously. "Did you hear anything you did not like in that owl hoot just now?"

"Aye," agreed Four Horses. "We were just talking about it."

"Too many hoots," amplified Iron Hand.

"And too close together," concluded Gray Bull.

Buffalo Ribs curled his wide lips. "We had better get over there, my brothers. We will not wait for Beaver-head."

"That is right," grinned Four Horses. "He is old enough to find his way in the dark."

"Yes," said Gray Bull. "And those teeth of his stick far enough out in front of him to keep him from running against any trees."

"Here is a bad time for jokes," warned Buffalo Ribs, straightening his mouth. "Follow fast, but be careful." The next moment the four Crows were circling the clearing's edge around behind the cabin at a silent dogtrot.

Inside the little building, Chickasaw cocked his head. "You hear that owl?" he asked Waco.

"I didn't hear nothing," said his companions. "Yes I did too, by God! There it goes agin."

The old man grunted, felt his way across the darkened room. "You hear that owl, Sal?"

"I heard it," came his answer from the lean-to. "You reckon it could be them?"

"With that damn Stark you never know. Pass it along. Look sharp. Moon'll be out in a minute. If it's them, they'll be coming in from the north."

Saleratus slid over to the crawlhole connecting the lean-to with the corral shed. "You hear what the old man said, Hogjaw?"

"We ain't deef. You ride yore 640. Me and Slim will hold down our section."

"All right. Chickasaw says look sharp. Moon's due over the ridge any minute."

"He's a hell of a prophet," admitted Hogjaw acidly. "Yonder she comes, jest topping out." As he spoke the climbing moon edged free of the surrounding hills, tipping the silent pines with silver, spilling past them to flood its startling light across the velvet black of the bench meadow. "Jesus Murphy!" gasped Hogjaw. *"Yonder they are—!"*

In mid-meadow Stark and his little band, trapped in the full glare of the winter moon, hesitated. At the back edge of the clearing, Buffalo Ribs and his three red shadows did not. They swung from their dogtrot into a full run, racing across the moon-bright grass.

Stark saw them a moment later. And the moment after that he was seeing something else.

Beyond the cabin, from the south timber, straining to cut them off from that direction, came Beaverhead and the remaining warriors.

The Montanan sprang toward Winter Boy, scooped him up, threw him aboard the travois mule with Broken Nose. "Hit for the cabin!" he yelled, and slashed the mule with his rifle butt. The Oglala lad held on, beating the overburdened beast with his guiding heels, yelling him onward with shrill Sioux courage words. Behind him, Stark and the two women ran like rabbits.

There was simply nothing else to do.

It is easy to tell about firing a rifle with deadly effect on foot and in a wild run. The unvarnished frontier truth was that no man ever lived who could do it. Much less any two women.

Even the cowboys, from their steadied rests inside the cabin and corral, could do no more than chew up the ground around the running Indians on the north side. They did succeed in this, however, forcing them to first slow up, then angle off and make for the shelter of the north timber, which Stark and his companions had just left. But the price came high. To pay it they had to leave the south side of the buildings undefended. Thus, as Stark saw Buffalo Ribs's bunch break off and run for cover, he also saw that Beaverhead's larger band was going to make it a dead heat at the unguarded cabin door.

With a tremendous burst of driving speed he passed the slowing mule, flashed by the door and kept right on going. The surprised Beaverhead found himself suddenly confronted with the apparition of a grizzly-big madman blasting away with a lever-action Henry rifle, held waist-high and charging his triumphant group, head-on.

It was one too many for the Crow subchief.

He was one Indian who always tempered his inherent

179

bravery with acquired intelligence. He hit the ground, rolling sideways like a crosswinded tumbleweed, sprang back to his feet, in reverse, and dug out for the safety of the south woods. His braves were as agile and alert, if not so bright. They took out after him. By the time Stark dropped the empty Henry to start working with the Colts, he was firing at nothing but the north end of eight Indians going south.

He did not pause to ponder how many, if any, of the stampeding bucks he had actually winged. He had, in fact, better than a poker player's hunch that he had run a powderburn, muzzleflash bluff—that none of the retreating Crows had even been nicked. But he was not going to let his curiosity kill him. He gambled just enough time to holster the smoking Colts and pick up the muddy Henry. The whole thing was over so quick that he was back and through the cabin door close enough on Nella's lagging heels that he had to give her a healthy shove on in and out of his headlong way.

"Thanks for the lift, mister!" she gasped. "I'd just about run out of oats."

"No extra charge," panted Stark, already at work re-barricading the door. "It comes with the regular room and board. Grab a sack and start stacking."

"All clear on the north," growled Chickasaw, coming in from the lean-to. "All we got to do now is stay awake and admire the moonlight." Then, in the same deadpan breath. "Enjoy your trip, Miss Nella?"

"Just dandy," straightfaced the girl, bucking the last floursack to Stark. "You-all miss me?"

"Sure did, ma'am." It was Waco, grinning his way up through the gloom. "Too bad you forgot yore toothbrush and had to come back."

"I know, I know. And I did so want to see the country down around Bozeman. They say it's lovely this time of year."

In the rebuilt barricade's black shadow, Stark's pale eyes warmed. He shook his head and moved out into the moonlight, grinning awkwardly. "I sure don't understand you people," he said enviously. "But I'm beginning to wish I could."

"How's that again?" asked Chickasaw, frankly amazed.

"The good fun you get out of things," said the big Montanan seriously. "And out of each other. I don't know. It's just something I'll never understand, I guess."

"Guess again, Mr. Stark," Waco stepped into the doorway moonlight with him, a slow, thoughtful nod cementing the strange new respect in his soft drawl. "I got a notion you will."

CHAPTER SEVENTEEN

THE FIRST twenty-four hours after Waco's prediction were too filled with Indian anxiety to allow his nerve-strung cabin companions to think about the little cowboy's friendly forecast of regenerative stirrings in Nathan Stark. And the following short winter days, stretching swiftly into the succeeding weeks and months, piled atop one another with such a pyramiding burden of continuing tensions that no fair, further chance was given the blond Montanan in which to demonstrate any beginning tendencies toward becoming a fellow human being.

There was constantly, from the first grim minute to the last, more work to be done than any six men, two women and one big-eyed Oglala boy could dream of getting around. With Stark, his disillusioned crew soon found, no love had yet alienated his affections for hard work. No desire had so far displaced his dedication to the dollar. No lesser ambition had undermined his fierce determination to found his first million on the winter gamble to build a cattle empire amid the lush Crow buffalo pastures of the Gallatin.

The unfolding of these certain facts began with daylight of the following morning, January 2, and did not cease from that time.

The watchful day dragged along with no sign of activity from the hidden Crows. The only exchange was Buffalo Ribs's cheerfully shouted refusal to accept Stark's bid of freeing Broken Nose in return for calling off the surround. Unable to bring himself to carry out the Texans' ugly advice to put a .44 slug through the back of the brave's head, Stark could only keep him tied up and hope the Crow chief would eventually relent and take the deal. He did not and the endless hours of waiting went on.

The chinook held steadily, drying the damp ground it had so recently denuded of snow into a perfect hard, clean underfooting for pony travel. The main Crow force showed up, led by the loudly bragging White Wolf and including Big Belly in a heavily padded saddle, shortly after noon of the third following day, the 5th. There were at least sixty of them in the first group and additional small bands continued to arrive until nightfall.

Counting their swelling number through the uncertain dusk of the brief twilight, old Chickasaw Billings estimated there were no less than a hundred braves squatted around the booming campfire in the south timber. Pretty Bird did her Oglala best to brighten the picture by assuring them there were more to come. Buffalo Ribs had boasted to her that his village was a big one—sixty lodges—and that every lodge held its full Indian count of trail-age warriors. That count was traditionally five to a lodge. Dividing the Crow chief's claim by half, a safe percentage with red reports, there still remained a minimum of thirty lodges. That left, in any mathematics, *Shacun* or *Wasicun,* a certain sum of 150 full-grown fighting braves to be taken into uneasy account.

Chickasaw topped the squaw's unpleasant prediction with one of his own: if any of them had anything to set right with the good Lord they had best get to it. The Crows would likely come in with their big rush like most other "hossback Injuns"—in the gray small hours of the false dawn just ahead of the true daylight.

But the rheumy-eyed old cowboy turned off a false prophet, and Pretty Bird still had the last word.

About 3 A.M. she got up and went to the cabin door. She sniffed the hot wind, quietly sought out Stark, off guard duty and dozing in the lean-to. He came awake at the first touch of her slim red hand on his restless shoulder.

"Go back to sleep, White Eyes," she smiled in Sioux, slender fingers lingering in the shy caress. "Rest well now, the danger is past." Then, the excitement of it quickening her whisper. "Do you not hear him out there, *Wasicun*? Listen. *Wasiya is coming back!*"

He went to the door, listened, heard no change in the constant, sucking draft of the chinook.

Yet he had only time to scowl his failure to do so when, for the first time in five days, the keening wind dropped dead away.

It seemed scarcely minutes before the Maytime warmth in the little cabin was gone and, in its place, the shivery chill of the Montana January was growing swiftly. Within the next hour the blizzard was back, but long before its first fat flakes stung the freezing ground Buffalo Ribs and his cheated braves, accompanied by the joyful Broken Nose whom Stark had at once ordered freed, had caught up their ponies and begun to curse their climbing way upward through Eagle Gap, homeward bound toward the distant Big Hole and the waiting safety of their snug lodges.

Hopo! Hookahey! as their Sioux cousins would have put it. It was no time for being heroes, or for proving a point of pasture possession. The buffalo grass would wait. So would the white interlopers who sought to steal it. But Wasiya, the Winter Giant, would not. It was a time for getting far out of that cursed place.

184

Buffalo Ribs paused only long enough to ride in as close as he dared to the silent cabin and shout a wind-tossed Crow farewell. He talked for thirty seconds, bellowing his bitter valedictory into the coming storm like a dust-tossing herdbull. But when he had finished and spurred his pony away and Stark had had time to ask Pretty Bird what he had said, the Oglala woman was able to reduce the blustery Kangi Wicasi oration to a simple Indian shrug.

"He said he would be back," she muttered.

But Buffalo Ribs did not come back.

When the great storm closed in this time, the gray skies did not open again. Within its first forty-eight hours seven feet of snow was piled on the level flats of the outer valley and drifts of twelve and fifteen feet were driven up and mountained over the low places between the Crow village and the sheltered haven of the Upper Gallatin. That the war party got home at all was entirely a tribute to its chief's angry acumen in breaking off the siege before the first flakes fell. That it would soon return, pony travel being the only transportation to which its horse-proud members would condescend, was completely improbable. The chinook had been the Indians' one chance for a winter wipeout of the white invaders. It had failed them by a miserable two hours. And Montana Territory was on its belated fierce way to being snowed in until the big spring thaw.

The Kangi Wicasi were too wise a people, too old and too respectful of their northern homeland's terrible winters, to leave their wind-whipped lodges. Man Above was really stirring up a deadly potion in his Medicine Hat this time. Until he quit mixing it and threw away his frozen spoon—until he poured it all out on the winter ground and let the new grass grow again—Buffalo Ribs and his Big Hole brothers would stay at home and count their buffalo chips.

The beginning twelve hours of the blizzard's return were mostly wind and driving sleet. Knowing his Montana weather almost as well as the Crow raiders, but not knowing it quite well enough to throw in and quit at its first warning whistle, Stark gambled on those opening hours.

The minute Buffalo Ribs said goodbye and rode off up the Eagle Gap gully, the Montanan went after his drifting cattle. Detailing Nella and Pretty Bird to go back after the starving Blue Grass and the sorrel mare, with peculiarly pointed emphasis on being sure to bring along the two Crow ponies as well, he led the shivering cowboys off up the Gallatin.

They had one winter-thin chance.

Stark knew where and what it was.

The returning wind, howling in from the north, would move the herd south, up the valley, into the deep snows at its head. Five miles south of the cabin there was a place where the river broke over an eight-foot rock and windfall dam. Here they might possibly swim its swollen crest by virtue of the relatively quiet water above the obstruction. Once across, they could string out to bottle up the narrowing neck of the valley floor. After that, providing they had beaten the cattle to that point, they could hope to turn a good part of them back toward the safety of the river timber which, in that upper end of the pasture, lay on higher ground and would not be under water.

It was the torn-shirt sort of a chance the westerner has proverbially granted the heathen Chinee in hell, but it *was* a chance.

To save the cattle they had guarded so jealously from Fort Worth to Virginia City, the Texas cowboys jumped at it as recklessly as their nerveless leader. And not alone jumped at it, but did a desperate good job of landing on their feet and bulldogging it as it went by.

They got across the Gallatin and into position minutes before the first of the wind-pushed herd followed old General Grant into sleet-hazed view from down-valley. By late afternoon and the start of the real snow, they had checked and gathered close to 400 of the original 500-head bunch. With time running out and the snow piling up under their tired horses, swift and shifty as hourglass sand, they could not wait for the stragglers. That 100 head would have to be left to drift to their quiet deaths in the deep snows above. It was a mercilessly hard decision, rough as chipped flint for any man to make. "Let's go, boys," was all that Nathan Stark said.

Chickasaw leading the way, with General Grant's ugly brindle bulk tailing the familiar bony rump of the old cattleman's gray gelding, they shoved the gather back down into the Gallatin timber. An hour later they re-crossed the now swiftly falling river to begin bucking

187

the full force of the blizzard back toward the cabin bench. Just before the last light went, Stark spotted the lofty beacon of the cabin cedar swaying through a momentary hole in the storm. He took a blind head on it and guided them in, not three freight wagon lengths short of the snow-covered horse shed.

After that, all they could do was pull the saddles on their own exhausted mounts and turn them lose, together with the others from the corral, so they could drift into the eastbank timber and dig for feed to stay alive. Only the two Crow ponies brought back by Nella and Pretty Bird were kept under fence. Stark himself saw to these, tying them hard and short in the horse shed where they could be gotten to from inside the lean-to. When questioned by the dead-tired Texas cowboys, he would only say that they had yet a little to learn about Montana weather.

To that forecast he added but one qualification.

Before the present big snow blew itself out those raunchy Indian crowbaits would turn into the two most beautiful horses any hungry cowhand ever tasted.

The Crow ponies lasted a little over three weeks. So did the blizzard. They were down to boiling the hock-bones of the second pony, and running low on stacked stove-wood when at last the weather lifted and let them tunnel out.

During the long days of their imprisonment Pretty Bird had fashioned three sets of Sioux snowshoes, using the poles and rawhide lacings from the travois bed to achieve the clumsy miracles. Stark had used them before and, after an hour of cursing, snowspitting tumbles on the parts of his chosen pupils, he had imparted enough of their secret to Chickasaw and Waco to allow the two old cowboys to follow him off up-valley for a field-glass check of the snowbound herd. Through the glasses they determined two things before the threat of another heavy flurry turned them back. There was still some open grass out in the middle of the amazing Gallatin; at least a part of the cattle they had pushed into the timber had survived and were starting to plow their way out toward the beckoning buffalo graze.

The ensuing months fell into a pray-and-wait pattern still familiar to Montana rangemen.

Whole days at a time passed in which they could not get out of the cabin. Short spells of clearing skies and quieting winds obtruded, during which they could. And, as winter wore away toward spring, there were a few longer stretches in which they were actually able to get to the loose horse herd, catch up mounts and ride out to the grazing grounds.

Pretty Bird and Nella, on these latter occasions when the men were with the cattle, served their hard turn as camp meat hunters, snowshoeing the lower timber of the Madisons in search of valley-wintering deer and elk. When the Texas girl's growing girth demanded it, Stark brusquely demoted her to cook's helper, a job formerly filled by the sulking Winter Boy. In the same move he promoted the Oglala lad to side his mother as an interim camp hunter, and Waniyetula's delight came embarrassingly close to hero worship. Before the winter was out, he and the big Montanan were separated only when the latter was driven to demand it in self-defense. During the same time and perhaps drawn by the white woman's condition, Pretty Bird transferred her silent attachment from the unresponsive Stark back to Nella. It was well she did, for the Texas girl, beginning with her seventh month, suffered a rough, frequently dogsick pregnancy. The Oglala squaw's patient, knowledgeable ministrations and, above all, her mere presence as another woman, were all that kept Nella fighting off the three-headed incubus of loneliness, cabin fever and the fear of having her baby without a doctor. But discounting the faithful Indian woman it seemed to the miserable girl that no one, least of all Nathan Stark, cared whether she lived or died. Or whether Ben Allison's baby ever saw the light of delivery day or not. Yet, in late February, Stark had done a strange thing—and despite the fact he had not moved to touch her, nor been encouraged to, since the night of his brutal attack, her heart took suspended pause to wonder.

In every herd of first-calf heifers, a few early breeders will drop late-winter calves. The Texas cattle were no exception, but the few head which calved prematurely in that wild northern winter had little chance to bring their babies through. Knowing this, Stark put out an order for the cowboys to rope and bring in any milking mother they might spot mooing over a down and frozen-dead calf.

Of the resulting number, over twenty head, if you could trust the notches on the delighted Waco's tally stick, Stark succeeded, after weeks of uproarious cowboy advice together with some little assistance, in making bossy-cow corral-milkers of exactly four. These pampered individuals were kept up in the horse shed, fed on hand-chopped buffalo hay and, when the weather was nice, put out on separate picket to graze the bench in front of the cabin. Yet in all the rough weeks of breaking the wild longhorns to the stanchion and bucket, Stark never once troubled to mention the project's purpose to Nella.

The only hint she got was from Chickasaw.

And even the old cowboy's testy reply was more defiant than explanatory.

"A baby's born, it's got to be weaned, goddamit! You cain't take it off'n its maw's milk on burnt venison and boiled beans!"

It was only incidental that the milking heifers served a sooner, less expected cause.

In early May, when eighty per cent of the calf crop was already on the ground, a late storm hit the spring thaw and froze-in a small bunch of about forty head on a river-bottom mudflat. There were over half of the bogged heifers nursing day- to week-old calves. The latter were easy to rope and snake out. But their 800-pound mothers would not come free. The new snow was piling fast. There was nothing to be done for the trapped cattle save to put a bullet through them. This was done.

On a pure whim, Stark ordered each of the riders to tie and pack a calf. "Pick the heifers," he told them, hard-grinning it and doing his stiff best to make it sound like

191

one of their rough-easy cowboy jokes. "We may need them to start a new herd next summer, providing this spring weather hangs on so beautiful."

There were six of them, Saleratus having come along to get a little fresh air. Each soon had his calf slung across his mount's withers, ready to hit for home ahead of the main blow. Stark led the way, packing not one, nor two, but three of the wild-eyed babies aboard Blue Grass—a pair hung heels-to-heels across the powerful bay's rump, the third carried, untied, in his own cradling arms. It was a handful even for the Montanan. A rumpful even for his thickmuscled stallion. Yet, together, and somehow, they brought it off. All hands, in spite of the face-cutting sleet and the constant struggle to keep the bawling calves aboard and balanced, salted the long ride home with many a cheerful laugh at themselves and their damn fool sentimentality in saving the spraddle-legged orphans.

It was as good a time as any to enjoy a free chuckle.

At least about those eight little longhorn heifers.

The day was on its way, and swiftly, when Stark's fumbling joke about using them to start a new herd was going to prove the unfunniest thing any young Montanan ever tried on five old Texas trailhands.

They say that Montana has twenty-four hours of spring, thirty days of summer, fifteen minutes of fall and eleven months of winter. Of course that is an exaggeration. Actually, spring sometimes begins as early as June, summer lasts almost through July and the first waterholes do not freeze until clear into August. Maybe it is true that the mountain valleys average out better than 5000 feet high and frost over nearly every night the year around. And perhaps it is so that a rancher's wife cannot raise anything but radishes and rutabagas and tall, tough sons. Nevertheless, Montana can be beautiful in May—and in that fifth month following the great blizzard of 1867 she was doing everything she could to prove it to Nathan Stark and his winterbound crew of transplanted Texans.

The snow was all gone in the low places before April was out. The last of the river ice broke free in the upper canyon and boomed off down the Gallatin the first week in May. By mid-month the new grass was coming an inch a minute and by June 1 the valley was carpeted, mountain wall to mountain wall, with the deepest green cow pasture the amazed southerners had ever seen. For men born and raised on the arid southwest plains, where the grazing capacity of land was reckoned in sections instead of acres, and where it sometimes took an entire 640 to support three cows and their increase, the sudden burgeoning of the northern meadows was a thing beyond belief.

Over the silky gray-blue curl of the true buffalo grass, which seldom grew above three or four inches, the sturdier blades of the blue grama, bunch, pine, June, foxtail and wheat grasses stood to two feet thick. While above the latter, the coarse stems of the hollowjoint and other rank forage plants shot up tall enough to hide a month-old calf. And as though the grass itself was not enough to drop an old Texan's jaw, the riotous wildflowers which came with it were simply overwhelming. The whole floor of the Gallatin was literally and all at once alive with glacier lilies, alpine poppies, columbines, white dryads, globeflowers, Indian paintbrushes, asters and arnicas. It was a sight to put a gleam in the eye of any old cattleman, and a pound of precious tallow a day on the ribs of any young Texas heifer.

Stark's cattle fattened mightily, his idle cowboys loafed in the spring sun and watched them do it.

The lengthening days came and went with no sign of a break in the bluebird weather nor, more to the increasingly uneasy point, any hint of Buffalo Ribs's promised return.

The rapid advance of June brought, as well, unspoken worries over another delayed arrival—Nella's baby was due and showing no desire to do anything about it.

The Texas girl was uncomfortably big. And as brave about being so as any twenty-year-old mother-to-be might be expected to manage under the isolated circumstances. Yet try as she might, and did, to hide her concern over the suspended approach of her time, she could not quite bring it off. She had reached the point of first-mother fear where sleep will not come at night and where the swift beating of that other heart pounded so fiercely beneath her own that it seemed her distended abdomen must actually burst before the new life could be otherwise and naturally freed.

Her tightlipped apprehension spread to the men, filling their simple thoughts with a nervousness as real, if not so painful, as her own. Stout Texas hearts that would not alter a pulsebeat in front of a charging steer or a full stampede jumped six feet every time Nella sneezed. Sun-squinted gray eyes that would not shift a crowsfooted wrinkle facing a Sioux surround or a howling head-on wave of feathered red horsemen winced in sensitive male sympathy at her slightest night groan, narrowed hurtfully each time she sighed or suppressed a soft cry of pain.

Even Stark, toward the last, was losing sleep.

And finding out, for the third time in his life, what it meant to fight something he could not see, nor get his powerful hands on. The first time had been this strange, shy friendship with Ben Allison. The second, his bitter, unreturned love for Nella Torneau. And now there was this third, worst time. This interminable, innocent, awesome time of waiting for a new baby to be born. It was more than any man could humanly take, to stand by in such an hour without suffering *some* fear. Stark suffered his. That was as certain as the fact he failed to show it. Where he had never known the feeling before, he now discovered how it felt to be *afraid.* And how fear, from the subconscious, daylong, false-proud way it held his teeth together, could make any man's jaw muscles ache.

Still, the big Montanan kept his concern for Nella's lateness to himself. As grimly, he confined his out-loud worrying to Buffalo Ribs and the Big Hole Crows.

And to what the red raiders were waiting for.

At 2 P.M. of a sweltering hot afternoon in the first week of July, he found out.

195

CHAPTER EIGHTEEN

SINCE MAY and the melt-off of the outer valley snow-packs had opened the way for pony travel, Stark had done what he could to get ready for the Crows. It was not much. A well-hidden spring, a short rifle shot up the gully behind the cabin, was dug out and its flow camouflaged as carefully as possible and trenched down inside the horse shed. Here a shallow pit was sunk and logged and tarred-in to collect the precious trickle. Additional rifle slits were cut into the cabin and lean-to walls. Meadow hay was cut, dried and stacked in the corral, against the time when the saddlestock and the nurse cows might need to be run in and handfed. The roofs were heavily sodded with green turf to prevent a burnout by fire arrows or close-in night sneaks with hand-thrown pitchpine torches. That was about it. These things accomplished, there remained but one last step of preparation—someone had to make the risky ride to Virginia City to contact Lazarus before he set out with the supplies promised Stark on his Christmas trip.

Typically, the Montanan elected himself. "It's not that you and Fentriss couldn't make it," he growled at the objecting Chickasaw. "I just like to do my own dirty laundry." But where the old cowboys could not argue him down, he next ran squarely up against somebody who could.

And did.

"Do you think you can set a horse long enough to

196

make it into town?" he asked Nella, coming to stand scowlingly before her where she rested in the cabin's shade just outside the door.

"I might," she replied, straightening on the plank bench Hogjaw had hewed out for her. "Why?"

"Get ready," he told her. "We can leave tonight and be in Bozeman come daylight. We can pick up a springbed wagon and a guard from there to Virginia City."

"I said *why?*" she repeated, green eyes hardening.

"I don't want you having that baby out here. Not if it can be helped. Get ready." He had already turned when she shot it at him.

"*Stark—!*"

He came around.

"I'm not going."

"Oh—"

"That's right. You once said nobody runs out on a deal with you."

"I did."

"Well, I'm somebody and I'm not running out!"

"Suit yourself. Esau will be in here with a wagon before long. You can go out then—in style."

"I'm not going, Stark! When *I'm* ready, I'll go! Meantime, don't push me!"

"Big talk, girl. You Texans are all alike. Mouth going a mile a minute to cover up the noise of your feet dragging."

She hated him then with that special helpless fury of the proud woman caught in the middle of a bad bluff by the one man in the world she would rather die than admit it to. Yet she could not find a solitary word with which to see his blunt call. And it was not until long minutes after he had saddled up and left that she was able to think up the twenty or thirty wonderful ways in which she could have burned his ears off, proper.

He was back in forty-eight hours, refusing to say anything of the success or failure of his talks with Lazarus. But two weeks later, with the Bozeman Road for the first time since the May thaw solid enough to hold a wagon wheel without letting it down to its hub-tallow in blue mud, the faithful old Jew showed up.

He came in a two-ton Pittsburg freighter, loaded to the top irons with essential camp supplies. In addition to the standard items—the flour, beans, bacon, sugar, coffee, blankets, lamp oil, veterinary and human medicines, horseshoes, harness leather, bellows forge, foot-treadle grindstone, axes, drawknives, shovels and the whole other rat's nest complex of handtools and mending materials necessary to an out-settlement ranching operation of the late sixties—Lazarus had brought along an outsized tailbox crammed with enough DuPont powder, bullet lead, multiple molds, primers, cartridge cases and blocks of paraffine fluxing wax to keep a Confederate regiment firing all summer. Nor was he quite through his bill of lading when the sweating cowboys had stored the last of the arsenal supplies in the far end of the horse shed.

Smiling happily, he unshaped the front seatbox to reveal the real treasure.

Even Stark's pale eyes lit up.

Snug in their original factory grease and the oily brown wrapping papers as familiar to gun lovers then as now, the ranch crew saw the dark steel and walnut gleam of new rifles.

They were unfired, mint-fresh Spencer Repeating Carbines—six of them—one each for the cowboys with one left over for the sharpshooting Pretty Bird. With Stark's and Nella's Henrys they made a battery of eight lever-action lead throwers, a formidable concentration of firepower in that still largely breech and muzzle-loading, single-shot time.

When Stark tried to object, arguing that they were not on his order list and that he could not and would not con-tract to pay for such deadly little luxuries, Lazarus palmed his slim hands in that eloquent, all-embracing gesture with which his people have deprecated their emotional generosity since the flight into the wilderness.

"They are a gift, Nathan. A wedding gift. Something as of a father to a son and daughter he never had."

"I can't take them," said Stark.

"Humor an old man. Take them, Nathan. They are little enough, far less than I owe you."

"I can't. And you don't owe me a thing. You've got that just backwards. The boot's pinching the other toe, Esau. You know that."

Lazarus's gentle eyes kindled, went to snapping excit-edly. He threw up his hands.

"Boots! Pinches! Toes! What am I? Your old friend or a shoe salesman? These guns—pahhh! Nothing! They won't even make them any more. Some smart Jew

199

named Winchester—the name's been changed, don't worry! I know a *landsman's* hand when I feel it in a deal—has brought out a new gun, eight shots, the finest yet. Everybody wants the new ones. All we hear now is Winchester! Winchester! These old relics? *Dschonke! Wertlos! Kitschig!* I am ashamed to offer them."

"So?" grinned Stark, not for a minute taken in by the overdone defense.

"So take them," huffed the other. "They're useless to me. I'm a banker, not a shopkeeper."

"We both know that, Esau."

"So!" It was Lazarus's sharp turn at the word.

"So," Stark answered softly, "you don't fool anybody with that put-on peddler's act." He reached for his hand, took it in silence, concluded abruptly. "I'll take the guns, Esau. And thanks until you're better paid."

"There is no better pay than the grip of a good friend's hand," said the little moneylender slowly. *"Will you never learn that, Nathan?"*

Stark's jaw squared. Did that mean what he thought it did? Was Lazarus deliberately trying to remind him of his bitterness over Ben Allison? Of his weakness in letting himself befriend the Texas trailboss? Of his subsequent harsh vow never to let another man be his friend? The Montanan's mind flashed back to the moment he had said goodbye to Ben in the Black Nugget's banking room, lingered on the strange, disturbing seconds in which the tall man's hand had gripped his. Angrily, he shook off the memory.

That was long ago. Ben was gone. There was no room

for another like him in Stark's life.

"You'll want to see Nella before you go back," he said belligerently. "She's lying down in the lean-to. I've got work to do."

"Yes," said Lazarus, watching him steadily. Then, quickly, to Chickasaw, "Please bring the small trunk behind the seat, Mr. Billings."

"What in hell's in it?" grumped the latter, shouldering the old-fashioned, brass-bound locker. "Nothing? It weighs fluffier'n a batch of Dixie's biscuits."

"Some little things from long ago," nodded Lazarus. The answer went to Chickasaw but his eyes stayed on Stark. *"For a man's bride, and for his firstborn son."*

He was not long in the little room with Nella.

When Chickasaw had put down the ancient trunk, he waited until the growing silence got to the old cattleman, letting him know there were places he was more needed than in the lean-to. Then he went to the low bunk and stood beside it.

"It's been a long time, Mr. Lazarus," Nella smiled. "I've gotten to be a big girl since you saw me last." She moved her hand hesitantly across the worn coverlet. He took it understandingly, seated himself on the edge of the bunk, answered her wearily smiled little joke with his gentle nod. "I'm glad, child. Nathan needs a son."

She grimaced, turning her head away. "If it was his, maybe."

"It will be his. No man can refuse a son."

"Stark can. He's not like any other man."

"No man is like another," shrugged Lazarus.

"It doesn't matter," she smiled tightly. "I'm going away as soon as this is over. My mind's made up now. Stark and I got started wrong. I've fought him and cheated him and hated him from the first. He despises me for it and I can't blame him. Yet, somehow, I still can't stand the thought of him touching me. He knows that and he'd rather cut off his hand than try it. It's been Ben, I think, back of it all. And all along. Him and the baby being his."

"No," said Lazarus quietly, "it's you and Nathan, no one else. It is each other you fight and hate, it is yourselves. Ben Allison was the only real friend Nathan ever had. You are the only woman he ever loved. He still loves you, he always will. An old man knows these things, you will see."

Nella shook her head, turned away again.

"I don't think so, Lazarus. I don't think I'll see anything. Not even my baby—"

He caught the fear in it, pressed her hand more closely. "You will, girl. The baby will be all right. And it will be a boy. I *know* that, too."

Something in his repeated, soft insistence went against the raised grain of her frayed nerves, setting her off. "Oh, you don't know anything!" she flared at him. "You're just an old man. What *could* you know! About me, or the baby, or Ben, or a single thing except your precious Stark! He's like a son to you. You can't seem to see anything wrong in him!"

202

"I can see *everything* wrong in him, my child. Believe me."

His patient kindness shamed her as quickly as his persistence angered her. "I'm sorry, Lazarus. I didn't mean that. Not about you and Stark. It was the baby. I only meant that you can't know about something like that—something you haven't gone through yourself. Nobody can."

Lazarus got up. "That's right," he nodded soothingly. Then, bringing the little trunk and placing it on the bunk at her feet. "Let me show you something."

"What is it?" she asked, eyeing the trunk dully.

"Don't you know?" said Esau Lazarus, and opened the dusty lid.

Her eyes widened. She came upright, leaned breathlessly forward.

The little trunk was piled, lidful, with the faded treasures of some forgotten bride's unused hope chest. The far-off fragrance of lavender and old rose, covered for fifty years, flooded out into the silence following Lazarus's question.

Nella saw the delicate linens and European laces, the damasks, silks, satin and cashmeres of a troth plighted long ago and in another land. And she saw, nestled among them in poignant, sad, small loneliness, the tiny, doll-like unrealities of the baby things.

"Oh, Lazarus, Lazarus! I'm sorry—"

"She was only a child. Seventeen that summer."

"And the baby?" Nella dreaded to ask it, knew she must.

"A boy. A son," said Esau Lazarus.

The silence again.

"It was why you said you *knew.*"

"Yes. And why I said I knew it would be all right with you."

"But that's it, Lazarus. That's what I don't understand. How *can* you know that?"

"An old man's faith in his God. *He* would not let it happen again."

Nella sank back. She could not look at him then, and her voice was hard from its fight against the tears she did not want him to see.

"If it's a son, we'll name it Esau."

"Nathan Esau," said the old Jew softly.

And got up and went out of the room without looking back.

July 3 dawned clear and windy. For the past three weeks, since mid-June, the buffalo pastures had shriveled under a succession of blazingly hot days. It was one of those freak spells of blistering daylong suns and dew-free all-night winds with which Montana can so witheringly take back the green promise of a wet spring. By early afternoon, lounging uneasily around the blowing ashes of their noon dinner coffee-fire five miles up the Gallatin, even the drought-wise Texas cowboys were kicking at the cracked earth, squinting into the brassy glare overhead, holding up wetted forefingers in frowning hope of finding a northerly switch in the desert wind, and popping small pebbles or loose bullets into their parched mouths to, as they put it, "salivate the situation somewhat."

It was one which could stand a little salivating.

The southern cattle, led on by the panhandle weather and loving every tail-switching, heel-fly-stomping minute of its nostalgic heat, were spread out across the Gallatin from the riverbank to the far foothills. There was no way, short of riding twenty-four-hour herd on them, to hold them in, either, and no chance to try even that with the Indians long overdue like they were. Could the herd have been held fairly close to the river timber below the cabin bench, the Crows would have been forced to ride within rifle range to get at it, giving a man at least one good crack at them with the new Spencers. But the way it was, Waco now cursed bitterly, "We got nursing heifers with calves, at foot scattered worse'n busted dimestore beads all over the twenty main miles of Stark's cussed Big Pasture!" And with not, Hogjaw scowlingly amended, "a Christian Cherokee's chance in Injun hell of rounding them up and running them in ahead of the lousy Crows coming back to take their second swipe at them."

At this point Slim Blanchard, who had gotten shut of something less than two dozen words since leaving Texas, spun away his brownpaper shuck, tongued his lower lip to soak loose the ragged tear of the paper glued to it, spat it away, sought the respected advice of the senior senator from San Saba County.

"What you think, Chickasaw?"

The old foreman tilted his tobacco-stained beard at the

yellow sky, pulled loose a clump of bunch grass, shredded its dust-dry blades, shifted his dribbling chaw, spatteringly drowned a passing chinch bug.

"It ain't what I think that's lathering me. It's what them damn Injuns think. Or might be thinking."

"I foller you that far, Old Paint," drawled Waco. "Keep acoming."

Chickasaw shot at, and missed, another chinch bug. He reloaded his cheek, fired again, got him on the second try. "Well, now, I say to myself, happen I was a Crow—which I wouldn't be on account of if I hadda been I'd shot myself for mortal shame sixty years ago—but just saying happen I was, what would I be thinking about, come this present hot spell? That is, saying last summer's dead hay was still standing three-foot high and dusty as punk, which it is, and this spring's new grass was already dried down to its ground joints, which it will be by sundown tonight."

"You're still rolling right my way," grinned Waco. "Don't stop now."

"Well," continued the old man, not grinning, "after that I remember that the wind's been blowing night and day three weeks straight. I figure I've waited on it just about as long as I dast. The grass cain't get no drier and a shower's like to blow up any afternoon and wet my tinder. So, along about three, four days ago, I saddle up my best pony, put on my warpaint and Sunday-go-to-meeting feathers, sneak into the south end of Mr. Stark's pasture and get myself set, *upwind.* Then I just hunker there awaiting for the breeze to lay just right, down valley, so's to be blowing square at them damn long-horns my white brothers have got spread out acrost my private buffalo range."

"Now, let's see," inquired the struggling Hogjaw earnestly. "Where's that bring you up to?"

"Right up to today. Or better yet, to tonight."

"Why tonight, oldtimer?" Waco, back in it again, sober and quick, not drawling and not grinning any-more. "You still just talking Crow maybe's, or are you giving us one of your goddam Comanche hunches?"

Chickasaw had a famous nose for Indian trouble. Nearly any of the old plainsmen, such as himself, who had managed to stay alive in hostile country past voting age, had developed some fair sense of "Injun smell." But the dirty-bearded dean of Ben Allison's trail crew could "catch the stink of hostile hossflesh" faster and farther away than a Kwahadi campdog. If he was presently riding one of his so-called Comanche hunches, it was high time his friends heard about it.

"I'm giving you a hunch," he growled, ending the sus-pense. "A prime big one."

"So why tonight?" prodded Waco.

"Wind's right, moon's dark, hay's ready."

"And—?"

"I smell a change in weather coming."

"Meaning so can they?"

"And will have to hustle to beat the rain."

Waco stood up.

"She's deep enough for me," he nodded. "I cain't smell neither the Injuns nor the wet weather, but I ain't arguing none. How about you boys?"

Hogjaw scowled, dumped out the coffee tin, dropped it in the grubsack. He was, as usual, three lengths off the pace of his companions' conversation, spurring hard to catch up. "Cripes Amighty, I dunno. I been choking on yore traildust for the past five minutes, but I'm damned if I can read yore sign. What in hell you two old Piutes augering about, anyhow? You know cussed well I cain't keep up with you when you go to throwing around that infernal Injun talk."

Waco and Chickasaw looked at him, but the answer did not come from either of them.

"Fire," said Slim Blanchard, dead slow and staring off south up the Gallatin, into the face of the sucking wind. "Injuns going to fire the grass, come dark tonight."

CHAPTER NINETEEN

WHEN THEY got back to the cabin, Stark was gone. After listening to their report, Saleratus told them he had taken Winter Boy with him and ridden off up the gully trail. "Seems you ain't the only one gets Injun hunches," he muttered to Chickasaw.

"Show them cards agin," interrupted Waco. "I didn't quite read all the spots on 'em."

Saleratus ran his tongue nervously over his snuff-colored gums. " 'Pears some of that special Injun savvy of Chickasaw's must of rubbed off on Stark somewheres along the trail up from Texas. Leastways, he got restless just after we'd et. Took me to one side and said he'd got a sudden feeling he'd ought to ride up and check Eagle Gap agin."

The cowboys looked at one another. Maybe it was just one of those things. Maybe it was not. Right after noon dinner was when Chickasaw had gotten *his* little Crow message from Man Above.

"It's yore hand," said Waco. "Keep adealing it."

Saleratus shrugged helplessly. "That's about the whole of it. He just allowed, in that deadpan way of his, that he didn't know near as much about *Injuns* as he'd like but that he figured he could hold his own in any color stud game and that a good poker player always bet his hunches, table limit. Whether they was red or white."

"Jesus Murphy!" stammered Hogjaw, catching up with the call faster than usual. "It don't never rain but what it cuts loose and comes a cloudburst."

"Sure enough," agreed Waco. "First Chicksaw stampedes us into hightailing for home to warn Stark he might be smelling his own beef burning before daylight. Then we get here and find he's already had his own private hunch and is out trying to see where they're going to stack the buffler chips to light the barbecue with. Looks like today's our day to get our bad news back-to-back."

"Sure does," nodded Saleratus. "And it sure is."

They caught the meaningful qualification, Chickasaw challenging at first.

"There's more?"

The dour cook checked the lean-to, jerked his head toward it.

"Her," he said.

"What about her?" asked the old man slowly.

"Right after noon dinner," answered the other, shaking his head. "Not ten minutes after he'd took off up the gulch. Like she'd been waiting for him to get out of sight—"

"Yeah?"

"She started having her pains."

In Montana daylight hangs on in July. There was still a good three or four hours of it left when Stark rode in at four o'clock.

"I hear you had a hunch," Chickasaw greeted him at the corral. "How'd she pay off?"

"One hundred to one. What are you doing back here? Thought I told you to keep trying to work the herd down this way."

"We tried," put in Waco.

"And?"

"They're spread too thin, Mr. Stark," Slim made one of his rare contributions. "Take ten men a month to make any kind of a gather."

"That doesn't say what you're doing back here."

"It don't," allowed Waco. "But try this. Chickasaw had a hunch, too."

Stark wheeled on the old foreman.

"Injun variety, same as yours," scowled the latter. "Hit me sudden today. Should of thought of it long before."

210

"Go on."

"First off, I reckon a Crow don't think no different than a Comanche. And down home them Kwahadi bastards never missed no bets when it come to ways and means of ruining a man's ranch."

"So?" said Stark, watching him closely.

"So they never thought up a better one than building a bonfire in his back pasture," grunted Chickasaw.

"Oldest Injun trick in the warbag," confirmed Waco. "And the damndest. Ever see 'em set a first-class prairie fire, Mr. Stark?"

"I've seen the Sioux do it to run buffalo."

"Uh-huh. Well, now you're going to see the Crows do it to roast beef. Leastways, that's Chickasaw's guess."

Stark was furious. His jawthrust thumbjerk singled out Chickasaw, but the black anger of his slow words included all of them.

"Do you mean to stand there and tell me that you left your cattle and cut for home just because this old fool decided it was a good day for the Indians to start a grassfire?"

The grizzled foreman looked him over.

"This *old fool,*" he said, just as slowly, "would have died a young fool, happen he'd made a habit of *not* cutting for home when he got sudden took with strong hostile smell, upwind." He paused, still eying the angry Montanan. Then nodded toward the gully behind the cabin. "You find anything up that draw to make a liar of me and my Comanche hunch, Mr. Stark?"

The latter thought about it. When he did, he cooled out

211

fast. He shook his massive head in honest admission. "No. I found heavy Indian sign just this side of the Gap. They had turned off the gully trail and followed down along the ridge."

"Sign was reasonable fresh?"

"Winter Boy picked up some of their pony droppings. He said there was still a little heat in them."

"Uh-huh. And they went *south* down the ridge?"

"That's right."

Chickasaw bobbed his head, tilted his scraggly beard, squinted up at him. "What way's this freak wind blowing from, Mr. Stark?"

Stark knew that the old cowboy had cut him out of the herd, and was not going to let him get back.

"All right, there was a big bunch of them. They *were* Crows and they were traveling south to get upwind. So what?"

"So fire," said Chickasaw. "Tonight. Before the rain comes."

Again Stark thought it over.

"You satisfied they'll hold off till dark?"

"Guarantee it. They got a real tender sense of beauty."

"They what!"

"What fire don't look purtier at night?"

Stark stared at him. "I don't know whether you're being funny, or feeble-minded. Fortunately, it doesn't matter. We've got three hours, either way. Grab yourselves some fresh horses."

"Fresh horses? For what?" demanded Waco moving forward, tightlipped.

212

Stark gestured across the river toward the farside floor of the Gallatin. "For getting over there and gathering what we can of the cattle while it's still light. I figure we can get around and bring in at least a hundred head."

"I figure you're right, Mr. Stark. Saving for one thing."

"Well, don't save it, Fentriss. Spit it out."

Waco nodded, hunched a shoulder toward the lean-to, spat as ordered.

"Your wife's gonna have a baby."

There was no easy grinning sarcasm in it, no rough-humored Fort Worth style cowboying. Stark caught and understood that. And he knew what it meant. Nella was not just *going* to have a baby, she *was* having it.

"When?" he asked quietly.

"Sal says the pains started right after you left. They still ain't coming fast though. I reckon we might get out and back, providing you want to chance it."

"Chance what?" Acutely sharp as he was in most matters, the Montanan still had occasional trouble following the drawling, off-tangent Texas way of putting things.

"The Crows being smart enough to have left their main bunch up on the ridge, yonder, to jump the cabin the minute the fire starts and pulls us out of it. Or the minute, meanwhile, they might catch us out of it for *any* reason."

"Waco's right, Mr. Stark." Chickasaw spoke in dead earnest.

The sun was far too low over the Madisons to leave time for injured feelings. "You got your choice. Try for

213

the cattle, or stick to the cabin and the gal. How you want to ride it?"

They all knew their pale-eyed employer by now. Nine months on the Texas trail, plus a long seven in a 12 x 20 Montana cabin, did not leave a man much room for secrets. Not even an unfriendly man like Stark. They waited for him, knowing the kind of dollar-counting fight that must be going on inside him. Knowing the killing high price and value he put on the precious herd of seedstock heifers. Knowing the hard, unfeeling way he had treated Nella from that beginning hour when old Judge Hacker had stumbled through the words in the Black Nugget's banking room. And thinking they knew which one of Chickasaw's choices the money-hungry Montanan would slap his saddle on.

The next minute they were being reminded of something they should never have forgotten in the first place.

With Nathan Stark, *nobody knew.*

"Forget it," he told them softly, and swung up on the still saddled Blue Grass. "I'll run the nurse cows in off the bench."

"We already brung the calves in," apologized Waco, with a lame nod to the corral and the twelve orphan heifers. "But their cussed foster mammas didn't aim to be brung along with 'em."

"I'll bring them," repeated Stark. He touched the stud with his knees, started him around the cabin. Hogjaw broke first. "Hold on, we'll go with you, Mr. Stark!" The young puncher was pulling his saddle off the toprail as he called out his awkward loyalty, but Stark spun the big

214

bay quick as a cat. He did not raise his voice, nor did he need to. *"You'll stay here,"* he said, *"with Mrs. Stark—"*

CHAPTER TWENTY

THEY WALKED slowly around the cabin, watching him lope the bay out across the bench. "He sets a heap of store by them damn cows," Waco observed. "They ain't ever been no particular use that I could see."

"Well, I dunno," offered Hogjaw soberly. "They brung up them little heifer calves slick as slippery ellum."

"Uh-huh, just what we need, ain't it? Another dozen heifers. Cripes, we got four hundred out yonder now that we cain't do nothing with but watch them burnt alive by them murdering Crows."

"Maybe it'll be like Stark said," persisted Hogjaw. "If they get the others, maybe we'll need them orphans for breeders next spring. Leastways we got 'em where the Injuns cain't get at 'em."

"Yeah." Waco's grin was tight at the mouth corners. "Leastways, not till after they get at *us*." He thought a moment, toeing the ground frowningly. "Damn it, it still don't figure. A stonehead like him, messing around making milkers out'n them pear-thicket scrubs. Nor, coming to that, wet nursing them cussed calves all winter through. It just don't add up. Not for Stark, it don't."

Chickasaw, who had not quit watching the dwindling horseman, broke in without shifting his careful gaze. "I told you once, way back. I'll give it to you agin. It ain't

215

got nothing to do with them dry-bag longhorns, nor with them lousy weaner calves. It's the gal, and it ain't never been nothing but the gal. He done it to make up to her. Her and Ben's kid that's coming in there now. If you cain't see that, and what it adds up to, your heads are a better granite than his."

"What the tarnal hell you talking about, you yaller-bearded old billy goat! Honest to Christ, sometimes I think—"

"And most times you don't," interrupted the old man quietly. "I'm talking about him and Nella."

"What about 'em?"

"You catch the way he looked when you told him her pains had set in?"

"Yeah, like he'd been kicked in the belly with a hob-nail boot. And why not? Likely he was weighing her agin a hundred head of longhorn heifers, plus a hundred fifty of Crow war ponies, and sick to his gut that we was no doubt right about the Injuns being laid up along the ridge just waiting for the bunch of us to cut away from the cabin and cross over the river. That's all, mister. He wasn't losing no fat over Nella, just heartbroke from knowing we dassn't risk our own dirty necks going after them cattle."

Chickasaw nodded slowly, his usual quick temper strangely absent. "Leave me put it this way, Waco. Supposing there wasn't no gal in that lean-to, yonder. And no baby cramping and tearing up her insides, till she's bit her lips clean through trying to hold down her yells. Supposing there was only them 'maybeso Crows' hid out up there on the ridge, or over in that fringe timber. You reckon Stark would still have figured we dassn't have a run at them hundred heifers acrost the river?"

It was a blind-corner question.

They all knew the pale-eyed answer to it.

Waco made it for them. "All right, so we'd be out yonder pounding saddle leather instead of standing here listening to you clacking your three good teeth. So then what?"

"So then," said Chickasaw softly, *"he loves her."* He waited a moment, watching their intent faces, then spread his gnarled hands. "There ain't no mystery to it. It ain't been no different right from the first, it ain't going to be no different clear to the last. That spell it out simple enough for you?"

"Naw—" Hogjaw was unable to imagine it.

"Yeah—" Slim Blanchard was. "I thought abouten it thataway since way down the trail."

Waco, not about to surrender to any notions of Montana romance, sought refuge in Texas cynicism. "Mister, if that's love I'd sure as hell hate to be the gal he sets his sights on!"

"Well, you ain't and it is—" muttered Chickasaw. He broke off the side-mouthed rebuttal, eyes narrowing suddenly. Before the others could follow the sweeping shift of his glance from Stark to the clearing's edge, he had thrown back his head and uttered a piercing, long-drawn Rebel yell.

It was a sound Stark had learned well in the wild-riding months of the traildrive, one that the Confederate-

217

bred cowboys put to three primary uses—turning a stampede, intimidating a trail town, countercharging an Indian attack.

There were not cattle enough in the whole Territory of Montana to start a decent stampede. The nearest trail town was Baxter Springs, down below the Kansas border. Stark had one guess left. He took it in a hurry.

In the same second he spun the bay stud and dug him out on a grass-flat gallop for the cabin.

The cowboys had never seen Blue Grass run. Not *actually* run. The Kentucky-foaled stallion could head the best cow-pony on the plains without breaking a hand gallop. Seeing him stretch now, even as they were grabbing their rifles from the door rack inside the cabin and hitting the dirt outside of it, they could not believe any living horse could cover ground like that.

The Indian scrubs, cutting in from the south-edge timber, seemed to be standing in one place throwing heel-sods. Where their riders had thought to easily cut the white man off 400 or 500 yards from the cabin, the best they could now hope for was to run him a dead heat at 200, and that putting them squarely under the belly-prone, elbow-propped fire of the four cowboys.

Beaverhead, who was leading the ambushing scout band, demonstrated his usual tact in such close questions of prairie protocol. Swinging wide, he took his followers on across the bench into the north-side timber, pausing only long enough to allow those among his braves who still favored the weapon, to get in a little offhand warbow practice.

218

They drove in on the four cows, cutting them apart and riding them out like rodeo team ropers, two braves to the animal, the hazer on the offside flank, the bowman on the nearside. The 800-pound longhorns were fast and scary as jumped-up brush wolves. But they were being run by Kangi Wicasi cowboys who thought nothing of siding an 1800-pound wounded bull on the dead gallop across a prairie dogholed pasture in the middle of a full-out buffalo stampede.

While Stark and the Texans watched helplessly, held speechless by the sheer admiration with which white frontiersmen, who were themselves among the world's finest horsemen, always received the incredible riding of their red betters, the Crows shot down the four milk cows.

Leaning crazily far down on the offside of their flying ponies, they drew their squat bows of mountain ash, full string, until the point of the gaudily feathered shafts almost touched the straining cattle. They fired only when just the right jump of both running animals narrowed the swaying range to actual contact. The broadhead buffalo arrows, less than two-feet long and tipped with as much as four ounces of cold hammered iron, went clear through the bawling quarry, channeling out a terrible wound which, if not instantly fatal, bled the stricken brute to death before it ran another hundred yards.

The entire action was over within thirty seconds. The last of the cows went down at the edge of the north timber. The Indians were gone as suddenly as they had appeared, and the late afternoon silence closed in once more over the cabin clearing. Stark and his Fort Worth crew blew out their rifle barrels, stared fixedly off down the bench.

It was Waco, the unquenchable, who found the first words for it.

"Matinee's over. Main show tonight."

And old Chickasaw, the irascible, who rang down the bobtailed curtain on the other cowboy's terse comment.

"Come early and bring your friends. It'll be a hell of a barbecue."

It was, too. And built over a bonfire that lit the Montana nightsky as far north as the Three Forks confluence of the main Missouri. But its Indian hosts made their white guests wait.

Hour after hour the black silence up the valley continued unbroken. The wind held from the south, soughing through the clearing-edge pines with a relentless due north draft that had the nerves of the sleepless whites dried out and popping like stepped-on twigs.

Midnight came. Off to the west, intermittent mutters of summer thunder and sultry stabs of heat lightning threatened but did not produce Chickasaw's predicted rain. The endless minutes inched toward one o'clock, began crawling past it.

On the rough plank seat in front of the cabin Waco and Chickasaw watched the south bay, talked softly of times gone by in Texas; of their boyhoods in San Saba and Uvalde counties, the war, their old regiments, friends long dead, comrades all but forgotten, and the myriad small things remindful of homes departed and happinesses lost which will rise up to plague a man's memory when he knows the coming sun will set on schedule— but not for him.

From the corral horse shed, Hogjaw and Slim, not long on talk at any time, peered wordlessly through the moonless dark of the clearing toward the edging blur of the timber and the black throat of Eagle Gap gully, straining to catch the first hint of detaching Indian shadows. Stationed at the north and southwall rifle slits, Saleratus and the wakeful Winter Boy kept the mainroom vigil; while in the lean-to Pretty Bird crouched beside Nella holding the Texas girl down on the sweat-soaked bunk when the pains became too great, giving her a twisted piece of mending leather to bite on for the lesser contractions and, all the meanwhile, muttering Sioux imprecations to a tiny *hanpospu hoksicala,* the grotesque buffalo-hide spirit doll carried by the Wikan, or ordained medicine women of the Oglala.

Between the three guardpoints and the suffering girl's bedside, Stark's tall silhouette moved without rest.

He had just talked to Waco and Chickasaw, out front, and started to recross the main room to look in once more on Nella when the old foreman's hoarse warning caught up to him from behind.

"Hold up a minute, Mr. Stark. Lookit yonder."

He stepped back to the door, narrowed glance sweeping automatically up-valley.

Far to the south, faintly staining the moondark above

the converging gaunt flanks of the Madison and Gallatin ranges, a glowing coal of firelight, in its first seconds and at the distance appearing no larger than a man's opened hand, was spreading its eager fingers skyward. Even as Stark watched, it reached hungrily outward and northward, sucked into instant, monstrous life by the furnace draft of the rising south wind. Within the following hushed minute the whole upper end of the Gallatin was glaringly walled off.

Nobody spoke. Waco and Chickasaw, siding Stark, stared tightlipped. Behind them, Saleratus, Slim and Hogjaw, drawn from their posts, echoed their hardfaced silence. It was Stark, finally, his flat voice wicked and mean and dead-end soft, who called the vicious turn of the Crow's hole-card.

"The bastards. The dirty, murdering, Indian sons of bitches."

"Amen," said Waco aimlessly. "What time is it?"

Stark pulled his stemwinder, scratched a sulphur pocketmatch. The yellow flame spurted, smoked, winked out.

It was five minutes past 2 A.M., July 4, 1867.

CHAPTER TWENTY-ONE

THE BRINDLE BULL was bedded with his small band in a lush swale ten miles south of the cabin bench.

He was an old bull, and wise with the dusty learning of many a dry summer on the sparse pastures of his native range. He was, too, by virtue of his six-foot horns

222

and six-inch temper, undisputed master not alone of his own surly forage habits, but of those of his jealously herded females. Accordingly, he kept his youthful mates close to the river, where the younger bulls, unmindful of the four- or five-mile walk to water, had theirs grazing in mid-valley. It was, perhaps, thus an accident of slothful old age which found him bedded so fortunately close to the Gallatin's bottom timber at 2 A.M. of that early July morning. It was no accident of any kind that he reacted as he did ten minutes later.

General Grant had seen his share of prairie fires, from the mesquite-studded flats of the Brazos to the cotton-wooded northern sweeps of the Canadian and the Cimarron. In his long-lived case instinct was hence amplified by experience. When he came lurching to his feet at the first warning of sifting ash and acrid smoke, his red-rimmed eyes were rolling with the ruminant's natural fear of the grass-fire smell. But in the same moment, with his females blundering up all around him in the flame-lit darkness and with his calves bleating piteously for mothers lost in the excitement of the mill, his savage memory flashed back to those other fires and those over riverbound pastures.

There was one way to go from fire. That was away from it. And away from it *toward* the nearest water and timber.

Be it sheltered by Texas mesquite, pear or cotton-wood, or by mixed Montana pine and alder, the grass always grew shorter and thinner and not so tinder-dry within a river's wooded fringe. Beyond that, beyond the safety of the trees themselves, there was the water; last natural haven to all four-footed creatures in their instinctive fire panic.

The General's hoarse bellow rose once and commandingly above the terrified lowing of his little band. That was all. Then he was lumbering confidently and straightaway for the nearby river. Behind him, the young cattle pushed and crowded frantically. Yet, under the old herdbull's unhurried example, they did not break and begin to run. When, minutes later, the fire wall exploded northward over their vacated bedding ground, they were standing belly-deep and safe in the ash-laden shallows of the Gallatin.

The cattle in mid-valley had no chance. Those which tried to reach the river were cut off by the race-horse speed of the flames. Those which stampeded ahead of the fire, down valley were burned over on the bawling run or trapped in the side draws and suffocated by the clotting strangle of the smoke.

Within the hour of its lighting by the Crows, the Gallatin holocaust had done its work. Within the following hour Chickasaw's rainstorm, drawn eastward by the vacuum of burned-out air over the smoldering buffalo pasture, swept in and drowned the last ember pockets.

It was too late.

In the dripping shelter of the south-valley timber, General Grant stood solitary sentinel over the survivors: thirty-four first-fresh and open heifers, twenty-seven weanling calves—the rain-drenched Montana remainder of Nathan Stark's great Texas trailherd.

Outside, the slash and winnow of the rain drove past the cabin door. Around the stove, Stark and his cowboys sat talking softly. In the lean-to, Nella was quiet, asleep for the first time in three days, her pains for the restlesss hour abated. Saleratus poured the last round for the hunched circle, set the empty coffee tin back on the woodbox. Stark stubbed out his cigar.

"Are you sure? Absolutely certain?" he asked the scowling Texans.

There was no answer beyond the little wash of silent nods, and he went on. "I just can't believe it. Some of them must have made it through to the river. Think again. Think hard. You were all up-valley yesterday morning. You must have spotted one bunch—some few head, somewhere—that wasn't too far from the timber. *Now where was it?*"

Chickasaw shook his head. "We keep telling you. It ain't nowhere. There wasn't none of them within two, three miles of the bottoms when she hit. It's why we didn't get nowhere making a gather earlier. They was just spread too wide and far out."

" 'Fraid that's it, Mr. Stark." Waco had taken deliberately to mistering the big Montanan since his last winter's prophecy that the latter was about to turn human, had drouthed-out and failed. "There wasn't none of them feeding near the water. Leastways, no bunch big enough to bother about."

Stark's flat voice pounced on the exception.

"What do you mean, 'no bunch big enough to bother about'?"

The small rider shrugged. "Well, we did see one little old measly bunch. Mebbe thirty head. Only reason we paid them any heed atall, was that they was with an old friend of Chickasaw's."

"General Grant," put in the old man dryly. "Him and Mr. Stark have met."

Stark thought a moment. "Good set of calves with his bunch?" he asked.

"Couple dozen." Waco, laconically. "Mostly brindles you can bet. The General's some stove up of late, but he don't leave it slow down his love life none."

Stark stood up. He did not raise his voice but even the gentle Slim winced at the bitterness in it. "My best herd-bull and better than fifty head of my last calves and brood cows might be alive up there, and you men sit there and tell me there wasn't anything worthwhile within three miles of the river." He paused, letting the acid of it eat into them. "Where were they?"

"That little heavy-grassed piece in the loop of the upper bend; place we call Seven-Mile Meadow." Waco got it out, headhung.

The Montanan went to the door, stood staring through the drive of the rain. He struck a light, cupped it, pulled his watch again. "Three twenty-five," he said. The match went out, burning his fingers. He did not drop it.

Back at the stove, he stood looking down at them. "Still a good hour till first light. Likely another two of smoke and fog after that. Maybe more if the rain holds." Again the long pause. Then, matter-of-factly as though excusing himself to go outside. "I'm going after them."

226

He was at the door rack, arming into his coat, when Chickasaw's reedy voice touched him on the shoulder.

"Reckon I'll keep you company."

He whirled around, angry denial ready. Waco's terse second beat him to it.

"Me, too, Mr. Stark. Let's don't auger it. That brindle bull thinks Chickasaw's his mother. He'll faller him faithfuller than Mary's lily white lamb. Saves a powerful lot of driving when you're in a hurry, Mr. Stark. *Which you will be.*"

It made hard cowboy sense. Stark admitted as much. "All right. Where does that leave you?" he asked Waco.

"Right where I've been for forty years—with the old man, here," said the wiry little rider, putting his hand to Chickasaw's thin shoulder. "Let's go."

Stark set his jaw. They had him beat and they knew it. He gave his orders to the others, then started for and held up at the lean-to door. Again Chickasaw was behind him.

"Leave her sleep, boy. There ain't nothing you can tell her now."

He looked at him, checking his reaching hand. He dropped the doorway blankets, letting them fall. The old man spoke the simple truth. There *was* nothing he could say to Nella now. The time he could have told her what his bull-headed heart had been fighting since the first thrilling minute she had kashed that smoky, slow, green-eyed look his way, was long gone. He had had his chance. Two, three, maybe more of them. Times when he could have given an inch of deadpan pride and gained

227

a mile of understanding gratitude. But no. Not him. Not Stark. Not the man nobody was going to stop or steal a march on, and who was going to make a million dollars no matter what. All he had done was gotten miserable drunk and gone after her on the one body-hungry way no man could take with a girl like Nella Torneau.

His wide mouth clamped shut, sealing off what was done and could not be undone. He nodded to Chickasaw, patted him awkwardly on the shoulder.

"You're right, oldtimer. Let's go."

They rode hard, south along the river. They found the General and his little band shortly after four o'clock, had them bunched and moving back by four-fifteen. With five-thirty and the first of the full summer daylight they had pushed halfway to the bench, had less than five miles to go. True to Stark's hope the rain continued, holding the fire's smoke low over the valley, adding the ground-stream of its own downpour to the camouflage. The weary cattle moved quietly, only the stumbling calves bleating a little. That small sound was quickly lost in the muffled beating of the rain. Forty-five minutes later they were within a mile of the river trail's final turn upward to the bench. They had crossed the cattle where they had found them, were now on the home-bank side of the Gallatin, would, in another few minutes, have them heading up the bench trail and into the temporary safety of the cabin corral.

But, as it will with all dead-end gamblers, when Nathan Stark's string ran out, it ran *clear* out.

Breaking around the last bend of the Gallatin, with the

cabin only 600 yards away, General Grant threw up his ugly head, halted, blew out explosively through his distended nostrils. The next moment he spun sideways and bounded like a giant cat into the trailside timber.

Chickasaw, hearing his alarmed snort and turning in the saddle in time to see him go, did not linger to question the old bull's motives. Throwing the startled gray hard right, he put the spurs to him. He had just time, before the wet trees slashed shut behind the ancient gelding, to accomplish two things: see the first of the Crow ponies loom up out of the smoke pall ahead; yell back a desperate warning to Stark and Waco, invisible, 100 feet away, through the dense fog.

The surprised Indian horsemen jumped their ponies forward, part of them splitting off after Chickasaw, the rest racing on past the herd after the unseen companions he had tried to warn.

By the sheerest sort of hostile luck Beaverhead, leading his prowling scoutband back up the Gallatin from an early morning check of the dead cattle along its middle reaches, had blundered squarely into the moving herd. Half an hour later his grinning warriors, having returned from their fruitless pursuit of the vanished white riders, began the systematic buffalo-lance and hunting-arrow execution of the last of the Texas longhorns.

Stark and Waco reached the cabin only minutes after the Crow attack, hand-leading their horses through the ghost world of the groundsmoke, step by breathheld step.

229

Chickasaw was not there to meet them.

An hour passed. Then, two. The rain eased up, stopped altogether. Still no Chickasaw.

About eight-thirty they heard the ponies in the corral whicker eagerly, followed by a delightful yell from Hogjaw in the horse shed. Shortly the missing oldster grumbled in through the lean-to crawlhole, none the worse for his three-hour absence.

In response to their questions he said that he had "doubled back and hid out to have a listen to what the red sons of bitches were up to." Holed-in a few feet off the trail, with his old gelding nose-wrapped and tethered safely back in the timber, he had gotten what he came after—a Texas-sized earful.

About an hour after Beaverhead's scouts had finished off the cattle, Buffalo Ribs and the main bunch had shown up. They had gutted and skinned a calf, built a big victory fire. With their buckskins stripped off and hung up to dry, they had squatted around, stark naked, listening to the meat spit and barking the Crow talk back and forth a mile an Indian minute.

During the long winter months of cabin confinement Chickasaw, claiming a professional Indian fighter's honest interest in learning all he could of his beloved Comanches' northern cousins, had put in a lot of time talking to Pretty Bird. Regardless of Waco's accusation that "the old goat" was a hell of a sight more interested in showing the comely Oglala squaw a few cozy cowboy hand-signs, than in having her teach him the fundamentals of "jabbering in Crow," he had, innocently or otherwise, acquired a considerable Kangi Wicasi vocabulary. Enough and to spare, as he cursingly spat it, "to fill them in on the immediate social schedule of them lousy cattle-stabbing bastards!"

Which, forthwith and bolstered by one of Stark's twenty-five cent cigars and six cups of Saleratus's "ash-felt tub-tar excuse for coffee," he proceeded to do.

The choice of transposing language was his own, and far from literal. But nobody needed a dictionary to follow him.

Buffalo Ribs and the main bunch had ridden clean around the east side of the valley, as far as the foothill pass, looking for live cattle. They had found a few singed strays, put them out of their blistered misery. With the nice job Beaverhead and his boys had done on General Grant's bunch, the Crow chief had proudly announced, they could figure that the upper reaches of the Gallatin Valley pasture had been safely put back to their rightful purpose of spring buffalo browse. And that, pending the little final matter of running the white cattlemen out of Montana, preferably baldheaded, they would have lived up to their agreement with Red Cloud's Sioux and all would again be right in the Kangi Wicasi world.

As to garnering the details of that latter arrangement, Chickasaw had not tarried overlong.

The rain had begun to let up and he had reckoned that the wind would not be far behind its slack off. And that, come that wind, a white man might find himself wishing he was a lot farther than forty feet away from 150 fog-

231

bound "spotted buffalo" hunters. Indian curiosity had killed a lot older cowboys than Mrs. Billings's favorite boy. The thought had taken him, sudden short, that he had used up the best part of Pretty Bird's language lessons and that he had better hit for home and turn in his report card.

"Which same," he concluded to Stark, biting off the end of the cigar and tonguing it into his cheek to chew the good out of its Habana wrapper, "you can now consider did. It's all yours and I allow even you can tally up close enough to figure our chances are in about the same shape as the baby's shirttail."

"How's that?" scowled the literal Montanan, in no mood for deciphering offtrail Texas references.

"Mighty short," translated Waco unsmilingly, "and full of brown stuff."

CHAPTER TWENTY-TWO

THE WIND came back an hour after Chickasaw's return. It set in from its normal westerly quarter, holding fresh and steady.

By ten o'clock the middle Gallatin was clearing and by eleven the sprawling valley's whole complex of backing ranges had been blown free of the fire's smoke and fog. From the pine-dark backbones of the Absarokas, eastward, and from the rocky spines of the Tobacco Roots to the west, the land of the Kangi Wicasi came awake under a golden wash of rain-clean summer morning freshness. But within the valley itself, between the charred bases of its own mountains and from the scorched flanks of the lower foothills to the blistered walls of the Gallatin's upper gorge, the Crow buffalo pasture lay black and lifeless beneath the climbing July sun.

At their stations in horse shed, lean-to and main cabin, Stark's silent men scanned the gutted grasslands and waited for Buffalo Ribs's last return.

There was full reason for their stillness.

And for their knowing that when the Crow chief came this time, he would not need to come again.

They were six against his 150. Though they had new copper-cartridge repeating rifles and virtually unlimited ammunition against his obsolete loose-powder breech and muzzle loaders, they knew that should he elect to attempt an all out four-side charge they could not expect to turn it back. Should he, on the other hand, choose to set up another siege, with a slant Indian eye to starving them out, they had even less chance.

Food? Yes. Lazarus had brought them supplies enough to summer a full-strength cavalry garrison. But water? No. Chickasaw's gully-washer had seen to that. The storm, cascading its upper Madisons' runoff down Eagle Gap's narrow defile, had taken out their painstakingly constructed lifeline from the hidden spring. They had only what water was left in the horse-shed tank. Enough, if carefully rationed, with allowance for unpreventable loss by seepage from the imperfectly tarred trough, to last them three, perhaps four days. After that, they could suck loose bullets until their tongues swelled

233

up and saved the Crows the trouble of scalping them.

Crouched at the lean-to's south-wall slit, Stark's mind wheeled and fought with cornered grizzly anger, seeking some way, *any* way, out of the trap which held him captive.

But there was no way out of that trap—*no human way.* If there was a way, it would have to come from some source higher than Nathan Stark. And Nathan Stark was a man who had gotten along without God's help for twenty-nine years. Had he wanted to, he would not have known how to apply for that help now. It only angered him the more, that the thought of doing so seemed to stare back at him from every blind turn his desperate mind sought to make in those final, waiting hours.

Behind him, from her darkened bunk, Nella's stifled cries tore at his heart with increasing frequency. Her pains were convulsing her repeatedly now, only minutes apart. Pretty Bird had told him the water had broken before daylight. She had begun to bleed, meantime. It would be an excruciating dry birth, perhaps a still one. For though the child was alive and moved far down, the Oglala woman feared that it was coming buttocks-first. She had tried, with all the rough skill of her medicine woman's training, to turn it in the canal. It seemed to be coming a little, she had whispered to Stark only minutes ago. But it was very large and its mother, very small. If White Eyes had a god, and knew how to talk to him—

He ground his teeth, cursed softly. The hell with that. It was way too late for a man to be looking for a better faith than his own in himself. He had made it this far, alone. He would go on in, from here, the same way.

Stark's way.

Somewhere out there 150 Crows were waiting to kill him. Somewhere in the cabin, hidden in himself, or in one of the others, was the answer to that deadly circle. It *had* to be there. And he had to find it.

But if it was there, it had not made itself apparent by nightfall.

Something else of Indian intent, however, had.

During the fly-drone, bird-twitter quiet of high noon, Buffalo Ribs had begun to move his forces into position. The warriors had loafed up from their riverside breakfast fire in careless, small groups. Guiding their ponies around the perimeter of the bench timber, just beyond sure range of the cabin rifles, they had dropped off group after group until they had the clearing completely sealed off. The defenders might easily have emptied a few saddles with lucky long tries, but Stark harshly forbade the attempt. The Montanan knew he was down to his last dollar in the toughest game he had ever sat to. He was not about to pitch that dollar away humoring any drawling Texas pleas to "leave us pour it to the red-gut sons of bitches!"

His patience was shortly rewarded.

By one o'clock the Indians had settled down again and it was clear that Buffalo Ribs had made his decision.

It was going to be a starve-out.

When the cookfires of the Crow surround began to dot the nightdark, putting the stamp of final certainty to

Stark's fear that they meant to take up where they had left off when the chinook had failed them the past winter, he realized that his own last decision had now been made for him.

If they were going to wait, he could not.

It was that belly-shrinking simple.

He called the men in from their various posts, laid it out for them in four-letter words.

Somebody had to go for help. That help might ordinarily be had from two places: Virginia City, which would take too long; Bozeman, which could not send enough men. There was a third, *or might be,* a third place. He paused, shaking his head as though already crossing off that dim possibility, leading Waco to prompt dryly, "Don't leave us hung up by our heels, Mr. Stark. Our levis might start draining."

"When he was here," Stark answered, "Lazarus said the army was thinking of setting up a post over east of Bozeman. Nothing much. Maybe a troop of horse and six, eight companies of infantry. Going to call it Fort Ellis, I think. Anyway, I remember one thing for sure— it wasn't due to be finished till sometime in August."

"Big help," growled Chickasaw. "Sure glad you thought of it. I was beginning to worry."

"Yeah." Waco was still able to grin. "Now all we got to do is hold out for thirty days."

"Ought to be easy!" snapped Saleratus. "Three from thirty is twenty-seven. No time at all for a good man to go without a drink."

Ignoring them, Stark plodded on. "I see a chance for

236

two things. They may have got the fort finished sooner than they figured. The garrison troops may have shown up ahead of schedule."

"Three things," corrected Saleratus, still concerned with his pessimistic arithmetic. "They may never have started the damn fort in the first place."

Waco bobbed his head apologetically toward the dour cook. "Don't mind him, Mr. Stark. It's why we keep him around, he's so all-the-time sweet and cheerful when the sand starts getting in the sourdough crock."

The Montanan did not mind Saleratus, nor any of the rest of them. "I figured I'd make a try for it as soon as our friends, yonder, have had a chance to get good and full of my free beef. That would make it about now."

"Mr. Stark, we ain't going to let you do it." Old Chickasaw's quiet statement caught him flatfooted. Before he could answer it, Waco had stood up to side the bearded foreman. "Not without you walk over the two of us," he said.

"The three of us," amended Hogjaw, stumbling to his feet.

"And one makes four," murmured Slim Blanchard, rising hesitantly.

"I'll stay with Stark and the women," gruffed Saleratus. "I been setting a wagonbox too long to be entering any hossback Injun races."

"You'll all of you shut up and listen," ordered Stark, and began to tell them how he meant to ride it and what they were to do when he was gone. As he went along, they waited him out in hard silence. But while they did,

237

other ears were listening. And not waiting.

Beyond the lean-to blankets, Pretty Bird stopped short. She had started in to tell Stark the baby was about to come. Now, hearing the terse discussion under way, she hesitated, her savage heart torn between new loyalties and old fears.

She knew the Crows. Knew what it meant to try and ride among them at night. Her own young man had died trying it. Of all the northern Plains tribes the hated Kangi Wicasi alone were unafraid of the dark. No mounted white man could hope to catch them napping. There was only one way that circle of cookfires might be broken—by an Indian, on foot. And right now. While they were broiling their meat and before they picketed their night guards.

Thus the third decision of that tense day was reached.

Calling softly to Winter Boy, she held him close. Then, releasing him, she talked calmly to him in Oglala, telling him what she must now do and what he must say to White Eyes when she had done it. That finished, and as quietly as she had called him to her, she kissed him and stood back. "Obey White Eyes, for we have given our lives to him. Be faithful to his woman and to the little one who now comes. Remember always that you are an Oglala. A Sioux. The son of a chief's daughter. A warrior."

She was gone then, before Winter Boy could think to call after her. He started to do so, but did not. The tightness in his throat would not let him, and talking through tears was too difficult a thing for a small warrior.

In the cabin room Stark came to his feet. He had said what he had to say, and he was all through with it. The time was now. "Don't tell Nella I've gone," he grunted. "She'll be all right with the squaw to help her." He started for the door, came back. "If it's a boy," he told them, "call him Ben."

He had already slipped into the outer darkness when Nella's frightened cry burst from the lean-to.

"Stark! Stark—!"

He made a deep sound in his throat, drove his clenched nails into his palms. Behind him, Chickasaw's shadow loomed in the doorway. "Go in to her, goddam it! One minute ain't going to make no difference where you're going."

"I cain't, old man. It's not in me."

"It's in you, all right, you blind bastard. Get in there to that poor gal."

He went then, stumbling in his hurry, feeling for the bunk and standing clumsily beside it in the darkness.

"Stark?"

"It's me, Nella."

"Oh, I'm glad, I'm glad." Her voice rose as he sank beside her. "Pretty Bird's gone, Stark! She's run away! I'm afraid, Stark, *real* afraid!"

"Be quiet, girl. It's all right. She's just gone outside."

"No, White Eyes." Winter Boy's piping denial jumped out of the blackness at his elbow, whipsawing his ragged nerves. "She has gone, like Sha'hin says. She will not be back."

239

"Gone! Gone where, for God's sake?"

"To the fort, to get the Pony Soldiers."

It hit him like walking into a stone wall in the dark, dazing him, confusing him. "When?" he asked gropingly.

"While you were talking about it," answered the Indian boy proudly. "She said to tell you a white man had no chance out there. That only a *Shacun,* a Sioux, could do it."

"Oh, Jesus!"

"What's the matter?" groaned Nella feverishly. "What's she done?"

"Tried to get through the Crows and bring help. She heard me telling the boys I was going."

Her hand reached out, found his. It was burning and sweaty and the weak, desperate feel of it made him suddenly very afraid. "Don't go now. Please, Stark. Not now—"

"All right, Nella. I got to see the boys." He pulled his hand gingerly away, finished the lie tight-voiced. "Just hang on, I'll be back." It seemed to quiet her, and he went swiftly into the outer room.

"Waco! Chickasaw!"

"Right here."

"The baby's coming in there. Have either of you ever—I mean, have you—"

"I pulled a calf once, coming wrong way too," Waco offered his crude best. "I'll side her."

Chickasaw followed slowly. "I seen my mother die having her last one. Nobody there but me and my kid

240

sister. But we got it out. I reckon I ain't forgot how."

Stark nodded, not knowing how to thank them, and not trying to. "If she asks for me, tell her I'm out checking the horses—or something."

"You still aim to try it?" asked Waco.

"I've no choice now, I've got to. The damn squaw's disappeared. Kid says she heard us talking and ducked out. God alone knows where or why, and I'd hate to guess."

"Injuns are Injuns," said Chickasaw bitterly. "Goddam 'em all."

Stark shook his head. "The boy claims she meant to try for the fort herself, figuring a white man couldn't make it."

"Well," said Waco heavily, "we'll know about that soon enough."

"About what?" gritted Stark.

"A white man making it through."

"Oh. Yes, I guess we will." The Montanan, moving for the door with his dry agreement, found Chickasaw there ahead of him.

"Waco didn't mean you, Mr. Stark."

Stark's big hand shot out, closing on the old man's arm. "What the hell are you talking about, Billings?"

"Slim. He beat you to it, Mr. Stark. We pulled straws while you was in the lean-to. Slim got the short one."

"He said he was glad," murmured Waco. "Allowed it was likely his best chance to get even with the red scuts for what they done to Curly."

Stark's face twisted. Curly Blanchard. Slim's

241

orphaned nephew and the youthful camp favorite of the hardcase Texas trail crew, had been killed by the Sioux while on night guard below Fort Kearney on the drive up from Fort Worth. The gentle soft-voiced cowboy had never gotten over it.

"He took that little roan mare of his," said Chickasaw, filling in the pause. "The one we pulled the shoes on the other day. He reckoned that riding her barefoot and with only a hackamore, like the Injuns, he might get away with it."

Still, Stark did not speak. He was trying to think of something a man like him could say at a time like this, to men like these. He had not yet found the humble words, when the first Crow shout echoed from the south timber.

After that, there was a wild minute of pursuing yells, rifle fire, and pony galloping, fading rapidly away down the river—then nothing.

"They got him," said Hogjaw.

"It's all right," replied Waco softly. "He always wanted to be with Curly, anyhow."

CHAPTER TWENTY-THREE

THE YOUNG BEEF had been sweet, broiled just right and with the warm blood running juicy with fat when you bit into it. Buffalo Ribs leaned back, belched graciously, eyed his five subchiefs with full-fed satisfaction.

For their parts, Iron Hand, Gray Bull, Four Horses, Beaverhead and Big Belly, had no complaints. They had come over from their outposts at the chief's invitation. A little celebration was in order over White Wolf's surprising coup in catching the white man who had tried to get away. It was the first scalp the garrulous brave had taken in fifteen years of futile boasting. But it was a big one. His companions therefore considered it only fit, though he was not the son, nor even the grandson of a chief, to honor him. Besides, the brief run after the foolish *Wasicun* had cut short their own suppers and it was but common courtesy that Buffalo Ribs should ask them over to finish at his fire.

They talked a little of the wonderful day just closed and of the fine prospects of those soon to come, but mostly they were content to sit back and listen to White Wolf, the great talker.

As they did so, it was hard to imagine that such a truly memorable day was not yet complete. However, it was not. They found that out barely an hour later when, drowsy with White Wolf's twelfth recount of his fearsome genius as a killer of *Wasicuns,* they received an unannounced visitor from the east who brought news of a real killing of the white brothers.

His name was Zincaziwan, Yellow Bird. He was a full-blood Oglala, well known to them from his visit of the previous winter, when he had come bearing Red Cloud's offer of a temporary truce. They greeted him with mixed feelings, glad enough to see him in general but concerned, in particular, with his ability to penetrate their pickets.

When this latter question was put unsmilingly by Buffalo Ribs, the hatchetfaced Oglala got the reunion off to a scowling start by replying haughtily that, "after all, he was a Sioux."

The clear implication was that they were only Crows.

This did not set too well, even on top of a belly swollen with white man's beef. But before their jealous grimaces could twist into anything more threatening, Yellow Bird gave them his news. After that, there was nothing to do but throw more wood on the fire and spit another strip of tenderloin.

Late in December—his Crow friends would excuse the delay, but the Sioux had thought it wise to stay very close to the tepees for a long time after it happened—Crazy Horse had trapped a rash young cavalry chief and eighty Pony Soldiers a few miles north of Fort Kearney. Only one man had escaped, a white army scout named Clayton, who had fought so well Crazy Horse had ordered his life spared and even taken him into his own lodge to nurse his wounds. This strange survivor had since married into the tribe and taken the name of Cetan Mani. Walking Hawk. He had become more Sioux than a Sioux, was a great warrior and a good friend of Zincaziwan's. But his Kangi Wicasi cousins must pardon him. He digressed. That was another story. Yellow Bird's news was of the Fort Kearney massacre, and all that it meant to the *Shacun*. The Pony Soldiers had abandoned the fort and the Sioux had burned it before their departing pony tracks were snowed over. There was no army post left within the Wyoming treaty lands of the Sioux, north of the Powder

River. Red Cloud wanted his Crow brothers to know of the great victory and to hear, in return, how their own fight with the hated *Wasicun* in Montana was going.

When Yellow Bird had finished and sat down to his smoking supper, Buffalo Ribs took his proud turn. He was not a boastful man, and brought his visitor up to date in far fewer words than the Sioux had used. But then his victory was not nearly as great and not even yet complete, so he told it modestly.

When the Crow chief had completed his brief report, Yellow Bird courteously rid himself of his stomach gas, wiped his greasy hands on his loincloth, stood up.

"Wait!" cried White Wolf, alarmed. "You have not heard how I caught the skinny *Wasicun!*"

"I will hear it another time," grunted the Sioux. "Makhpiya Luta has ordered me to return at once." It was an honest Indian lie and demonstrated that Red Cloud was careful in his selection of couriers. Yellow Bird was no fool. Truce or no truce, the less time a lone Oglala spent with 150 Big Hole Crows the better his chances of getting home with his hair all in one piece.

"Well, we are sorry," said Buffalo Ribs. "But a good warrior has no choice when his chief commands. Tell all our Sioux brothers and sisters that our hearts are big for them and that we promise this business of driving the *Wasicun* from the buffalo pastures will soon be done."

Yellow Bird nodded hurriedly, turned to go, thought of a social note which might interest his hosts, stepped back to the fire.

"By the way, speaking of Sioux sisters, I saw one of

my own just now. A full sister, too, one who left the lodge of our father in disgrace many years ago. I believe you know her. Zincahopa, Pretty Bird. At least she mentioned you. Spoke well of you, too. Said you had spared her life once. How was that?"

As he spoke, the six Crows had come to their feet, slant eyes glittering.

"That cursed squaw!" blurted White Wolf. "By my mother's navel, I will—"

"Be quiet!" snarled Buffalo Ribs. "Take your big mouth and your mother's navel and get out."

White Wolf knew when he had made just one speech too many. "Come with me, cousin," he smirked at Yellow Bird. "I will show you an easy way along the river."

"Wait a minute," frowned the Sioux messenger, eying Buffalo Ribs. "Do you know my sister, or not?"

The Crow chief shook his head. "No, the woman is lying. We have seen no Oglala here since you came last winter."

"It may well be," Yellow Bird wisely conceded. "Her tongue was always a little crooked. *Woyuonihan,* I salute my Crow brothers." He touched the fingertips of his left hand to his forehead respectfully, and followed White Wolf away toward the river.

When he had gone, Buffalo Ribs wheeled on Beaverhead. "Take ten warriors. Pick only the fastest ponies. Do not come back to me without her hair."

Beaverhead nodded, scowled. "All right, but you should have taken it the first time. I warned you to. Remember?"

246

"My memory is strong. I hope yours is as good."

"How is that?"

"If you do not bring me *her* hair, your own will do."

With his chisel-toothed subchief departed, Buffalo Ribs squatted again to the fire. He was very quiet while he loaded his stone pipe, and his companions had the good sense to fill their own and let the silence do the talking. Buffalo Ribs was not by nature a surly man, but when he got quiet like that a sow grizzly with caked breasts was a safer thing to disturb.

The smoke from the fragrant mixture of red willow bark and trade tobacco drifted upward. The coals in the fire popped fitfully, slowed their scarlet winking. The stillness deepened.

Suddenly, startlingly, it was broken. But the tiny sound which snapped its taut threat was one so familiar and tepee-close to their Indian hearts that even Buffalo Ribs had to raise his angry head and grin. It came from the darkened cabin across the meadow, quavering through the starlight, high and thin and squalling resentful. There was no other sound in the world like it, and it was guaranteed to kindle a response in the breast of any man lucky enough to have heard it in his own lodge, or old enough to regret that he had not.

"It sounds strong," said Four Horses admiringly. "Brave and lusty, like a man child."

"I am not so sure," murmured Iron Hand, listening raptly. "My firstborn sounded like that and it was a girl. I say it is a girl."

"And I," rumbled Big Belly, the proud father of four

sons. "A man child would not complain so much."

Gray Bull said nothing, for he was a bachelor and not qualified.

Buffalo Ribs, too, kept quiet. He was also, though in a less excusable way, disqualified. He had three wives and six daughters, but no son. Who was he to settle an argument about the way a man child sounded when it came into the world?

He was not to be let off, however.

"What do you think, brother?" Four Horses asked him grinningly. "What does it sound like to you?"

The glowering chief started a short answer, then was taken with an impelling thought. He held his silence a moment longer, the idea turning in his savage mind.

"I think," he said at last, "that a son is a son. If that is a man child over there, I will take it with me."

There was no decent light for tracking. The summer stars, big and fat and flashing white as antelope flags, lit the Bozeman trail enough for good riding but the new moon, first-night pale and sickle-thin, was of no trailing use whatever.

Beaverhead had a problem, and a reputation to defend. Not to mention two glossy braids of blue-black hair to protect.

The Oglala squaw had an hour's start, was undoubtedly a powerful and tireless runner. Being an Indian, there was no chance they might ride up on her, unawares—not from the rear at any rate. One pony might do it from the front and moving at a walk, as

Yellow Bird's had apparently done. But ten ponies going in a group, at a gallop, could not hope to surprise a Root Digger, let alone a Sioux chief's daughter.

No, if they caught that squaw it would be by brain sweat, not pony lather.

Easing his mount to a rolling lope, he spoke to Paints Red and Little Man, his lieutenants. "Well, brothers, how would you say to ride it?"

Little Man shrugged. "I would make a fire and wait for the sun. The ground is very soft from the rain and we would have no trouble following her. But then it is not my hair that you are worrying about."

"Nor mine," growled Paints Red unsympathetically. "So what can we tell you? I would ride it much like Little Man. Where can she go? What harm can she do? Why wear the ponies down running this cursed river in the dark?"

"I will tell you why." Beaverhead's voice was thoughtful and he took his time in answering. "It has just come to me. We will ride hard to get between her and the white man's village on the Wagon Road. That is where I think she is going. And what I think she means to do there, is tell them we have White Eyes and his Big Hats in a bad trap. What do you think of that?"

Paints Red nodded approvingly. "A good plan, brother. If you are right, we have but to wait down there and she will run right into us."

"Aye," agreed Little Man. "And if we should miss her going into the village, we have only to watch for her to come back out of it."

"That is the way I see it," said Beaverhead. "*Hopo,* let us go." He turned and barked the order back to the others, kicked his pony into a flat gallop.

By daylight they were confidently waiting on a pine-clad rise overlooking the open sweep of the outer Gallatin grasslands leading into Bozeman. But when an hour had passed with no sight of the fugitive squaw, their assurance began to waver. It fell apart altogether when, about eight o'clock, Paints Red and Little Man returned from a scout up the Gallatin's bank to report no prints in the rain-soft earth save those of Yellow Bird's pony going south, upstream. The squaw was gone and they had no choice but to assume she had gotten around them in the dark and was now safely in the village.

They were thus left with two apparent courses. They could stay where they were, sitting out Beaverhead's guess that the woman would come back this way when she had spread her warning. They could fan out on a ten-way blind scout to pick up her vanished trail somewhere in the limitless maze of the open grass below them. The first way was bad, but the second was worse. And neither was worth a Pawnee's chance in the middle of a Crow horse herd. The whole situation was bad, very bad. It had been one big guess from the start, and if Beaverhead had been wrong to begin with and the Oglala woman had not even tried to reach the village, they were all in trouble. Perhaps their hair was not in actual danger like Beaverhead's, but Buffalo Ribs had very small ears for listening to failures and they could depend on him to be very unhappy with all of them should the squaw get cleanly away.

At the moment, however, lacking a better idea of their own, they had to trust to Beaverhead's opinion that they should wait where they were.

Grimly, they settled to the long watch.

High noon came and passed. The sun dropped an hour. Then two. Still nothing.

Suddenly Paints Red sprang to his feet. "To the east there, to the east! Is not that a loping pony?" They narrowed their slant eyes, studying the moving dot. "It is," decided Beaverhead, "and coming our way."

"He rides like an Indian," said Little Man.

"*She* rides like an Indian!" hissed Paints Red, who was an Eagle Medicine Dreamer and could see the color of an enemy's face paint a full mile. "That is a woman out there!"

They waited another long minute to make sure. Then Beaverhead moved for his sleeping pony.

"She will pass around this hill. We will meet her down below there, where the pines grow dark and close to the river." As the other braves ran for their ponies, he nodded to Paints Red and Little Man. "You stay up here. She might change her direction. Watch her to see that she comes to us. But do not ride down yourselves until you hear my gun. You might frighten her off."

The two braves scowled their disappointment but did not argue. A man might be upset at missing the fun, yet he had to admit that that damned Beaverhead thought of everything. Small wonder that he was second only to Buffalo Ribs in the Big Hole band.

251

They returned their attention to the approaching rider. "Where do you suppose she got that pony?" asked Paints Red. "There are no white men over that way."

"No," puzzled the other, "and it is not an Indian pony, either."

"Well, we will soon know."

"Aye, there she goes around the hill."

In the forest below, Beaverhead and his seven red shadows waited. "Don't shoot right away," the subchief told them. "Give her a little time to remember us." As he spoke, the Sioux squaw rounded the river trail's bend and rode into them.

"Good afternoon, sister," grinned Beaverhead. "What is your hurry?"

Pretty Bird said nothing. She was an Indian. She knew what was coming.

"Do you want to say where you have been?" asked the Crow. "Or perhaps give us some little message for White Eyes?"

The Oglala woman kneed her mount toward him, until its nose was touching his riding blanket.

"I have a little message for Buffalo Ribs. You may take it to him for me."

Beaverhead's leer slackened yet more.

"By all means, sister. What is it?"

Pretty Bird looked at him, straightened proudly, spat full in his face.

He shot her through the belly, the muzzle flash of his gun muffling in her doeskin campdress. Her mount leaped away, out from under her nerveless body. The merciful concussion of the fall brought the blessed blackness. She lay unconscious and without pain and was dead before they could dismount to take her hair.

Beaverhead had his knife poised when one of the braves cried out sharply. "Wait a bit! This horse is marked with the Pony Soldier sign!" They moved swiftly to where he held the animal, their eyes leaping to the feared cavalry brand. "I do not like that," said Beaverhead quietly.

"No," gritted another of the braves, "and I do not think you will like *that* either!" With the words he pointed up the hill. Racing their ponies headlong down the slope were Paints Red and Little Man, shouting and waving the warning sign. They slid their mounts to a dirt-showering halt gasping the incredible news. "Pony soldiers! Walk-A-Heaps! Coming from over there, where the squaw came from! *Hookahey! Hopo!*"

Beaverhead was stunned. Cavalry troops? And foot soldiers, too? Here? A hundred and forty miles from Fort Smith over in the Big Horns? Impossible Yet Paints Red was an Eagle Dreamer. His eyes could not lie. "Quickly!" he snarled. "Get that woman's body and tie it on the soldier pony. We cannot leave it here where they will find it."

Two braves sprang to the ground, seized the body, lashed it on the cavalry horse. Seconds later the river-trail clearing was empty and Beaverhead, galloping at the head of his nervous band, was consoling himself with hard Indian philosophy. From the fact she rode a branded army mount, it was certain the Oglala squaw had somehow found and warned those soldiers. But other facts were equally, and more hopefully, certain. Moving at the foot-pace of the Walk-A-Heaps they would not reach White Eyes' cabin that day. *Beaverhead would.* And with three long hours of good fighting daylight to spare. Time, and plenty of time, for his gaunt chief to scalp six *Wasicun* settlers!

"*Hookahey,*" he grunted to Paints Red and Little Man. "Ride faster."

CHAPTER TWENTY-FOUR

IT WAS Chickasaw, on watch at the barricaded door, who saw them come back. His chronic squint drew in sharply. They were sure in a prime hurry about something, cutting straight across the bench like that. Eight, ten—no, by thunder!—eleven of them, ponies lathered to their sweat-slicked hocks. But it was not Beaverhead's eleven braves who put the final crowsfoot to the old cattleman's eye corners. It was the twelfth Indian.

Waco, answering his low call, came over from the southwall rifle slit. "Fetch Stark. Don't say nothing in front of Nella or the Injun kid. *They got the squaw.*"

The little cowboy winced, stepped to the lean-to hangings. "Mr. Stark, you got a minute?" As the latter replied, he put his head in past the blankets, adding a deliberate covering wave for Nella. "How you feeling now, gal? You sure sweated the lot of us for nothing, didn't you?" His crinkly grin broadened, forcing the put-on banter. "You're a sure enough four-flusher, Miss

Nella. You didn't have no more last-minute trouble than a six-kid Comanche squaw!"

"Thanks to you and Chickasaw," she smiled wearily. *"And you,"* she added, her eyes finding and holding Stark's.

He took her hand, patting it clumsily. "I'll be right back. Don't try to get up now." She smiled again, shook her head wearily. "Don't worry, mister. I couldn't out-pull a sick cat." He nodded, transferred the pat to Winter Boy's shaggy head. "You watch her, son. And keep an eye on your little brother."

Joining Waco and Chickasaw at the door, he watched and listened to the flurry of activity in the main Crow camp. In five minutes he had seen and heard all he was ever going to need to. For some reason the Indians had changed their minds. They were going to attack, and not tomorrow.

He called the other men in from the horse shed. When they were all standing embarrassed and boot-shuffling under his intent, strangely disturbing look, he dealt it to them in the same way he always had—straight out and face up.

"I don't have to tell you what's coming up over there. What you don't know, you can guess. What you maybe wouldn't guess is what I mean to tell you now." He paused, the struggle to get it out beading his forehead with sweat. "You boys have taught me a lesson. One I should have learned a long time ago; from Esau and Ben and likely others before them. It's too late for it to do any of us any good now, but it's in me and I've got to say

255

it—I wish we could have been friends." Again the awkward pause. Then, hard-voiced. "Hold low and get their
ponies down. They hate to fight on foot."

Strangely, it was Hogjaw who started it. Slouching
forward, the gangling youth put out his hand. Stark took
it. Neither man spoke. Nor did any of the others, as they
fled by in wordless turn, to grip the big Montanan's
hand.

The Crow attack began ten minutes later.

Captain Sanderson pulled in his horse and waved the
halt back to his troopers. Riding off the left flank of K
Troop's lagging column of two's, Sergeant Martin
Barkis picked up the signal, bawled it back to the following infantry. At the head of the latter, Second Lieutenant E. J. Forbes sighed gratefully, told his first
sergeant to keep the men on their feet and in ranks, rode
forward to find out what the captain had on his mind.

What Sanderson had on his mind was Section 23,
*Field Manual OA-342, Combat & Service Regulations,
Infantry.* What he had in his hand was his double-cased
German silver pocketwatch. And the two items were not
coming out even.

Section *23* said that foot troops under forced march
made four miles an hour. The big and little hands of the
watch said they did not. It was 5:07 P.M. In the past hour
his column had covered less than three miles. They
were, by the rough description given them by the
missing Indian woman, still ten or fifteen miles northeast of the Gallatin Valley ranchhouse. By the Almanac

256

Table, sunset was 7:42. At their present rate even the long summer twilight would beat them to their objective by several miles.

It was no good, and he let his young lieutenant know it the moment the latter cantered up.

"Let me see that damn map again, Forbes."

He spread the worn document across his saddle pommel, studying it frowningly. It was a service copy of John Bozeman's survey of his ill-fated wagon route from the Montana diggings to Wyoming's Fort Laramie and the Oregon route—the only field chart the army had showing the Gallatin River drainage—and it was rough enough to lose a local settler, let alone seventy-eight raw recruits and a company commander who had yet to fire his first shot in anger at a horseback Indian.

"I don't like it, Forbes, I don't like it a damn bit."

"Neither do I, Captain, but I don't know what we can do about it. My men can't march any faster and not very much longer."

"I know, I know. And this infernal map doesn't tell us a blessed thing except that we're in Montana Territory. Look at this, will you! He's got this damn river dotted off into those hills ahead in a straight line. We can certainly see that's impossible!"

"Your guess is as good as mine, sir. I'd say all we can do is keep following the river like the squaw said—straight or crooked."

Sanderson stuffed the map in his shirtfront.

"We've got to do better than that, boy."

"How in hell can we, sir? My boys are done in right

now. They've already made over twenty miles under full pack. Regulations say—"

"I think I know the manual, Lieutenant."

"Yes sir, I'm sure you do. Beg pardon, sir."

Sanderson ignored him, shaking his head and trying to think. He pulled his watch again, checked it against the reddening sun, stared off up the Gallatin at the rearing granite walls of the canyon far ahead. The seconds ticked away. Somewhere far back in the hills a coyote began tuning up. From the river meadow, downstream, a dog fox interrupted his mouse hunting to bark back at him. After that there was only the sound of the watch, and of the wind, soft and sad and lonesome through the restless pines.

"Jesus," shivered Lieutenant Forbes. "What a godforsaken place."

Sanderson looked at him, lips tightening.

"What do you think it is for those poor devils up there?"

"Beg pardon, sir."

"Nothing. I'm going ahead, Forbes. Fall your men out and set up camp."

"But, sir—"

"That's an order. Barkis!"

"Yes sir." The sergeant shoved his horse forward, salute snapping.

"Close up, column fours, no flankers. We're going on."

"Column fours, no flankers. Yes sir." He wheeled his mount, galloped back, shouting ahead to Corporal

Gates. "Close 'em up, Jimmy, we're going on."

The troopers shifted up in column, talking nervously. Sanderson flagged back the "Forward ho!" and K Troop moved out. Riding with Barkis in its lead, Corporal James Gates peered into the forest darkening so swiftly on all sides, gulped noisily, got his tightening adam's apple worked free.

"I don't mind telling you, Marty, I'm scared. Bad scared."

Sergeant Barkis was a twenty-year regular and had ridden out after Indians before. But he only looked back at him, hawked at the dry mucus webbing his own throat, spat dustily.

"Move over, soldier. It ain't exactly joy that's making my spit stick."

In his hurry and overconfidence, Buffalo Ribs made a mistake. It was a very bad mistake to make against four old Confederate cowboys and as many new Union carbines. Not to mention one young Montanan and a well-worn Henry Repeater.

Not troubling to split his forces, the Crow chief led the first charge straight across the meadow from the south timber.

It was a beautiful, breathtaking charge, too. Full of all the gaudy feathers, garish face paint and bloodcurdling war cries so dear to the hearts of the old western storytellers. Replete, as well, with all the wild horsemanship, incredible daring and crazy personal courage which was to lead such professional Indian campaigners as Crook,

Bourke, Clark Custer and Major Anson Mills to remember them as "the finest light cavalry in the world."

But the old storytellers were still young men and the murderous battles of the Washita, the Rosebud, Hat Creek Bluffs and the Little Big Horn had not yet been fought.

And Nathan Stark and his Fort Worth Irregulars had been given a ten-minute warning.

They were ready.

They fired fast and held close. The first ponies began to stumble and go down clear out past 200 yards. At 150 yards their howling masters were growing big enough to be separated from the motley-colored mass of their mounts, and riderless ponies started to quarter frantically across the front of the charge. At 100 yards, a crouching buck filled the rearsight of a Union Spencer pretty as a painting in a picture frame. In the next 50 yards there were suddenly more empty than occupied saddles heading the Crow assault. Inside the last 50 yards—some of the screaming braves so close their floundering ponies crashed into the cabin walls—the charge fell apart.

Buffalo Ribs, raked once across the jaw and ripped twice through the fleshy part of his right side by the Spencer slugs, led the retreat on into the north timber without breaking his gallop. There he held up to count his losses.

In the cabin, cursing and grinning despite the fact they had only delayed their executioners, and knew it, the

Texas sharpshooters totaled up their own version of the same Crow census.

Those Yankee carbines held seven rounds in their tubular buttstock magazines. Those rounds were caliber 52-56 Spencer, rimfire copper case. Four times seven was twenty-eight, and there were twelve good Indians lying out there in that meadow. Giving Stark his fair share, they had still averaged better than one Crow dead and down for every three shots fired. "And, mister!" announced Chickasaw, blowing out his barrel, "I don't care how you count it, that's shooting!"

"Comanche or Crow, Texas or Montana," drawled Waco, "it sure as hell is."

"Load up," said Stark, peering from the south-wall slit. "They're coming back."

The return charge was mostly excitement left over from the first. They did not really mean it and broke it off well out beyond effective range. Wheeling and yelling, they swept into the old Plains Indian wagon surround gallop, circling the ranch buildings hanging on the far sides of their ponies and firing under their necks.

They kept this up for ten threatening minutes and until Chickasaw, getting tired of it, stacked his Spencer and hauled out his old Sharps bullgun and drilled one of them clean at 450 yards.

The estimate of the extreme distance was the old man's own, but as Waco charitably allowed, "Leave him stretch it a mite. It wasn't a bad shot." For truth it was not, and nobody knew that better than the diminutive Uvalde County cowboy. That buck had been so far away

261

he looked like a tickbird sitting on a buffalo chip. And the way he grabbed his guts and bounced off that piebald pony was not brought on by belly cramps or stomach gas.

That was for sure as a dead Crow did not crawl anymore.

For the next interminable two hours nothing happened. They could tell a big powwow of some kind was going on in the south timber from the way the ponies kept galloping across the bench toward it, from the encircling posts around the clearing. But the usual signs of horseback Indians working themselves up for a final attack on a cornered and outnumbered bunch of whites where unaccountably missing. There was no big shouting of courage words for themselves, nor of taunting insults for their victims. Just that brief gathering of the ponies toward the main camp then ominous silence.

After that, the powder-smudged cowboys were left to listen to their own sounds: Ben's baby crying—Stark and Nella talking low-voiced in the lean-to—Chickasaw reloading a fresh chaw and firing liquid tobacco shots out of his rifle slit—Saleratus lugubriously lipping and inhaling his snoose—Hogjaw muttering of chinaberry trees, red haws ripening, the welcome cool of pear-thicket shade at high noon, how low the water might be in the Brazos, the smell of roundup dust, cutting horse lather, irons burning in the fire, breakfast bacon, blue bonnets after a summer shower—and Waco cheering him up with the thought of how much prettier his bright red hair was going to look hanging down a Crow lodge smokehole, than his own or Chickasaw's or Saleratus's dingy gray headpieces.

But shortly the taste went out of Chickasaw's quid. Stark and Nella quit talking. Hogjaw gave up on Texas. Even the baby got quiet. Then there was nothing for them to do but squint through their rifle slits and try to put their tired minds to guessing how Buffalo Ribs meant to finish it up.

About seven-fifteen, with a good deal more than plenty of clear sharpshooting daylight remaining, they found out.

The second attack came without a single Indian sound. One minute the clearing was mountain-meadow quiet. The next it was filled with a slithering, muffled rush more terrifying than any human-throat noise—the pounding drumfire beat of almost 150 barefoot ponies' hooves slashing through dead brown July grass.

The hostile mounts, bursting simultaneously from all three sides of the flanking timber, were halfway to the cabin before the stunned defenders levered off the first volley. This time there was no turning them. The front-running ponies screamed and pitched and squalled and went down like buffalo stampeding into a hide hunters' ambush. Following ponies fell over them, stumbled, sprawled, got up riderless, ran free. But there were too many of them, coming from too many ways.

Hogjaw and Saleratus fired their last rounds at the west wave, broke from the horse shed, ran for the lean-to crawlhole. Stark was waiting for them. As they dove through, he jammed Nella's dressing table into the opening, yelled into Waco and Chickasaw. "Hold the door! They're into the horse shed!"

"We cain't do it!" bellowed Chickasaw. "We're empty!"

The Montanan leaped into the main room, shouting back for Hogjaw and Saleratus to watch the crawlhole. He fired from the hip with both Colts, over the top of the floursack barricade, and the heads of the crouching Texans as they reloaded desperately.

Three Crows were driving their mounts straight at the opening. He got two of them at about ten yards, the third, so close to the cabin that his crazed mount, rearing to avoid colliding with the wall, threw his stricken rider across the barricade and into the room. Waco killed him with the stove ax, with Stark's guns still blasting across the piled sacks to drive back the rush of braves who sought to follow their dead comrade in.

Again the sheer swarm of their numbers broke through. As his .44's snapped empty, Stark heard the roar of Saleratus's and Hogjaw's handguns opening up. The Crows were at the crawlhole—and Nella was in there—!

He wheeled for the lean-to, but his time was out. Five more paint-slashed faces loomed above the barricade, firing point-blank into the smoke-filled cabin. He seized the ax, where Waco had dropped it, feeling their lead go into him as he did. He went crazy then, with the pain and anger of the wounds. He was back at the barricade driving the clotted blade into the nearest braided head, bare

264

red collarbone, reaching arm, climbing leg or leaping groin—anything that was Indian flesh and Crow blood.

Other savages were at the rifle slits on all sides now, poking their guns in through the narrow openings, firing blindly into both cabin and lean-to. Their random shots began to tell. Hogjaw groaned chokingly, staggered back from the crawlhole, a smoothbore slug through his lungs. Waco, reloaded at last and jumping to Stark's aid, was hit high in the shoulder. He spun like a spiked top, crashed over the stove, fell into the empty woodbox.

Chickasaw, still loading furiously, went to pieces when he saw the little cowboy go down. He leaped to side Stark, rifle-clubbed, crying with blind rage, "You bastards! You lousy, filthy, no-good Injun bastards—!" His steel-butted Spencer caved in the skull of a brave who had scrambled over the barricade and was swinging a war ax on Stark; broke the face bones of another tumbling in over the bloody sacks behind his fellow. The next moment Stark was down with the two dying braves on top of him and the berserk old cattleman was driving for the dirt in slackmouthed surprise and reflex obedience to the high-pitched furious cry from the lean-to.

"Get down, you old fool, get down—!"

Nella Torneau, faded cotton nightgown framing her gaunt figure, Henry Rifle clutched in her thin hands, stood swaying in the blanket-hung doorway. Her wild warning was still echoing above the entering, triumphant Crow shouts when she began to fire. But when the Henry lever had spun the last empty into the lean-to doorjamb there was no more Indian noise, and the only

Crows still across the barricade were those who hung dangling there in midfall, or who lay forever quiet below it in the dirt of the cabin floor.

The moment of following great stillness was broken by the most beautiful sound in any Indian-fighting rancher's world.

It came, high and thin and trumpet-bell clear, from the far, Gallatin, edge of the bench meadow.

Boots and Saddles. Played in A-flat, brass. To the accompaniment of an unknown West Point baritone sounding "Forward ho!" offkey, in a full gallop.

"It's the first time," said old Chickasaw Billings slowly, "I ever enjoyed hearing a northern bugler blow a blue-belly charge."

"Amen," sighed Waco reverently, lying gratefully back and making no effort whatever to get out of the woodbox. "God bless the little Union sons of bitches, one and all."

CHAPTER TWENTY-FIVE

HOGJAW WENT HOME to Texas that night. They buried him the next morning on the sunswept point of the bench above the river and in full view of the cabin. It was the way Stark asked that it be. "I want him where I can see him," said the big Montanan. "It may be that I'll need reminding someday."

They found Pretty Bird still laced to the tethered cavalry horse in the abandoned Crow camp. She was put to rest beneath the ashes of Buffalo Ribs's last council fire, her long braids untouched by the fleeing hostiles. Her terse eulogy was furnished in five words by Chickasaw Billings, standing back in hard-eyed silence following the last tamped shovelful of returned earth. Somehow it seemed to put it better than a prayerbook full of fancy praise. *"She was a good Injun,"* said the old man, and took off his hat.

K Troop left at noon after helping clean up the Crow dead. They were put in a common trench, covered up without white regret or Christian comment; twenty-seven brave and decent men who died fighting for what they believed their God had given them to fight for—but they were Indians.

When the cavalry had gone, trailing the red survivors westward through Eagle Gap, the afternoon stillness closed in once more over the cabin bench. Waco, Chickasaw and Saleratus saddled up quietly and rode off up the valley to, in their restless words, "get the good smell of hoss sweat and fresh wind back in our noses and maybe talk a little about old times in Texas."

Stark had understood that and had watched them from the cabin door a long time and until their mounts were small with distance and slow riding. When he went in to Nella and the baby there was a compelling look of lonely sadness in his broad face, which the Texas girl had never seen there. "Where's the boy?" he said, glancing around and coming to stand beside her. "With his mother," she told him. "He asked if I would let him stay with her 'until the sun died.'"

He nodded, wide mouth tightening. "Poor little devil. I hope he's going to be all right."

"Stark—"

"Yes."

"He can stay with us, can't he?"

When she said it she looked up at him with a strange intensity not inherent in the question itself, her green eyes clear and steady, yet half shy and uncertain, too.

He knew then how she had meant it, and knew that in the simple query about the Indian boy she had at once stated all her own haunting doubts and answered his. She had told him what his heart had been afraid to ask, or even dream, and was waiting for his reply.

"With us, Nella?" he said softly, taking her hand and following its gentle urging down onto the bunk beside her.

"With us, Stark—always and forever."

It was a tender kiss, long and slow and cool, soft-lipped and lingering. The calm and quiet and blessed peace of it flooded through him in a way no heated embrace ever could. It was a final promise for the future; one that would be kept, that was given willingly, with a full and a free and a gladly surrendering heart. And one that said beyond any words which might have faltered to frame it half so well that Nella Torneau and Nathan Stark would never be lonely again.

Lazarus came late that afternoon, riding a lathered horse and gray with fatigue. Alerted by a Bozeman settler who had met Sanderson's column early the previous day and spread the alarm to Virginia City, he had gathered a big posse of hard-rock volunteers from the Alder Gulch camps and started in across Eagle Gap. At the top of the divide they had encountered the cavalry troops and turned back with them after the Indians, leaving him to go on to the ranch alone.

Shortly after his arrival the cowboys returned from the upper valley, their spirits much improved by an accidental meeting with an old friend, found calmly grazing the west-bank fringe of the Gallatin timber. The reunion had been one of mutual, if unspoken, delight. And to prove it, General Grant had ambled all the long way back with them, unbidden and rope-free. The old herd-bull's contentment was gratifyingly completed when they turned him into the pony corral with the dozen wide-eyed, curiously sniffing heifer calves Waco and Chickasaw had brought in from the bench pasture before the fire.

Saleratus, clearly inspired by the way things were working out, inhaled a mighty charge of Copenhagen and set out to put on a feed that would be remembered in Montana for a long time to come. "At least," he hedged growlingly, "as long as the goddam competition is limited to soda biscuits and salt sidemeat!"

There was still a half hour of daylight left after they had sopped up the last of the pan gravy and emptied the four-quart coffee tin. Stark, when the first smokes had been lit and the talk beginning to trail off accordingly, got up and went outside. He walked slowly around the cabin to the pony corral, his thoughts his own and reaching far back through the past months.

His thirtieth birthday lay short weeks ahead and he was still long, tough years away from any small part of his million-dollar ambition. But he had fought for the Big Pasture and won it. He had old General Grant and his twelve little orphan heifers with which to begin rebuilding his great dream of a Gallatin Valley empire. And beyond that, safe in the log-walled vault of the lean-to behind him, he had a fortune waiting far greater than any ever imagined in terms of yellow dust or banknotes.

With the last thought a slow smile softened his wide mouth. He leaned gratefully back against the good strong feel of the pony corral poles, a man at final peace with his hard-won world.

It was there that Lazarus found him long minutes later; still smoking, still looking off across the sleepy rustle of the bench grass nodding to the sunset stir of the night-wind.

He came to stand beside him and to look with him, letting the evening stillness grow. At last, finding the words he wanted, he spoke.

"A long time ago, Nathan, I said you would make your million but that you would never be wealthy. I was wrong."

Stark moved his head, pale eyes still looking far off. "Yes, old friend, you were. I haven't got a hard dollar to my name and I'm the richest man in Montana." He paused, his dry voice deepening with a humility as warm and real as the fertile meadow earth upon which he stood. "I've found many things since last we talked;

three good men to be my friends, a wonderful woman to be my wife, a fine son to carry my name, the loveliest virgin valley in God's western creation to call my own—and theirs. No man can hope for more. Few find half as much."

"Yes," said Lazarus slowly, "that is true. You *have* found all these things. But you have found something else far more important than any of them."

The big man looked at him, puzzled, interested.

"And what is that, Esau?"

The old Jew returned his look, nodded, let his gaze go back to the fading Gallatin twilight.

"Yourself," was all he said.

Center Point Publishing
600 Brooks Road • PO Box 1
Thorndike ME 04986-0001 USA

(207) 568-3717

US & Canada:
1 800 929-9108